Taming Her Mate

Also by Kathy Lyons

The Bear Who Loved Me

License to Shift

For the Bear's Eyes Only

Alpha Unleashed

Bound to the Bear

Taming Her Mate

Book Six of Grizzlies Gone Wild

KATHY LYONS

FOREVER
YOURS

New York   Boston

Copyright © 2019 by Kathy Lyons

Excerpt from *Alpha Unleashed* copyright © 2018 by Kathy Lyons

Cover design by Brian Lemus. Cover images © Shutterstock. Cover copyright © 2019 by Hachette Book Group, Inc.

Forever Yours

Hachette Book Group

1290 Avenue of the Americas, New York, NY 10104

read-forever.com

twitter.com/readforeverpub

First published as an ebook and as a print on demand: March 2019

Forever Yours is an imprint of Grand Central Publishing. The Forever Yours name and logo are trademarks of Hachette Book Group, Inc.

The publisher is not responsible for websites (or their content) that are not owned by the publisher.

The Hachette Speakers Bureau provides a wide range of authors for speaking events. To find out more, go to www.hachettespeakersbureau.com or call (866) 376-6591.

ISBNs: 978-1-5387-6216-5 (ebook), 978-1-5387-6217-2 (print on demand)

I am so grateful to Amy Pierpont and Madeleine Colavita for their amazing work on this series. They've taken it to places I could not have gone on my own and I'm so thankful. This book is dedicated to them and everyone at Hachette for being awesome.

Chapter 1

How did he get himself into these situations?

As the only shifter cop on the Detroit police force, Detective Ryan Kennedy knew there were some things he had to investigate without backup from his fellow officers. But he shouldn't be here in the sewer, about to face a paranormal threat, without his fellow shifters by his side.

Except he was because the alpha of the Detroit grizzly bear clan was an asshole. Or rather, he had been. Nanook was dead, Simon was the new leader, and Ryan was getting really tired of being betrayed by everyone in his life.

So he hadn't trusted the new alpha and now here he was, alone in the sewer, and considering his meager options.

He was soaking wet and stank as he followed a pair of werewolves through the Detroit sewer system. He had a hunch that the asshole wolves who were poisoning the city water were down here somewhere. All the cops who weren't at home puking were scouring the water supply for where the crap was being poured in. Ryan was the only idiot looking at sewage because he guessed the damned dogs were using this system to get around.

He was right.

Two werewolves trudged ahead of him. They were men dressed in hip waders and tees; their scruffy jaws worked as they groused about carrying boxes of something through the sewer system. Ryan would bet his grizzly hump that the boxes contained jugs of the poison. More than half the city was at home sick, many hallucinating. A bunch more were outside rioting thanks to the aggression the poison caused, but that was nothing compared to what it did to shifters.

Regular shifters became like the Hulk, with aggression and strength to match. Then there were the unlucky few who became hybrids, neither animal nor man but some hideous combination of both. Most went insane within a couple days. And these two bastards were the perpetrators who had brought Detroit to the edge of destruction.

He had to stop them. The only problem was that he was alone down here, his phone couldn't get a signal through all the concrete, and the passageway narrowed ahead. No way could he follow the werewolves without being spotted.

It was only luck and good hearing that he'd found them in the first place, and now regulations said he should head back to safety and a cell signal to report what he'd found. He'd rather arrest them and get them to confess everything. Problem was that he was alone because he didn't trust his fellow shifters and he'd taken sick days because he couldn't tell his captain about shifters. Worse, there was no guarantee he'd win against the wolves. It was two to one and being able to shift into a grizzly bear wasn't helpful in the narrow spaces of the sewer system.

How did he get himself in these situations? Answer: He didn't trust anyone but himself, and that meant he had to take these guys down by himself.

He pulled out his gun and tried to judge angles. A miss in these tunnels could mean death by a ricocheting bullet, but he'd have to risk it. Or maybe the wolves would be smart and just surrender.

Yeah, right.

"Police. You're under arrest. Stop right there!"

His voice boomed over the sound of the water and echoed impressively. The wolves didn't care. One took off, box in hand. The other pulled out a gun.

Shit. Ryan ducked back. Wolves didn't tend to carry guns. They preferred to use their animal bodies to attack, but it was just his luck that this guy would be the exception.

But instead of shooting at him, the werewolf shot through the cardboard box. Pale green liquid gushed from the hole in the box. The poison. And the guy held up the box to guzzle some of it.

Oh hell. Ryan had never seen what the undiluted stuff did to shifters. The werewolf had no sooner swallowed twice than suddenly he was busting out of his waders in full animal mode. The thing let out a roar and launched into an attack. Ryan got off a few shots—only way to handle a hopped-up werewolf—but then he was out of time.

His human skin couldn't take the attack, so he shifted straight into bear. He was in grizzly form by the time the werewolf hit him square in the chest. Or what would have been his chest if he'd remained human.

The werewolf had enough size and speed that Ryan slammed against the curved tunnel wall. His head was forced down, right onto the bastard's neck and he bit with all his grizzly strength.

The wolf howled and scrabbled with his feet against Ryan's belly, claws raking through the fur. Pain sliced across his thoughts and he threw the wolf off him rather than get disemboweled. He tried to slam it as hard as he could against the wall. If Ryan was lucky, the creature's neck would break.

He wasn't lucky, but Ryan was free. The wolf spun around, teeth bared as blood dripped from his neck. Ryan's belly burned, but he wasn't ripped open, so he faced off as best he could in the narrow space. He tried to think of a better way to do this. He was excruciatingly aware that the first wolf was long gone, and the dropped jug of poison was pouring into the water. But his biggest problem was the super-crazed wolf who wasted no time in attacking again.

The creature was strong for a wolf, thanks to the poison, and Ryan struggled to grapple with him. The thing had launched straight at his face, mouth open, claws extended. Ryan kept himself steady, never breaking eye contact. He needed to see if the wolf was rational. The snarls suggested no, but the relentless attack said yes. He could handle a rational werewolf, fight and not kill it so he could question the guy later. But if the creature was all animal, then there would be no end except in death.

On and on, the wolf kept coming while Ryan grew tired slamming the thing aside and hoping for a lucky blow. The creature was expending ten times more energy than Ryan, and yet still seemed as ferocious as at the beginning.

Ryan was gasping for breath as he kept batting the wolf aside. Eventually, the creature would be too beaten up to rise again. But so far, the wolf wasn't slowing down. And it was lightning fast. Ryan's arms ached from the steady impact. His bear claws had scored a half-dozen hits, there was blood splatter all over the walls, but the werewolf would not stop.

Damn it, why wouldn't the thing tire?

Ryan caught the wolf hard under the jaw, slamming him to the side. The impact reverberated in the space as the creature slid to the floor, legs twitching. Was he down? The creature's eyes opened slightly, and Ryan saw madness there. Damn it, there was no man left inside. Only an insane determination to keep fighting. That meant—

Two shots exploded nearby, the echo deafening. Ryan flinched when the wolf's head exploded in a gory mess.

Thank God.

Ryan's arms dropped to his sides while his lungs worked like bellows. The fight had taken a lot out of him, and he needed a moment to recover. Eventually, his breath eased enough for him to face his rescuer. He turned and saw a man aiming his gun straight at Ryan.

No!

He started to shift back to human. He needed to show that he was sane and not a shifter hopped up on the poison, but he didn't get the chance.

Two impacts like sledgehammers, straight to the torso, and he collapsed against the tunnel wall.

Pain.

He had to get up and move or he was dead for sure. He knew that, and yet every part of him was swamped in agony. Blackness surged forward, offering him the escape of unconsciousness. He couldn't. So he fought it, using every ounce of discipline he had to stay conscious.

The greatest mastery is a mind that lets go.

The mantra filtered through his thoughts. He'd barely started the meditation regimen that his pack mate Hank had given him, and yet it came to him now when his mind was pounded by waves of misery.

Let go.

He fought the words. He needed to hold on, to stay awake, to…

Let go.

A wave of agony rolled through his mind, obliterating everything. He couldn't do it. He couldn't fight something that huge, so he gave up. His grip on consciousness floundered, his thinking mind went silent, and pain became everything.

Or nearly everything.

Agony battered him, but a part remained separate, no longer fighting. It was as if he stood on a cliff above the surging pain and watched what was happening without participating in it. And it was that part of him that heard the woman.

Chapter 2

*N*o! No! No!

Francesca Wolf felt like she was screaming those words a lot lately, but she'd long since given up voicing the sentiment aloud. She'd been in the sewer tunnels trying to reason with two of her father's most loyal people when she'd heard a gunshot. They'd turned away from the sound, heading for safety, but she'd run toward it. She might disagree vehemently with her father's men, but she was there to back them up in a fight. It was what the daughter of an alpha did.

She got there in time to see Jayce Davis in hopped-up wolf form grapple with a grizzly bear–shifter. It was a vicious fight that looked like it had been going on for a while, but as she skidded to a stop just out of range, the bear managed a heavy blow to Jayce's head. The wolf went down, and she exhaled a slow breath while she tried to think of what to do.

Wolf law said she had to help her pack mate no matter what, but Jayce had been an asshole before he started guzzling the green goo. In its purest form, the serum turned shifters into amped-up super beings, while burning out their neurons; in its diluted form, it was poisoning all of Detroit. Jayce was addicted to the stuff, and she wasn't going to help a guy who had probably gone psycho on some equally hopped-up grizzly. Not when it looked like the fight was over. The bear was standing there, his breath heaving as he recovered, and Jayce lay—

Another gunshot boomed through the tunnels. The sound pounded at her eardrums, but it was the sight of Jayce's head exploding that would haunt her forever.

No!

She didn't scream the word out loud, but in her head it echoed over and over. Jayce had been down. There was no need to kill him. Damned grizzlies were killers, pure and simple, and they didn't stop to assess the situation before they went lethal.

She forced herself to crouch low. The need to be seen, to tell the bastard bears exactly what she thought of them, burned in her blood but she held back. Since becoming a hybrid she'd had the compulsion to let everyone see her and damn them if they hated her just because she was different. But that was the serum talking and not her thinking mind. Until she took control of the werewolf pack, she had to keep hidden no matter how much it chafed.

Meanwhile, the bear's arms dropped to his sides in relief. She didn't know grizzly expressions well, but if ever a bear looked exhausted, this guy did. Must have been one hell of a fight. And now that she had a different angle, she could see his gun-happy companion.

And did a double take.

That wasn't a bear with a gun. It was Brady Joe Bailey brandishing a Glock. Damn it! The one wolf she was trying to find was gunning down one of their own. What the hell?

Two more shots rang out, and Frankie watched in slow motion horror as the grizzly slammed back against the wall. Blood burst out of his chest, and this time her words wouldn't be denied.

"No!" she bellowed as she jumped forward. "Brady, no!"

The man jerked in reaction, his gun aimed at her chest. She threw her hands out wide, her head cocked slightly to the side in surrender. It was a trick she'd learned young to keep the larger wolves off her. She surrendered immediately so their instincts stopped pushing them to kill her. And once their wolves were satisfied, she engaged their reason. Or she surprise-attacked right when the animals were at their weakest.

It worked like a charm.

Brady's shoulders eased down, and his lips released his animal snarl, but he didn't say a word. Which meant it was up to her to get him talking so the rational man could take precedence over the wolf.

"Hey Brady," she said. "It's me, Frankie. Don't know if you can see me. It's dark in here." It wasn't that dark, but it gave him an excuse for aiming a gun at the alpha's daughter. "So this is a bit of a shit show." She glanced down at Jayce. "I saw the end of that fight. Jayce looked hopped up for sure."

Brady's chin jerked down in a nod and his eyes darted sideways for a second before coming back to her. She followed his look and saw a cardboard box on its side. Even in the half-light, she could see the plastic jug inside it dripping green goo into the sewer. Shame swamped her at the sight of that poison, but she couldn't succumb to it now. She was not responsible for her family's sins, and yet every part of her felt guilty. Her brother claimed that the goo made the pack stronger and it would help partial shifters kick over into their full potential. That was his reason for putting it into the water supply. He thought there'd be dozens of wolves out there who didn't know they were shifters who could finally discover the truth.

No one expected the weird hybrids or that it would make most of the city hallucinate. And he sure as hell hadn't told anyone that most of the pack would end up addicted to the stuff.

"Jayce was an addict, pure and simple," she said, her hands slowly lowering to her side.

"Feels damned good as it kills you," Brady said, his voice heavy with yearning.

Shit. He was an addict, too. No one else ached for the poison like a shifter who had tasted the pure stuff, but he didn't go for it. Instead, he stood there with his gun still up while his gaze kept darting to the dripping jug.

"That's what happens when you drink that shit. You end up dead like Jayce," she said.

Brady nodded. "He should have run when the cop showed up. He should have taken off like I did. But instead, he shoots the jug and starts drinking. I came back as soon as I could, but it was too late. He'd already drunk it. They were already fighting."

It took a few moments for her to understand Brady's words. "You and he were transporting the goo?"

"Yeah."

"And then a cop showed up?" Her gaze went to the grizzly. Sure enough, she could see the chain around his neck that held his police badge. It was the only part of his clothing that wasn't in tatters on the floor. But she still couldn't quite believe what Brady had done. "You shot a cop?"

Brady nodded, his expression miserable. "I didn't know what to do. Jayce was crazy. I had to stop him."

Holy shit! There was only one grizzly-shifter on the force, and that was Detective Ryan Kennedy. Goddamn it! He was one of the good guys, and now Brady had shot him? She headed for the downed bear, barely remembering to move slow. She didn't want to spook her pack mate.

"Keep back!" Brady ordered. "He's drugged, too!"

That didn't track. First off, the bear hadn't acted crazy. A shifter on the green goo would have kept beating on Jayce, even after the wolf was a corpse. Second, the grizzlies were the first ones to figure out that the Detroit flu was caused by a contaminant in the water. The No Drink order had gone out immediately, and word was the new guy Simon kept a tight rein on his people. The bears were the most sober shifters in the city right now, and that included her own pack.

"He's a cop. We have to help him."

She made it to Kennedy's side and was close enough to see that he was breathing. Still alive, so that was good, but he was also bleeding sluggishly from the two holes in his chest.

"He's a bear," Brady said, his tone stubborn. "Wolf said to kill any of them that we can corner in secret."

Frankie's head snapped up. Emory Wolf was her father and the alpha in the pack. He couldn't possibly have given so stupid an order. "He did not."

Brady's expression didn't waver. "He did."

Damn it. Her father had gone off the deep end then. She didn't want to believe it, but it had happened. A kill order on all bears was insane. Why go to war with The Griz? This had her brother Raoul's fingers all over it, but what the hell had happened to her father that he'd gone along with it?

She sat back on her haunches, pretending to obey her father's orders. In truth, she was trying to buy time to reason with Brady. She had to get him on her side so he would tell her where the serum stash was and she could end this nightmare forever. But she couldn't do that while appearing to help the bear.

"He's a cop," she said as she looked at Brady. "We don't hurt cops, remember?"

Brady winced. "Your father won't see it that way, and you know it."

A loyalist. She knew as much. Wolves were pack creatures and they remained loyal to a fault. Fact is, once a werewolf heard a direct order from his alpha, he or she was genetically conditioned to carry it out. Brady wasn't a killer, but once her father had ordered him to kill bears, his instinct drove him to do exactly that. It was a measure of his humanity that he kept himself from finishing the job.

"Okay," she said. "We need to talk, but we can't do it here. Let me take care of this, and we'll meet—"

"I can't talk to you. Raoul's orders. If he even smells you on me, he'll kill me."

Shit, shit, shit. Brady was her only chance to find out where her brother kept the serum supply. "I can call you."

"He's got bugs on our phones. He said so."

And her brother probably did. Then she hit on an idea. "Noelle. You can talk to Noelle, right?"

"'Course. She's my wife's sister."

"Then I'll send her. Tonight." She looked to the dark tunnel behind her. "I got people coming," she lied. "You don't want to be here when they show up."

His eyes widened. "What people?"

"Cleanup crew." She looked down at the cop. "We'll take care of this."

Brady shook his head. "I did it." His gaze cut to Jayce. "I need to face the consequences."

Well, that was decent of him especially since her father was going to skewer him—literally—for killing a pack mate.

"Don't be an idiot," she said. "Jayce was killed by the grizzly. You weren't anywhere near." Then she pretended to hear a noise behind her. "They're coming," she lied. "Go! I'll finish him off."

He wavered for a moment, then gave in. With a quick nod, he hurried over to the downed jug of goo, grabbed it, and then ran off into the dark tunnel. Which left her alone with the bear.

Finally! Now it was time to save the cop.

"Okay, Detective Kennedy—"

He attacked.

Chapter 3

Ryan surged forward, and the woman cried out in surprise as he tried to press his arm against her throat. His plan was to choke her until she was unconscious, then escape.

But he didn't have the dexterity and pain ate at his control. Plus, she wasn't just lying still. She fought him, her body slippery as she wriggled. Her knee came up hard between his thighs, but he barely noticed amid his other problems. His vision was going, which meant significant blood loss. Every breath was agony and his arms wouldn't work right.

"Trying. To help!" Her words were sharp explosions of sound right by his ear.

He didn't believe her, but it didn't matter. He couldn't incapacitate her, which meant his only hope was in running before her friends arrived.

"Shift!" she gasped, clearly struggling beneath his weight. "Human!"

It was the right move. If he shifted human, then his wounds would heal. That would stop the blood loss, but he'd be running around with two bullets in his chest. That was a recipe for disaster, but a later kind of problem. He'd also lose his fighting advantage, which was why she wanted him to do it. Much easier to kill a man than a grizzly.

"Hold. In between," she gasped. "Bullets. Will fall."

He didn't want to hear her. His attention was on forcing his body to do what he wanted despite the pain. But her voice triggered a softness inside him. He didn't have the time to understand the reason; he only knew that the notes of her voice became a kind of touchstone to safety. Some part of him knew this woman and admired her. So her words filtered in, and he chose to listen.

"Hold in between," she repeated, and he tried.

Shifting to human was a skill learned on the first shift. Not every shifter managed it, and he'd had more than the usual difficulties given that he hadn't had a clue what he was. But he had years of experience now, so this part was easy. He pictured in his mind exactly who he was. Well, more like an idealized version of who he wanted to be: strong, powerful, and a master of his fate. The physicality of that was clear. After all, he'd been studying bodybuilder magazines since he was ten.

He held that image now. Sculpted muscles, hard jaw, and power in every line of his body. Then he changed into exactly what he saw.

"Go slow!"

Her words caught him just at the moment of transition. Weird since he wasn't even sure he had ears to hear, but he knew her meaning. He tried to reach for the in-between state, that place where his body was energy, neither bear nor man. Normally, the transition lasted a second at most, and he'd worked hard to shorten that time. But this time he stretched it out.

He held himself in the in-between as long as he could. A second? More? How long would it take gravity to pull the bullets out of him?

He solidified as a man. No longer buried in pain, his mind grabbed on to details. Sounds first. Her breath against his ear, his own heartbeat, then hers. A wave of weakness hit him, a sure sign that he'd been shifting too much lately. And then another nearly buried him, but he pushed it aside and focused on something else. A smell hit him, hard and nauseating. Blood. His blood on her body. She was covered in it.

His bear surged forward, dark and ugly. It was pure instinct and he didn't have the energy to hold back the animal drive when it was set on survival. It believed she was a threat, and the most he could do was keep it from killing her. He had to subdue her so his bear would feel safe. And then he could figure out his next step.

He felt her move, shoving against him. His muscles contracted, breath flowed in, and then—finally—his vision solidified. He saw her clearly. Bright green eyes, light brown curls shorn short, and clear skin except for a mole high on her left cheek just to the outside of her eye. It looked like a brown teardrop on a face that otherwise would be deemed perfect. Damn it, he was sure he knew her!

The mole told him she wasn't a shifter. She might be related to one since she was obviously in on the shifter secret. But those who could change into an animal rarely came back to human with moles. It didn't help him place her identity, but it meant he could beat her man against woman.

He attacked. His rational mind said she was a friend, but instinct burned hot and his bear felt very vulnerable.

He caught her by surprise, and though his hand slid on her wet skin, he was able to grab hold. But he wasn't able to keep it as she jerked her elbow forward, missing his nose, but nailing his forearm. He lost his grip, then rolled with the movement to brace himself on the ground. Then he shoved hard, pushing himself upright. A split second later, he had his feet under him, but she was standing as well. A quick scan of the sewer told him no one was near, though his nose told him there was a hybrid close. The things smelled worse than the sewer, which was saying something. But the best news came when he saw two bullets on the ground.

His bullets. The ones that had been shot into his grizzly body were now on the bloody floor. Which meant no lead inside his human body.

Hallelu—

She hit him broadside with a kick faster than should be possible for a normal human. His breath gusted out of him, but he was already countering the move with one of his own. She blocked it—damn she was *really* fast—but he followed up with more. Blow after blow, she kept countering his punches. Part of him struggled to think. Why was she here? Did he know her? But he was at the end of his strength with nothing but animal instinct keeping him upright. Fortunately, this fight wouldn't last long. She didn't have the strength to keep up the fight. Not when every one of his blows had more weight behind it. She could block him, but his power was taking a toll on her.

She started to visibly flag. Her blocks were slower, her body collapsed more with every impact. Just a couple more hits and he'd be able to pin and handcuff her. Then he could think. He redoubled his efforts, trying to end this quickly. There were others coming. She'd said so, but his peripheral vision told him they were alone for now.

Last hit and she should go down. He put everything he had into it, swinging with all his might.

And caught air.

What?

She'd been fooling him, pretending to tire. He watched in horrified shock as she zipped out from under his swing, pivoted, and slammed him in the back when he was off balance. She didn't need power to topple him. He was doing that all by himself as his momentum kept him driving forward and down.

He hit the tunnel's concrete hard enough to see stars. And then she was on him, pinning his back with her knee as she slid a very sharp knife to his throat.

"Move and you're dead," she said, her voice a low growl.

He wasn't moving. And though his animal was screaming for him to fight, he hadn't the strength. Only a dull pounding in his head as he sucked air, and the gray fog of confusion.

"Fucking grizzlies never think," she said. "I was trying to help you."

Bullshit. That response was pure instinct. He'd learned not to trust anyone.

"Are you sane?" she pressed. "How much tap water did you drink?"

Yes and none. But he hadn't the breath to respond.

"Damn it, Kennedy. You're supposed to be one of the smart ones." She shoved her knee into him hard, and he grunted from the sudden pressure. "I need you to get a message to your alpha."

It took a moment for her words to penetrate. His rational mind was holding on by a thread. Fortunately, she didn't need his response to keep talking, and he used her voice to keep himself conscious. There was something about her voice...

"There's a kill order on bears, but only if you're caught alone. Tell your people to stay together until this is over. Nobody alone."

He was alone, and she wasn't slicing his throat. "Who...are you?"

"Somebody who is trying to help." She eased up on his back. "You were supposed to figure that out by now."

He had to buy time until he could think. Keep her talking until he figured out who she was. "Anonymous tips are dangerous," he mumbled.

She straightened off his back. He forced himself to get up, recruiting all his focus to shove onto all fours then scramble awkwardly to his feet. His head was pounding, his body weak, and he kept expecting to be clocked in the back of the head. He wasn't. She even stepped back enough to give him room, but when he finally turned to look her in the eye, he saw that she was as wary as he was.

"Well," she drawled, "I can see that you haven't been drinking the water. You look like shit."

That's what came from being shot and pushing how often he shifted. He'd gone grizzly so much in the last week, it was a personal record. "You look familiar," he said.

She ducked her chin. "I just have one of those faces." She sounded mournful about that, but he didn't believe it for a second. She was trying to hide who she was, and that made him want to pay ten times more attention.

Her face was sweet looking. Very girl-next-door, but with a hard edge to go with her ruler-straight nose. In fact, the only softness in her face was her full lips, which she pressed tightly closed as if holding back her words. And now that he looked at her closely, her entire body seemed compressed, like a super ball just before the bounce. So much restrained energy. It made him want to poke her just to see how big the explosion would be.

"Whoa there," she said as she abruptly gripped his arm.

He frowned down at her relatively small hands, wondering what she was talking about. But then a wave of dizziness hit, and he had to grab her arm just to keep upright.

"Great," she said as she guided him to lean against the wall. "I get the one shifter in all of Detroit who is about to pass out."

"I'm fine," he said, but the words came out slurred. Oh hell. He really was fucked up.

"And I'm Annie Oakley. Come on. Let's get you topside."

Sounded like a great idea to him, except when he took a step, it was all he could do to keep from tipping over. She caught him with her shoulder, planting it square into his chest. He grunted as she connected, but he was able to take a few more steps this way.

Then he inhaled. Oh hell. He could smell it clear as day. "Hybrid. Coming."

She looked at him, and her expression shut down even more. "This way."

He didn't bother nodding. It took too much energy away from putting one foot in front of the other.

Chapter 4

$\mathbf{A}$re you crazy?"

Yes, she was, Francesca thought as she stood outside her car. It was crazy to bring a man to their secret "book club" location. Worse that the man was a grizzly-shifter and a cop. But when Detective Kennedy had passed out in her car, she could think of only one safe place to take him. Here. Hazel's secret dojo PLACE, which stood for "Private Library and Cosmetics Emporium." And then she'd begged Hazel—the closest thing to a mother she had—to come out of the dojo to help her.

Except Hazel had been more worried about the blood on Frankie's clothes than the unconscious man in the front seat. Hazel had reason to not like men.

"Why's he naked?"

"Because his clothes were ripped off when he shifted." The remains of his shoes, pants, and boxers were in the sewer. She hadn't seen any shirt, but that was because it was probably in fragments in the water. All that was left on his body was the detective's badge dangling from a chain around his neck. It had remained on the bear and the man, though it was barely recognizable now beneath all the blood.

"He belongs in a hospital," Hazel stated.

"Are you sure?" Francesca pressed. The woman had once been an army nurse and had medical experience. "I think it's exhaustion. You know, from shifting too many times." She winced. "He also got shot by, um, someone who shouldn't have shot him."

Hazel grimaced as she gingerly stretched forward to take the detective's pulse. "You wolves are shooting cops now?"

"I'm not. I'm trying to save the guy."

"A cop shifter." Then Hazel gasped as she put the pieces together. The woman was sharp as a tack. "Is this Detective Kennedy? Your idiot crush from three years ago?"

"He was not an idiot crush! He's a smart shifter who was helping the community, and so I told people. He was doing—"

Hazel pointed an arthritic finger at her. "Right there. That's the idiot part. Good God, what you did to that poor man, and he didn't even know why he was a target."

She blew out a breath, her temper fraying. It had already been a long day in a very long few weeks. "Are you going to help me with him or not? He just needs a place to rest."

"He's a cop! I can't have him here."

Fair point. PLACE often housed runaway wives and children. The organization survived in part because she and Hazel kept law enforcement and crazy husbands completely in the dark as to its real nature. Everyone referred to it as a "book club," the sign read "Private Library and Cosmetics Emporium," and no one ever brought an adult male here.

Until today.

"We'll just keep him away from everyone. That's what the attic's for."

"You going to haul him up there?" Hazel blew out a breath. "Why didn't you take him back to the Griz?"

"Because I would have been spotted. Now are you going to help me—"

"All right. All right. Go get the wheelchair." She grimaced. "And a blanket to cover him up." She looked around the parking lot. Francesca had slid her Prius into a secluded area surrounded by fences and topped by trees. But you never knew who might be spying, and they had reason to be careful.

She started to head back inside while Hazel unbuckled Detective Kennedy. She was halfway to the door when the woman grunted.

"Make it a really big blanket. Geez, bears are huge."

Frankie snorted. She'd been the one to half carry, half drag the guy to her car. She knew exactly how impressively he was built. He'd make a great ally, if she could get him on her side. If not, then she'd…what? Kill him per her father's orders? She shuddered in horror at the thought. War or not, she was not going to kill anyone. She'd just have to convince Kennedy to help her all while keeping him off her pack's radar.

By the time she got outside with the wheelchair and the largest blanket they owned, Hazel had maneuvered his legs out and was trying to wake the guy with none too subtle slaps on the face. "Come on, fuzz face, wakey wakey." She turned to wink at Francesca. "'Cause he's the fuzz."

Francesca laughed at the old-fashioned term for cop. "You know the sixties were a really long time ago."

"Not in my heart. Come on, Detective Fuzz."

"Stop it," Francesca said as Hazel was getting more aggressive with her face taps. "I can get him." As the child of a shifter, she was slightly stronger than the average woman. As a newly formed hybrid, she was scary strong. She edged Hazel out of the way, braced Detective Kennedy against her, and hauled him out of the car.

"Don't do that out here!" Hazel said in an urgent whisper as she held the wheelchair in place. "Someone could see that you've changed."

Anyone with a good nose could tell. It was only because they'd been down in the sewers that Kennedy hadn't realized she was the newest form of shifter monster. She set him down in the chair then they wheeled him inside, but she balked at climbing four flights of stairs with him as deadweight. She was strong, but no one was that strong.

"We'll just have to wait until he wakes."

"Put him in the back of the coat closet. It's summer. No one goes there now."

Francesca complied, though she worried about what he would think—and do—when he woke. Hazel peered over her shoulder.

"That's fine. Shut the door and get ready for class."

Francesca jolted. "Class? The city's on lockdown. No one's coming for class."

Hazel pinned her with a heavy stare. "You're here. I'm here. That means we have class."

Frankie shook her head. "I need to talk to Noelle." She was the only one who could convince Brady to go against Raoul. "Can you text her? Ask how she's doing? Something innocuous that doesn't reveal—"

"That you're the one asking. Yeah, I got it." Hazel pulled out her phone and whipped off a text. A moment later, she grunted as she got Noelle's response. "Says she's going to bed, and she'll kill anyone who wakes her or the boys right now."

"Yeah, the twins have the flu. Not the Detroit Flu, just the regular one." Frankie did some mental calculations. "I'll visit her in a couple hours and—"

"Excellent. You have time to train."

"I've been running nonstop," she said with a sigh. "Let's skip, okay?" It was a vain hope. She knew Hazel's answer long before it was spoken aloud.

"Your brother is stepping up his insanity. That means you train."

"I'm not fighting him. That would be suicide."

"You don't have to fight, just—"

"Delay," Francesca said the word with her. That was Hazel's mantra. Don't fight, delay. That meant getting in a surprise attack before getting the hell out of Dodge. It was the smart way to survive and had saved many of her students' lives. But that kind of strategy only went so far, especially with wolf-shifters like her brother. Escape worked in the short term, but he always found a way to get even. Always.

Best option was not to fight him at all, just manipulate everyone else to keep him in check. Then she was just one of many, not one standing alone in a dark alley against the most vicious werewolf she'd ever known.

She consciously relaxed her shoulders. That image alone was enough to terrify her into practicing. Because deep inside her nightmares was the sure belief that one day she would have to face Raoul, and she would die.

Chapter 5

Save me!

Pain burned through Ryan's ribs. His neck throbbed, his leg was on fire, and he was going to die. He knew that with a horror that choked him. Four hybrids were closing in on him. They were crazed and carrying a stench that made it impossible to breathe. Each sliced him with claws or teeth, their blows impossibly strong, and they never rested. Rabid animals sent to attack him by the one person who had sworn to protect him.

Save me!

He looked past his attackers to his alpha. Nanook stretched back against his chair with a bored expression on his face. Nanook was the Griz alpha and the person who'd promised to keep the Detroit bear-shifters safe. He was their leader and defender, and he alone had the mental power to control the crazed hybrids. But instead of pulling them away, Nanook had sent them to attack. Ryan's alpha had given the orders to kill him.

Why?

He knew the answer. It was because Ryan was a cop and he'd just discovered that Nanook sold guns and drugs to the Detroit gangs. Ryan had demanded he stop, had threatened to expose the whole organization. He'd gambled that Nanook's bond to his fellow shifters was stronger than his greed.

He'd lost that bet. Nanook had sent the hybrids to attack.

Save me!

Ryan couldn't fight anymore. He couldn't breathe, couldn't stand, and the smell. God, the smell! It didn't matter. No dead man breathed anyway. With his last strength, he submitted to his alpha. Even as he did it, he was ashamed of himself. What Nanook was doing was not only illegal in the normal sense, but anathema among shifters. No alpha betrayed one of his own, and yet, it was happening. And Ryan chose to submit.

His head dropped and tilted to the side, exposing his neck. It left him open to the hybrids, but Nanook controlled them. If he chose, he would stop them. And Ryan was too valuable to kill, right?

Right?

Nanook looked straight at him and did nothing.

Pain burst through his chest, explosion of impact. Bombs of agony. And then fire sliced through his thigh, ripping open muscles and vessels. Next came the cut to his arm, nearly tearing it off at the shoulder joint.

Betrayed.

Ryan collapsed, but the pain kept coming. The hybrids descended, eating him like the beasts they were. Nanook looked away. Ryan didn't even have the breath to scream.

He tried anyway.

He woke with a garbled cry. It came out as a gagged choke, but it jolted him awake. His gaze roamed wildly looking for a touchstone. Everything was dark, and he heard the grunting sounds of a fight. Not full dark. Light seeped around the seams of a doorway.

He closed his eyes and tried to breathe. It shamed him that he didn't want to go out into the light. Better to hide in the dark and heal. His ribs were on fire, his chest pulsing with a dull ache, and he couldn't move his neck. His head hung like a sack of potatoes, and he whimpered in shame.

Betrayed.

The word echoed in his head while he sat in agony in the dark. He needed to get his head on straight. He needed to figure out where he was and come up with a plan. But first, he needed to get the memory out of his head. He couldn't do jack shit while fighting ghosts.

He forced himself to relive the slash that had gutted his thigh, the impact on his arm that nearly ripped open his shoulder, and the way he had looked to his alpha Nanook, submitting to the bastard even though it would expose him to one of his attackers. And he remembered how Nanook had looked away.

His own alpha had betrayed him. Ryan had been a naïve idiot to think the shifter bond would overcome the bastard's greed. Nanook chose to kill his own clan mate rather than stop selling shit to the gangs. And now Ryan was stuck with nightmares and the absolute certainty that no one would ever have his back. Because no one ever had.

Thankfully Simon, his mate Alyssa, and the sane hybrid Vic had intervened and now Simon was the new head of the Griz. All done, trauma over, stand up and take a bow. Except Ryan didn't trust any of them. And now he was beaten all to shit and he didn't even know where the hell he was.

"The greatest mastery is a mind that lets go."

He whispered the mantra as he tried to release the echo of his nightmare. The same nightmare that haunted him every fucking time he closed his eyes. He hadn't slept more than an hour since Simon had taken over the Griz.

The chest pain was new. He pressed his hand to his torso and felt the impact of the two bullets from when he'd been down in the sewer. Hell. Now he had fresh trauma to add to his nightmare. And even though his human body was whole—he felt all around his chest to be sure—the mental ache was still there. And mental pain could feel damn real sometimes.

But at least he could breathe now. Which meant it was time to get off his ass and make an escape plan.

As prisons went, this was a piss-poor one. Now that his eyes had adjusted, he realized he was in a closet and sitting in a wheelchair. The last thing he remembered was the werewolf woman asking him if he could walk. How had he'd gotten from the sewer to here?

He pushed up from the wheelchair, his entire body aching and cold. A blanket fell off his naked body, but at least his badge still hung around his neck. It was the only piece of attire that had survived him going grizzly in the sewer. Lord, he felt like he carried a thousand extra pounds. He half stumbled, half walked to the front of the closet. It was a slanting one built in the space beneath a staircase, and the door hadn't been shut properly.

He listened closely before pushing it open. More grunts and then a thud.

"You need to use your strength," a woman said. "You're holding back."

"I'm being stealthy," someone else snapped in reply. He knew that voice. It was the woman from the sewer. And he knew her, not just from the sewer, but from before. Who was she?

"You're being a coward."

Ryan winced. Those were fighting words among werewolves. They were the smallest of the predator shifters, but they more than made up for it in viciousness. Being called a coward was one of the worst things one could say to a werewolf, but the woman just snorted her response.

"I'm not as strong as they are. It's stupid to attack that way."

"It's stupid to have strength and never use it." He heard the heavy stomp of a foot on a mat. "Again!"

Combat practice, probably hand to hand. And while they were busy beating each other up, he'd slip away and call for backup. He eased through the door, stepping silently on the hardwood floor. The slats were uneven and probably creaked. He chose to step right next to the wall to minimize the risk.

Narrow hallway, old home. Front door to his right, studio to his left, stairs behind him. He smelled a kitchen and old spaghetti sauce. Also books. There was traffic noise and light coming in around heavy curtains. Whoever lived here valued privacy.

The combat training was in the back, so best he ease out the front. He'd taken two steps when he heard a voice.

"Where you going, Detective Kennedy?" The wolf woman's voice.

He straightened and turned to see his captor. She stood with her hands on her hips in the studio doorway. She'd been the one training. He could tell by the sheen of sweat on her skin, much of which was revealed by her outfit of tight sports bra and sleek leggings. Her short-cropped hair curled about her temples and her eyes were alight with humor.

She looked like one of the porn pictures he'd particularly enjoyed as a teen. Athletic body, full breasts, beautiful skin, and dripping with sexual hunger. Well, this woman wasn't exactly dripping anything but amusement, but her body was built along the same sexy lines, and his mind couldn't help but supply the details of what was currently covered in Lycra.

Her eyebrows went up in surprise as her nostrils flared. And then a fit woman in her sixties stepped into the light and blew out a low, appreciative whistle.

"And here I thought I'd seen everything," she said. "Never expected to see a naked cop with an erection in my front hallway, but there you go. I can die happy now."

Ryan had been focused on his injuries, on the echoes of pain that were almost as real as the dull ache throughout his torso. He wanted to be able to fight if he needed to. It didn't bother him that he was naked. Shifters tended to forget that stuff, but the way the two women were looking at him made him feel like a teenage boy who'd walked into the wrong locker room.

He jerked his hands down to cover himself, but the abrupt movement set off a wave of dizziness that made him stumble. He felt his shoulder hit the wall and he grunted in pain.

"Whoa there, Five-O," the older woman said as she grabbed his arm. "No need to be embarrassed. That's a mighty fine penis you got there."

"Hazel!" the wolf woman snapped. She'd made it to his other side with lightning speed. Or had he blacked out there for a moment? It was hard to tell. "You're dead on your feet, Detective. You need to sit back down."

"You're wanted for questioning," he said, imbuing his voice with all the strength he had. "Call the precinct. Tell them I'm here and call it a…" What was the code for emergency? Or officer in trouble? Hell, why couldn't he remember? He'd memorized all of them by the age of eight. "Tell them—"

"Let's get him upstairs," the wolf woman said over him. Then the two women started maneuvering him toward the base of the stairs.

He tried to resist, but he hadn't the strength. Damn, his head was spinning. "No!" he said, pleased that his voice had some power to it. "I need to make a call."

"You can do that upstairs," the wolf woman said.

"God, he's heavy," the older woman said with a grunt.

Yeah, he was. Close to 240 pounds, most of it muscle and bone. And right now, he wasn't supporting himself. His damn knees kept folding like wet origami. Which meant the bulk of his weight was on the wolf woman who was handling him as if he were a ninety-pound weakling. That didn't make sense, but then nothing did right then. He thought he smelled hybrid, but that couldn't be right. She was obviously a shifter—had to be—but she wasn't in wolf face now. As a human, she shouldn't be able to manage him so easily.

Then the older woman stumbled. Tripped over something in the hall, and her support was gone. He tried to help. If his legs didn't work, then he sure as hell could use his hands.

No go. There was nothing to grip and nowhere to go but down. Except he didn't. All of his weight was on the wolf woman and she kept moving him steadily toward the stairs.

That was scary strong.

"Set me down," he huffed. "I'm going…to crush you."

"Climb the stairs," she ordered.

She wasn't going to give up, and he didn't have the brainpower to figure it out. "Call. Cops." Or maybe… "The Griz."

She shot him a hard look. "Climb!" There was command in her voice, an authority that would not be disobeyed, and he felt a surge of strength in his body as he rallied. But he wasn't going up the stairs. He needed out of here. Back to safety.

His head swam. "No. Call the Griz."

"It's not like I have their number on speed dial."

She paused and leaned him against the wall. She wasn't even breathless, and that should tell him something. Something important, but he couldn't hold on to it. He was too busy holding on to the wall.

"I would love to call the Griz and have them pick you up, but they can't come here and you're in no shape to go to them."

"Put me in a cab."

She nodded. "That would work, but I need your help. I want you to stop the person responsible for the Detroit Flu. And you can't do that if you're laid up in the back of Griz Hardware."

The Griz home base used to be an Ace Hardware store, so the nickname had some merit. He still didn't like it.

"Who's responsible?"

"Raoul Wolf."

He grimaced. "Nanook was right. It is the wolves."

"Not the wolves. *One* wolf. Raoul."

"Proof."

She threw up her hands. "If I had the proof, I wouldn't need you, now would I?"

He dropped his head back against the wall. The clunk added to a headache he hadn't even noticed before. "What can I do?"

"Arrest Raoul before the war starts."

He frowned. "What war?"

"Wolves against bears. You're going to die, then we're all screwed."

He snorted. "Bring it on, wolf. We'll see who gets bloody."

She stepped backward to lean against the stair railing, her eyes infinitely sad. "I thought you were different," she said quietly.

Meanwhile, the older woman snorted. "Told you. I don't know why you're messing with him. Only chance is with the Griz women."

"They're all snobby bitches who won't lift a finger against their men."

Ryan frowned. Protecting your man was a good thing. Man, woman, holding together against the storm. But his mind was churning on her earlier statement. "Different than who? How do you know me?" He straightened as much as he could against the wall. "Who the hell are you?"

"Don't tell him!" the older woman huffed. "Let's put him in a cab and send him away."

"I need him!" the wolf woman responded. "He's the only shifter cop in Detroit. Anybody else is going to require proof against Raoul."

He narrowed his eyes, really focused on her face. His memories were foggy, but he was able to put the pieces together. She was a wolf-shifter. She was high enough in the werewolf hierarchy to know who was responsible for what. And since he made it his mission to know his adversary, he ran through the wolf family tree to find a woman. Someone who hid in the background but was—

"You're Frankie, the bastard daughter." How the hell had he missed that before?

He'd only met her once, but she'd stuck out. She'd been the driving force behind a new community center in the heart of werewolf territory. She'd lobbied the city, raised money for it from all over the state, and put together a design with careful forethought. He'd met the staff and had been impressed by their qualifications, but none had held a candle to the quiet efficiency of Francesca Wolf. She was charming, beautiful, organized, and determined. All qualities he admired. When he saw her at the ribbon-cutting ceremony, he'd been struck with a physical need to be with her.

He'd planned to ask her out right then and there, but he hadn't had the opportunity during the festivities. He'd been willing to break normal shifter lines and date a werewolf even though he was a bear. But that was also the day his work problems in the robbery department began. Before long, he had too many of his own issues to deal with to think of adding romantic entanglements on top.

"I'm not a bastard," she stated with force.

Touchy subject? The rumor mill said she'd never shifted and therefore had to be a bastard. Since Emory had never contradicted the rumor, the idea stuck. Well, Ryan now could say with certainty that Frankie was no shifter slouch. Anyone who could support his body weight had to be a full shifter.

"And that doesn't matter," she said, her voice tight with anger. "Do you want to stop the Detroit Flu or not?"

That was an easy answer. "I do."

"So, arrest Raoul."

"On what grounds?"

"I don't care. Make something up. Whatever it takes, just get him off the streets for a few days."

He arched his brow. "And then what?"

"And then I'll get the proof you need to lock him up forever. He's the cause of the Detroit Flu. I swear it." Then when he didn't say anything, she pushed it further. "That's why I was in the sewer. I was getting proof, but then you got shot and I had to save your ass."

He stared at her, fury boiling up. Detroit was in crisis. There had been at least a dozen deaths, a ton more injuries, and the National Guard surrounded the city to keep it in quarantine. The entire city had been brought to its knees by this poison. And why? For a fucking wolf power play.

He didn't know if Raoul had indeed poisoned the city or if it had been werewolves working in concert. Didn't matter. As far as he was concerned, the whole pack was responsible. That's how shifters worked. The pack took responsibility for every member's actions. And that Frankie here would use a citywide crisis to make a play for power within the werewolf ranks made him sick to his stomach.

But that was wolves for you. The Borgias had nothing on the machinations inside a werewolf pack. He straightened to his full height. At least the dizziness was over. He felt stronger now.

"Sure, I'll help you. Tell me where Raoul is." It wasn't a lie. He absolutely intended to arrest Raoul, her, and any other werewolf he could charge.

She grimaced. "I don't know."

Of course not. "Get me a phone. I'll call it in anyway."

She blew out her breath. "You need to do it. He's a werewolf. He's too dangerous for normal people."

Plus, over half the force was out puking up their guts from the Detroit Flu. "I'm hardly in a fit state here." He sagged against the wall for effect, then realized that he really did appreciate the extra support.

She winced. "That's why I brought you here. So you can rest in privacy. I need to explain things to you. And you need to tell the Griz not to go to war yet." She sighed. "And not get caught alone. The wolves are going to attack you."

That was a lot of information coming at him fast, but he got the gist of it, especially since he remembered hearing some of it when they were in the sewer. "We already know you're responsible," he said. "And we figured any pack insane enough to poison a city was going to be crazy enough to attack the Griz for exposing you." He paused. "So get me a damned phone and I'll take care of Raoul for you." What he was going to do was get the Griz to come take this woman and this house by force. And then, when he wasn't dead on his feet, he could arrest the whole pack for their idiocy and watch them get prosecuted to the fullest extent of the law.

"Ah hell," the older woman interrupted. She'd been hanging back, letting him and Frankie have their say, but now she was looking through a crack in the heavy curtains beside the front door. "It's too late. We got wolves already here."

Frankie jolted. "What? Who?"

"Like I know one dog from the other? I just know that walk and that car."

Frankie quickly peered through another break in the curtains. "That's Delphine, Raoul's woman, and she's come to bring you in." Her expression turned anguished. "Hazel, you have to get out of here. They know you're my friend. They know—"

"They know jack shit. Now get him upstairs. I'll deal with Miss Fancy Pants."

Chapter 6

Frankie grabbed Detective Huge Disappointment and started dragging him upstairs whether he wanted to go or not. The last thing she needed was for Hazel to be caught harboring a naked grizzly bear. And damn it, Delphine was likely to kill the guy on sight—or at least try to—and then Frankie would be forced to defend him, and the shit would really hit the fan.

She drew on her hybrid strength to haul him upstairs. She didn't go ugly-faced to do it, but it took all her focus to keep her abilities under control. Didn't the man have an ounce of fat? No, the guy was all muscle, which was lovely to look at but he weighed a ton. By the time they reached the top of the stairs, they were both panting. But then she looked at his face.

Oh hell. He wasn't being stubborn. The guy really was holding on by a thread. His face was pale, and his breath came in sketchy pants. But the real tip off was that he felt unnaturally cold. That was a telltale sign of a shifter who'd burned through way too much of his energy. He didn't have the strength to heat his own body. "Just how often have you been shifting lately?" Not to mention that brutal fight with Jayce and getting shot a couple times. It was a wonder the guy was standing at all.

He didn't answer, not that she expected him to. There was no way they could get to the attic now. She'd just have to pray that the second floor was hidden enough. So she maneuvered him into the nearest bedroom, recently vacated by an abused mother and her three kids. She and Hazel had managed to get the family out before the quarantine, thank God, so that left the large bed and two cots conveniently empty.

She helped him sit on the nearest cot, then took a moment to check his pulse and study his gorgeous blue eyes. Well, those were still pretty, and at the moment they were focused on her face. How could a guy on the verge of passing out have eyes that seemed crystal bright?

"I'm trying to help," she said as the doorbell rang.

"Then get me a phone."

Her cell was downstairs. She'd taken it off to spar with Hazel, and now she was up here without any way to call for help. "It's a delicate situation. I want us to work together."

He arched a brow. He looked like Spock in a very sexy Vulcan moment. Which was when she was forced to see the logic of the situation.

She'd wanted to manage this carefully so as to get the fewest number of people killed. But maybe that was walking too fine a line. And bears were not known for their finesse, though she'd hoped Detective Kennedy was different.

"Fine," she finally said. "Right after Delphine leaves, okay? But you have to listen to the full story."

He nodded, though it might have been because he was too weak to keep his head upright. The doorbell rang again, and she heard Hazel respond like the old woman she definitely was not.

"I'm coming! Geez, my knees don't work so well anymore, you know?"

That was total bullshit. Hazel's knees worked fine, even though she'd just celebrated her sixtieth birthday. She was giving Frankie time to hide the detective. Plus, she probably enjoyed making Delphine wait. Frankie liked it, too, since she knew Delphine was a two-faced, backstabbing bitch.

The doorbell rang a third time and Hazel started undoing the locks. Every click sounded loud to Frankie's enhanced hearing while she maneuvered herself to see everything that went on downstairs. Hazel had set up a large mirror in the hallway, angled just right so someone in the bedroom could watch while still hidden behind carefully placed furniture. She saw clearly when Hazel opened the door to confront Delphine. The woman's expression was vaguely bored as she stood there dripping with costume jewelry and wearing skintight leggings and a loose blouse that accentuated her curves. It had one more advantage, too. Clothing that stretched or ripped told everyone she could go wolf anytime. Sure, the witch had shifted only once during her teens, but that put her well ahead of Frankie who—until recently—hadn't done anything more than stand there and look stupid.

"Yes?" Hazel asked, her voice weaker than usual.

"You're Hazel Smith, right?" Delphine asked. Then she continued without waiting for an answer. "You're supposed to come to the community center. And where's Frankie? She needs to hightail it there, too."

Frankie's body tensed. Her compulsion to be seen was pushing her to boldly confront Delphine and tell the bitch what she thought. But that was stupid, especially if Hazel could handle things herself. Still, the need was like a physical itch under her skin.

"We're supposed to stay inside," Hazel said. "There's a quarantine on. Don't you listen to the news?"

Delphine pursed her perfect lips. "Of course, I listen to the news."

Frankie rolled her eyes. "Not unless *The Real Housewives* counts."

"That's why you're supposed to come to the center. So we can protect you."

"I can protect myself," Hazel said, as she tried to close the door.

Delphine was faster than that. She caught the closing door with the flat of her hand and held it open. The woman may have shifted only once, but she had a shifter's strength. Hazel wasn't going to win that fight.

"You're a valued part of our community," Delphine said, her voice so bored, she sounded like she was reading off a cue card.

"I'm sure I am," Hazel snorted. "Thanks, but—"

"You're coming, Hazel. No argument." Her expression didn't change, but her tone was chilling. "Now go get Frankie. I've wasted enough time on that girl's silliness." She made it sound like she was waiting on a petulant child.

Frankie muttered under her breath, "We're the same fucking age, bitch."

The detective chuckled, his voice equally low. "You kiss your mama with that mouth?"

She shot him a glare, but he just raised that sexy eyebrow. Damn Hazel for making her watch *Star Trek* reruns. That expression totally worked for her. Meanwhile, Hazel was standing her ground.

"Frankie left to make the rounds of the Galster apartment building. Most folks there are pretty sick. She's helping out."

"Bullshit. She's here. I can smell her."

Hazel nodded. "She was here, then she left. Check with Noelle, apartment 6E. Those twins are tag-teaming the vomit."

Delphine's response was to sniff in disdain as she stomped inside the house. Hazel could have stopped her, but she was playing weakling right now. She always said to pick your fights carefully. Apparently, she wasn't ready for a showdown with Delphine.

"Why does it smell like a sewer in here?" Delphine asked.

"Probably because Frankie's been helping out with the sick kids."

Detective Kennedy's voice rumbled in her ear. "Or crawling through the sewer."

His voice sent shivers down her spine. Something about the note of humor in his gravelly voice was really sexy. In an annoying kind of way. "*And* helping out with the kids," she said in a low whisper. Last thing she wanted was for Delphine's shifter ears to hear her. But it was hard enough to stay hidden upstairs, she couldn't keep silent when Kennedy pushed her. "Do you know how many times I've been thrown up on lately?"

He wavered where he sat on the cot. Damn, he was really in a bad way. There was perspiration on his upper lip, and she reached out to steady him. Meanwhile, Delphine was sniffing her way deeper into the house.

"Who else is here with you?"

"No one now," Hazel said. "I'm still cleaning upstairs. Norma puked up an entire pizza. I sent her home yesterday, but it's hard on my knees to climb up there." She grabbed hold of Delphine's arm.

"You'd do me a kindness if you'd help me clean it up. I got a bucket and mop in the closet. I just got too tired, you know?"

The detective shifted uncomfortably on the cot. Probably preparing to fight if Delphine came upstairs.

"Don't worry," she whispered. "Delphine's got an uber-sensitive nose. She won't come within a hundred miles of vomit if she can help it." It probably helped that neither of them smelled fresh. She'd cleaned up after putting Kennedy in the closet, but Delphine's nose was really sharp.

Sure enough, the woman turned her perfectly sloped nose toward the stairs and immediately looked away. "No thanks," she huffed. "Look, just call her, will you? Her brother's worried about her."

Not true. The only brother who ever worried about her was dead under suspicious circumstances. That was two years ago, and soon afterward, Frankie had learned to make herself scarce.

"You want Frankie, you go get her." Hazel gestured down the street. "It's just a couple blocks away."

"Call her."

Hazel folded her arms over her chest. "I'm not the one who needs to talk to her." That, plus, Frankie's phone was downstairs. Leaving it there had been a major mistake.

Delphine sniffed again. "Why does everyone have to be so difficult?" She pulled out her cell phone and stabbed at it with a blood red nail. Eventually, she put it to her ear. "She's at the Galster Street property. Apartment 6E. Go get her."

Frankie winced. Noelle would not thank her if Delphine's goons woke the twins. Meanwhile, Delphine gestured to the front door. "Come on, Hazel. Get in the car. I'll drive you."

"I'm staying right here."

Frankie felt her hackles rise at Hazel's tone of voice. She'd lost the quavering old lady act and had shifted into bring-it mode. She was obviously tired of the supercilious bitch and was ready to kick ass. And not being stupid, Delphine recognized the change in attitude.

"Don't be an idiot," Delphine said. "Raoul wants to talk to you." She made an attempt at charming with a pretty smile that didn't touch her eyes. "Look, this really is for your own safety. We consider you one of us, so we protect you. But we can't patrol blocks and blocks of territory. It's too dangerous for both you and our men. Much better for everyone if you come with me, okay?"

"I don't know…" Hazel blew out a breath as if she were considering it.

Frankie wasn't fooled, but Delphine was. She was just rolling her eyes when Hazel shoved her hard. The door was open, so Delphine went stumbling backward in her designer sandals. Not bad enough to fall, but enough to get her past the threshold and onto the concrete steps. Then Hazel grabbed hold of the door and slammed it shut.

Or she tried to. Hazel was fast, but apparently, Delphine was faster. She blocked the door with one hand. She didn't have the strength to send Hazel flying, but the door sure as hell didn't slam shut. Frankie tensed, raising up onto her feet. She could be down there in a shot, but Hazel bellowed straight into Delphine's face.

"Stay back!"

The message appeared to be for Delphine, but Frankie knew it was meant for her. Hazel didn't want her running to the rescue. And given that the older woman was a master in Aikido, not to mention a few other martial arts, Hazel probably had it under control. Still, her muscles twitched with the need to confront Delphine. Detective Kennedy, too, apparently, because he was already on his feet.

"Stop," she hissed right in his face, the words as much for herself as him. "She can handle herself."

His eyes blazed into hers, but she completely blocked his path. If he wanted to go downstairs, it would have to be through her. And then they heard a thump on the stairs, hard enough to rattle the floor where they stood.

As one, they turned to see what was going on, and Frankie couldn't resist an inner grin. Delphine lay sprawled on her side on the stairs. Her blouse was untucked, and her eyes were wide with surprise. Hell, even her makeup was visibly smudged.

Frankie could guess what had happened. Hazel had abruptly released the door. Given the pressure Delphine was putting on it, she must have flown forward, tripped over Hazel's perfectly placed foot, and landed on the stairs.

"I said, no," Hazel said calmly. Then she adjusted her position so she was framed in the open doorway. Frankie knew what was going to happen next. In a fit of pique, Delphine was going to surge forward to grab Hazel by the throat. Hazel would duck at the last second, and Delphine would be out on her ass. Door slam, bolts thrown, then Hazel would threaten to call the cops. It wasn't much of a threat since the cops were overloaded, but no way would Delphine go to more drastic methods to take Hazel. She'd stomp away to fix her makeup in the car.

No problem.

Frankie even relaxed, anticipating the show.

She saw Delphine's body tense while Hazel's grew calm and centered. And then—

Oh shit.

Delphine shifted. Where one second there had been a prissy bitch sprawled on the stairs, now there was a golden-brown wolf in a loose blouse and leggings flying at Hazel's throat.

Hazel dodged, mostly because she'd been prepared, but she hadn't expected Delphine's speed or that she'd use claws, not hands. Hazel's jump landed her hard against the door, but there was no time to react. Delphine had already pivoted. Wolves were a hundred times faster on their feet than humans. She sprang at Hazel before anyone else could move.

If Delphine had wanted to go for Hazel's throat, Frankie's best friend would now be dead. Apparently, she wanted Hazel alive, so she clamped down hard on Hazel's upper arm. Hazel howled and beat down on Delphine's head with her fist, but it had no effect. And all the while, Hazel kept screaming.

"Stay back! Stay back!"

It was the only thing keeping Frankie upstairs. *Logic. Strategy.* The words had been burned into her since birth. It didn't help anyone if she ran to the rescue and exposed herself and Kennedy before she had the proof she needed to take her brother down. Besides Hazel could handle this, right? She was a martial arts master.

Except the more Frankie watched, the more terrified she felt for the older woman. No matter how much Hazel struggled, Delphine just kept her jaws clamped tight. Blood and saliva flew as Hazel tried one attack after another. Not just her free hand, she kicked as well, but the wolf hung on. Who knew the bitch could take a beating like that?

Hazel had to stop. Delphine was ripping the shit out of her arm. It was only a matter of time before she tore something vital.

"Stay back! Stay ba—" The last word ended on a scream as Delphine must have bit down hard. Had she broken bone?

Frankie lunged forward, but was stopped by Kennedy. He gripped her arm and spoke in a low tone. "Can you take out both of them? Are they going to kill her? Or just talk to her?"

Both of them? What the hell—

He gestured to the open doorway where Frankie's third cousin Wade was standing with a gun. He had it pointed casually down at Hazel and was obviously waiting for a pause in the action to shoot. The break came all too soon as Hazel froze, panting hard.

"Do I carry you, Hazel?" he asked. "She can snap your arm in half right now if you fight her. And she will."

"Stay back," Hazel said, and her words held strength for all that she was out of breath. "You can't drag me out of my own home." Oh God, the quiet defiance in those words broke Frankie's heart. Because they obviously could.

"You want to walk on your own two feet?"

There was a long pause as Hazel obviously considered her option. "Stay back," she repeated.

Damn it, the woman was fucking stubborn, warning Frankie to stay away, but she had a point. Even with all of Frankie's new abilities, she didn't think she could take on a werewolf and a gunman at once. Certainly not from all the way up the stairs. Wade would shoot her before she got three steps.

Then Delphine had to go and make it worse. She shook her head—teeth still deep in Hazel's arm—making the older woman cry out in pain.

"Come on, now," Wade said, his voice calm. "Please help us keep you safe."

"This is safe?" Hazel asked, her voice bitter. The community center couldn't be any worse than getting her arm torn up, but Hazel despised being told by anyone where to go or what to do. She created PLACE so women couldn't be forced to do anything they didn't want.

"You're the one being stubborn," Wade returned.

Eventually Hazel nodded. "I'll go. Just…let me get my purse."

"You won't need it," Wade said. Then he held out his hand as if he were a gentleman instead of a brute.

Hazel wouldn't touch him, so he grabbed hold of her free arm without her consent. And then Delphine released her jaws. Hazel hissed in pain, but she glared at the wolf.

"Stay back," and this time the message might have been for the wolf. Didn't matter. Wade hauled her to her feet, then all three marched out the door before Wade pulled it shut behind them.

Damn it!

Frankie twisted out of Kennedy's grip then rushed downstairs. She got to the door in time to see Hazel climb into the backseat of Delphine's car, her expression pale but still defiant.

Damn, damn, damn! What the fuck did Raoul want with Hazel? She was still considering her options when she heard a heavy clatter upstairs. Oh hell.

She dashed back upstairs to find Kennedy toppled half on the cot, half on the floor. His strength had finally given out.

Chapter 7

Frankie dropped down next to Ryan and saw that he wasn't just out cold. He looked like he was dying. His skin was gray, his breath shallow, and…she tried to feel for a pulse. Damn it, her own was racing so hard, she couldn't figure out what was his and what was hers.

Hazel was the one with medical experience, and she'd just been taken for God only knew what reason. Probably to get leverage on Frankie. She was the only one who threatened Raoul's control of the pack. Imagining the things Raoul might do to her had Frankie fighting panic, but she couldn't help her best friend right now, and she could help Kennedy.

But how?

He was just exhausted, right? She'd seen shifters push themselves too far. Hell, it was practically routine among the teenagers in her pack. So what was the procedure there? It took three breaths before she could remember. Her mind kept skittering back to what her brother might be planning for Hazel.

Focus!

First step, get Kennedy into a comfortable position. That meant rolling him onto his back, elevating his feet, and making sure he was warm enough. It took her a moment, but she managed it. Even got a pillow for his head and a blanket to cover him. A shame to cover all that muscled glory, but conserving his heat was important.

Second, check his vitals. He was breathing, but shallowly. When she pressed fingers to his neck, she couldn't find a pulse. But he was breathing, so his heart had to be beating, right?

She needed help. There wasn't anyone of her own pack to call. They'd kill him immediately and then tell her father that she was disobeying orders. She looked at the detective badge still around his neck. She wondered if the man slept in it. She ought to call the police or 911 for an ambulance, but exhaustion like this was unique to shifters. The wolves had learned long ago that what hospitals gave for exhaustion didn't help shifters. There was a nutrient or enzyme or something that shifters needed, and it wasn't in normal hospitals.

She had to call the Griz. His own people would know what to do, but the moment she did that, her anonymity was shot. Worse, it would mean publicly picking a bear over her own pack. No way would the bears keep her secret. They had no discretion.

At best, she'd become a werewolf outcast. At worse, they'd kill her for the aberration. Either way, she'd have no power whatsoever in her pack. No way to stop her brother or the poisoning of Detroit. She'd already garnered a lot of support to end her brother's influence on her father. She was close to a tipping point in numbers. But if she threw in with the bears, all of that would end. Worse, anyone who ever supported her would become suspect, and her brother would be vicious in pressing the advantage.

God, how the hell had it come to this? That she was choosing between a bear's life and stopping her brother? She swallowed. She should let him rest and hope for the best, except he didn't look like he was getting better. And every minute that she sat here with him was another moment that Hazel was left to manage on her own.

This was insane. She'd been raised from birth to weigh consequences, to check loyalties, and to never, ever betray the pack. Problems were managed from within, never from outside.

His breath rattled in his chest. Oh shit. That was bad. That was *really* bad.

She dashed downstairs to get her phone, her heart pounding in her chest. She hadn't even consciously decided to act when she found herself already doing it. She snatched up her phone and started dialing. It was a stupid phone number, a leftover from the old Griz alpha, but maybe it would still work. It was her only hope because she didn't know any other way to contact them.

1-800-THE-GRIZ.

A woman answered on the third ring.

"Hello?"

Frankie spoke low out of habit and because she was panting from sprinting back up the stairs. "Is this the Griz?"

"Yes, who's this?"

"You have to come." She rattled off the address as she set her hand to Kennedy's neck. Was that a pulse? "I think he's still breathing," she whispered. Yes, there was a definite rise to his chest. Maybe. "It's Detective Kennedy. Exhaustion, I think, from shifting too much. You know how to deal with that, right?" Wolves had an IV concoction specifically for that. Nutrients, calories, she didn't know what all was in it, but it worked great for their teenagers. She didn't have any of it here. "You have to bring an IV. He's bad. He's really bad."

"What IV? I don't understand."

Frankie winced. Didn't the damn bears know anything? "A nutrient IV for shifter exhaustion. Don't you have doctors?"

"I'm sending an ambulance."

"They can't help!" God, just how backward were these bears? "He needs the shifter IV with the enzyme or whatever. He'll die without it!" She was practically shouting at the end there, grabbing at the words that would most spur them into action. But the moment she'd voiced it aloud, she knew it was true. He was dying. Right there in front of her. His skin was ashen. There was more and more time between breaths. She couldn't feel a pulse.

She knew what she had to do. Even if the bears had exactly what he needed, there wasn't any more time. He was dying, and she had no choice. But, God, he was going to kill her when it was over. Assuming he survived at all.

"We're on our way!" the woman on the other line said.

They wouldn't get here in time. Not unless Frankie did what was necessary.

She thumbed the phone off. She'd need two hands for this. She waited a moment longer, scanning him from head to toe, praying that she would see signs that he was getting better. That he would hold on.

Was he breathing? Didn't look like it.

She ran into the back bedroom and used her nails to dig up the floorboard. Even Hazel didn't know this was here. A pouch with a vial and a hypodermic needle. The green goo in its injectable form. Earlier formula, thirty times more potent than what was being dumped in the water.

She knew the dosage. At least what it had been for her. So, with shaking hands, she inserted the needle and drew out the goo. She gave him a few more cc's because he was a lot bigger than she was. Then she ran back to his side just in time to hear the rattle. The body's last attempt to breathe on its own.

No more time.

She twisted Kennedy's arm and injected it straight into his vein. Then she dropped the hypodermic to the side and started CPR.

"Come on, you stupid bear," she huffed as she pushed down on his chest. She stopped and dropped down to his mouth. Was he breathing? She tilted his head, sealed her mouth over his, and breathed. Once. Twice. Back to chest compressions.

Was he breathing? Was his heart beating?

She was sweating as she tried to check. Pulse? Breath?

Come on, Kennedy!

She cupped his face again, tilting his face. One breath. Two. Then back to chest compressions. The goo couldn't help if his heart didn't pump it to every part of his body. She would have cursed him if she had the breath. Curse, threaten, plead, anything to keep him alive.

Fight for your life!

Back to his mouth. One breath. Two—

His gasp was dramatic as his whole body arched with the inhalation. He banged his head against her, and she reeled backward, her eyes watering from the pain.

She saw his body ripple as the blanket fell to the side. His naked body pulsed, and she watched it glow with a shift, even sprout fur, but the bones and structure of a man were visible beneath. That didn't happen normally as he seemed to be everything at once:

bear, man, and some in between state of energy. Fluid. Changeable. Beautiful.

His eyes found hers. She met his gaze, thinking to look for intelligence there. She had to know if he retained his mind. Was there sanity inside?

Instead, she found herself sinking into the golden depths. Swirls of blue and gold, patterns of energy coiling into infinity and bursting back out. She saw it, but she couldn't believe it. She remained transfixed by the sight.

What had she done to him?

Then came the roar. Agony made sound. His mouth stretched wide as his body convulsed. Grizzly furor, human aggression, an energy that jangled and beat at her skin. That was new, too, and it pervaded the entire room, but it was centered on her.

She scrambled backward in terror. She wanted to help him, but she didn't know what *he* was. Man? Animal? Something else entirely?

"I'm sorry," she whispered. "I'm so sorry."

The glow faded, and he looked fully human, but she saw his nostrils flare, and his expression tightened into something predatory. She'd lived with animals, and she knew the look. Hunger, desire, need—it all compressed into a single expression of body and mind. He stalked around the room.

When had he found his feet? When had he stood up while she cowered against a wall like a child?

"Kennedy," she bellowed, "get it together!"

She wanted to sound forceful. She wanted to declare her birthright as the daughter of an alpha. But no matter how strong her voice was, the power was an illusion. She was nothing when compared to him. He was prowling toward her. She could barely find the strength to stand. Her knees were shaking, and her heartbeat was spiking with adrenaline.

She would fight him. She had to.

He lunged for her, and she dodged.

"Ryan!" she cried. "Ryan!"

She had to reach the intelligence inside the beast, but he didn't seem to be listening. And while she took breath to say something else, he leapt again.

She scrambled, but he was faster. And he'd been expecting it.

He caught her around the waist and caged her against the wall.

Trapped.

No holding back. Not with his body pulsing with a new energy that seared her. Not with his mouth open and teeth that seemed to elongate with fangs. She let loose. Every part of her that she kept carefully hidden, every secret she held under strict control, every restraint she had for her safety and everyone else's—she let them all go.

Her body seemed to explode with power. Her face changed, her arms furred, and her hands became claws. The room filled with her scent—a defensive smell that would make him ill—and she roared in his face like the monster she was.

Full hybrid. Full fight.

He grinned—the joy of a man with normal teeth—as he inhaled the scent deep into his lungs.

WTF?

Then he came for her. She fought. She was well trained, and she gave it all to him. She began with swipes with her claws, which he batted away as if they were nothing. She punched with her elbow, ducked and kicked at his vulnerabilities. He blocked her. And when she was too fast, he simply absorbed the impact as if it were no more than a pesky fly.

He kept coming. Closer with his mouth stretched into a grin. Faster with legs that were stronger and quicker than she expected.

She redoubled her efforts. She landed blows on his chest, drew blood on his forearm, and she damn well slammed down hard on his foot. It was what she'd been taught. When he tried to grab her, she rolled with the flow of his attack until she'd twisted free.

And when she came up, she was grinning. Her animal was in full force now. Her human mind told her to run. It was the safest choice, but the monster inside her wasn't going anywhere. It wasn't afraid. It was happy, and that threw her human mind for a loop.

He sprang forward, she dodged. Or she thought she did. Instead, he caught her feet with his. Fouled her footing and entangled their legs until she crashed down on her bottom.

He pinned her before she could draw breath. And though she squirmed and fought, he was larger, stronger, and he…

He was licking her neck.

Instead of taking out her throat, he was scraping his teeth along the underside of her jaw.

WTF?

The shock of understanding briefly stilled her frantic movements. This wasn't an attack. This was animal courting, and now he was skating tiny licks across her collarbone. Nips as his teeth went lower.

Primitive urges surged forward, meeting and matching his. She was new to being a shifter, and when the animal exploded in her mind like this, she didn't know what to do. Hard enough to fight him, but when her own wolf nature tried to take control, she ended up fighting herself, too.

"Let go of him!" a voice bellowed.

Her gaze shot up to the doorway while Ryan bared his teeth and growled. He leapt off her and launched himself at the intruder. Another pair of footsteps sounded heavy on the stairs. Ryan already had the intruder plastered against the wall.

"Don't you fucking do it!" the other voice bellowed.

Frankie was on her feet now, too, rushing to face the other intruder. She had no thought except to defend herself and Ryan. She was nearly on him when she saw the gun, but it didn't stop her. She simply batted it aside as she closed with the enemy. The scent told her he was a hybrid. The shock on his face said he hadn't expected her to attack. And all of it was about to go ugly.

Chapter 8

Ryan fought against a cyclone of forces that tore at his mind and body. Words like "protect" and "mate" whispered through the maelstrom, but they were a pale shadow compared to the feelings that gripped him. The meaning was the same, but the reality of his needs was so much more powerful than two tiny words. He tried to fight the onslaught. At least beat it back so he understood what was happening.

He failed. The best he could do was ride the wave and hope to come out the other side.

He'd been on top of her—his mate—and then they'd been interrupted. He attacked, launching himself at the interloper. Some part of him heard the words. Something about getting away. Staying back. He didn't know, and it didn't matter.

He protected the female, and no rival was allowed near.

More sounds. Another male, this one a hybrid. He would take care of that one, too, but there was no need. His mate was strong, and she leapt upon the second interloper. She would dispatch him, and he would praise her with his body and his seed.

A sound cut through the air and his mate screamed. Electrical charge. A Taser. He knew the word and its meaning, but the message was drowned out beneath the fury. They attacked his mate. They would die.

He saw her crumple to the floor, her body twitching while the smell of ozone gave a bite to the air. He roared and rounded on the one with the Taser, but he had underestimated the first one. He'd thought the first one was defeated because the defense was weak. But the moment Ryan turned, strong arms gripped him about the neck and squeezed.

He fought. He snarled. He meant to kill, but the two worked together to stop him. One blocked his attacks, the other continued to choke him. And they both boxed him in tight in the hallway so that there was no room to maneuver. No way to fight. And all the while there were words.

"Calm down! Ryan!"

"I'm your alpha. Shut down. Damn it, stop!"

Part of him heard the words, but the forces gripping him were too strong. He had to protect his mate and he couldn't do that with them on him. He couldn't save her with his breath choked off.

Stars gathered around the edge of his vision. Sounds echoed weirdly. Darkness crept in.

He surged forward. Nearly escaped.

And then electricity shot through his body. He didn't even have the chance to scream.

Black.

Or maybe not so black because though he couldn't see or move, he could hear. And he could smell. The interlopers were breathing hard, but they didn't seem to be attacking. And she was breathing as well. Quiet, but strong. As if she were asleep.

He fought to make his body move, but it was like a dead weight. Nothing did as he willed, so he had to use his mind. The forces that drove him poured into his thoughts. No longer pushing his body, they helped him think as long as he protected her.

"What the fuck?" one of the men was saying. "I thought you said he was dying?"

"That's what she said," the other huffed, and he finally recognized the voice. It was Simon, his alpha. "She said come fast. She sounded panicked."

"He doesn't look dead to me," the other one groused, and in that tone, he remembered the person. This was Vic, Simon's beta. He was a hybrid and both men were his friends. Or so they claimed.

Why then had they attacked?

"How is she?" Simon asked.

"Fine. Coming around, I think. Do we tie her up?"

Ryan growled at that. In his mind, he bared his teeth and he tore out Vic's throat for even suggesting it. But his body didn't move, though there was a sound. A deep, throaty sound that he knew he'd made.

"He's not out," Vic said. "Ryan, can you hear me? We're not here to hurt you."

"Or her," Simon stressed. "We're not going to touch her."

A moment's pause, then Vic spoke again, his voice slightly more relaxed. "Is that what happened? Did we interrupt—"

"I don't know. I thought she was hurting him. Look at her. I thought—"

"Not all hybrids are insane, you know," Vic said. He should know. He was one of the sane ones.

"But most are. And if Ryan was hurt—"

Vic snorted. "Don't think that was the problem." Then Ryan felt someone nudge his foot. "Come on, Ryan. We know you're awake."

"Stay away from him," she said. His mate. "Stay back." Her words were slurred but everyone heard her.

"We're not here to hurt him," Simon stressed. "We're here to help."

"He'll hurt you," she said, her words getting clearer. "He's not rational right now. Give him time."

A pause then Simon spoke. "Why not? What did you do to him?"

She blew out a breath. "I saved his life."

Which is when Ryan at last got some muscle control back. It came to his face first as his lip curled, exposing his teeth. Then he lifted his head. His arms and legs were still useless, but his face wasn't. Let them see his teeth. And he would see exactly where everyone stood.

Simon was crouched over Frankie. Vic remained standing, his gun out and his gaze trained hard on Ryan. He was the one who spoke.

"Keep it together, man. We aren't here to hurt you or her."

Simon kept his focus on Frankie. "What did you do to him?"

"Only way."

"What was the only way?" Simon hadn't raised his tone one decibel, but there was threat in his voice and Ryan reacted to it. His arm twitched. It wasn't much, but he was coming back.

"Easy, big guy," Vic said. Then he looked at Simon. "He's protecting her."

Simon didn't relent. "We need to know now. What did you do to him?"

She sighed. The sound filled Ryan's head with the bitter taste of defeat. He didn't know why. She'd fought valiantly; he was the one who had failed to protect her. And yet the sound he heard was painful in its darkness.

"The serum," she said.

"What?"

She gestured weakly with a finger. Simon turned to look into the bedroom. A moment later, he stepped over Ryan's body to grab something from the floor. A hypodermic needle.

"You shot him up with this?" Simon demanded, anger a tangible force in the air.

"You prefer him dead?" Her voice was stronger now, and she'd lifted her head. She looked first at Simon, but then to him. Her words were entirely for him. "You needed adrenaline. You weren't breathing, and I couldn't feel your pulse. It was the only thing I had." Then she shrugged. "But it worked, right? You're alive. You're okay."

The last words were as much a question as a statement. Was he okay? No. He couldn't fucking move. But he was breathing, his mind was clearing, and truthfully, he felt stronger than ever before.

He curled his fingers. They were stiff, but they moved, clenching slowly into fists.

"Keep it together, Ryan," Vic said. "We're not here to hurt anyone. We came because she said you were dying."

His tongue worked, as did his jaw. Which meant he was able to speak. "Stay away from her."

"What does this shit do?" Simon asked as he held up the needle.

She swallowed, and her eyes never left Ryan's face. "Amps them up. Like a thousand percent. But he did something more. Something I've never seen before."

"What?"

She shook her head. "I don't know. One second, he was dying. The next, he was on top of me."

"He attacked?"

She nodded. "But not to hurt me." She moved her arms to cover her breasts. Damn it, her upper body was naked, and they were looking at her.

Ryan growled, and Simon shot him a look. A second later, he pulled a blanket off the cot and draped it carefully around her shoulders. She clutched it weakly, and he saw that her feet moved. His did, too, but he held himself back. He wasn't going to attack them yet. Not until he had more strength. Not until he could take them both down.

"Ryan," she said, her voice soothing. "Can you talk? Do you know what happened?"

"Tased." Then he glared at Simon and Vic. "Stay away from her."

Vic threw up his hands. "We got that, man. We're more worried about you. Where the hell have you been? First thing we heard from you in a day is her begging us to come save your ass."

He sorted through his memories. Things were coming back in focus now. "Sewers," he said. "Shot. Saved. Wolves." His eyes narrowed on her. "Enemy." No, that wasn't right. "Mate."

Well shit, that made no sense. And the looks on both Simon and Vic's faces echoed the thought. He remembered specifically not trusting her. And then he remembered—still felt—the burning need to claim her.

"What did you do...to me?"

She shuddered as she breathed, her eyes completely on his. They held his, grounded him. "You were dying. I gave you a stimulant."

He looked at the needle in Simon's hand. "The poison?"

Her gaze slid away to the floor.

"Answer me!" he bellowed.

Her eyes locked back on to his. "Yes!" she spit back. "You were dying, and it was the only way." Then she shuddered as she clutched the blanket tighter around her shoulders. "It's addictive," she said softly. "You should know that."

He stared at the needle, his mind revolting at the thought that she had shoved it into his arm.

Meanwhile, Simon dropped it into a plastic baggie that Vic held out. "How did you get it?" he asked.

She shot him a glare. "I told you. It's addictive."

His gaze abruptly sharpened. "You're an addict?"

"No." Then she winced. "Yes." She blew out a breath. "I want it, but I haven't had it. I'm clean."

Simon squatted down right in front of her. "I think you better start talking. Who are you and what do you know about the serum? How did you get it and—"

Ryan surged forward. He didn't quite have his full body together. His movements were sluggish, his power unsteady, but he had enough to catch Simon unawares as he barreled into him broadside. Simon stumbled, but didn't fall. Vic reacted quickly as well, his gun out, and his eyes narrowed. But rather than further the attack, Ryan crouched there beside Frankie. "Stay back," he growled.

Simon threw his hand sideways to hold Vic back. His eyes narrowed and his skin flushed, but he didn't attack. He just held still and watched. Ryan knew that if he made a move toward either of them, Vic wouldn't hesitate to shoot. So, he made a deliberate choice to turn to Frankie. If anyone was going to interrogate her, it was him.

"Where did you get the poison?"

She lifted her chin. "How do you think I became like this?"

He only now realized that her face was part wolf. Fur was on her ears, her mouth was elongated and showed sharp canines. Arms and claws were definitely wolf, but her legs were human. Odd how the sight pleased him. In fact, he reached out and stroked the fur along her arms.

"It wasn't the water?" he asked.

She shook her head. "Injected. Straight into my veins. Multiple doses starting three months ago."

"So you chose this?"

"I was unconscious the first time. But then…" She shrugged.

"Addiction kicked in?"

"My brother said I needed more to complete the change." She held up her paw. "I agreed." Then she let it drop into her lap. "Plus, I wanted it. It made me feel invincible."

"How many doses?"

She swallowed. "Eight in total. By then I'd felt the addiction, knew it was making me reckless."

"You stopped?"

She nodded. She took a deep breath, and as she blew it out, her body reverted back to human. Still beautiful, but now 100 percent human. "I wasn't changing into a full wolf. I was just getting hungry."

Vic spoke from the top of the stairs. "Hungry? Like for food?"

Ryan shook his head, already knowing what she meant. It was a dark need, not even noticeable until he looked. It was a desire for more. More food, more sex, more attention, more power. It didn't even have a focus until he saw her, and he wanted all of her. His thinking mind reminded him that he didn't know her well enough to want her, but the need just burned hotter.

"What do you want, Frankie?" He made her name a caress, and her eyes burned bright as she looked at him.

"To be seen."

"I see you."

"And you nearly killed me."

His entire body rebelled at that thought. He hadn't been trying to kill her. He'd been trying to have her, to catch and hold her. To mate. "Never," he whispered.

Her eyes widened. Did she understand what he meant? He wasn't even sure, but he felt like she was the most important person in his life. He'd been attracted to her before. She was a gorgeous, powerful woman, and she'd saved his life. Who wouldn't want her? But now there was an extra drive. An obsession even, because he couldn't tear his eyes from her. If it weren't for the potential rivals standing behind him, he would be content to just sit here and look at her.

Especially, since she was looking back. She was holding his gaze and not wavering, though he caught shifting emotions as they skittered across her face. Fear, interest, anger, desire. Or maybe he was just projecting his own emotions onto her because he absolutely was afraid of whatever she'd shot into his veins. Angry, too, that she'd done it. But overriding all was an interest in her, and a desire to have her as intimately as possible in every way.

"Does the obsession fade?" he asked. He couldn't imagine the possibility, but then who knew what happened with this drug?

She shrugged. "It's different with each person." She held his gaze. "It hasn't with me."

"So you crave the spotlight?" That didn't fit with what he'd seen from her. Hell, it had taken him forever to figure out her name. And from everything he'd heard about her, she worked hard to stay in the shadows.

Her jaw tightened, and he could tell she was fighting herself. Wolves didn't talk to outsiders, but she wasn't a typical werewolf. Eventually, she spoke, her words clipped and angry. "I want people to listen to me. I need it." She lifted her chin. "So will you listen?"

"Of course."

"Arrest my brother, Raoul Wolf. He's the one poisoning the city."

He felt rather than saw Simon stiffen, but the words were clear enough. "You're Emory Wolf's daughter?"

Her gaze shifted to Simon and Ryan felt his insides clench. He didn't like her looking at anyone else. "I am, and I'm trying to stop this."

"You're the ones who started this!" Vic said stepping around Simon to glare at Frankie. "You may have picked becoming a hybrid, but I sure as hell didn't." He squatted down. Not close enough to hurt her, but so that he could look her in the eye. "I had a perfectly sane life before." He nodded. "That's right. I'm a hybrid just like you. Only I didn't shoot it into my veins on purpose."

"Neither did I," she growled. She was getting movement back into her body, shifting her legs as she straightened off the wall.

"You wolves sure as hell are doing it now! You want us to arrest your brother? Great. Tell us where he is, and I'll go—"

Ryan interrupted. "Not your job." It was his. He was the cop here, but everything was jumbled. His priority was to the people of Detroit. He'd sworn that oath and he lived by it. But right now, everything in him was trying to protect Frankie and everyone else be damned. That wasn't him, and he didn't like the conflicting loyalties, but he couldn't deny that she came first.

"Can you stand?" he asked. He didn't like her sitting half naked on the floor while Simon and Vic grilled her.

She shook her head. "Not yet, but soon."

Meanwhile, Simon was focused on the larger picture. "Why not arrest Emory? Isn't he your alpha?"

"He is, but he's not thinking right. I'm pretty sure my brother has poisoned him. If you take Raoul out of the picture, then I can get my father clean and thinking clearly. I can also get you enough proof to lock up my brother." Her gaze returned to his, her green eyes cutting right through him. "Please."

It was on the tip of his tongue to agree. The urge was powerfully strong, but he recognized how irrational that was. He couldn't just arrest someone without charges on her say so. Truthfully, he'd wanted to take in the whole damn pack two days ago when the Griz had raided the wolf lab and discovered the poison, but Simon had talked him out of it on a purely logistical basis. More than half the cops were out with the Flu. The rest wouldn't be able to handle werewolves hopped up on poison.

This was a shifter problem. The best thing to do was find and destroy the wolves' stash of poison, then make the ones responsible pay. That's what his original plan had been when he'd started tailing the two werewolves through the sewer system. He saw no reason to change tactics. At least he didn't until he looked into her eyes and saw the crystal clear purpose in her. She believed her way was the best, and part of him agreed with whatever she wanted.

"Where are you keeping the poison?" he asked. "And how are you getting it into the water?"

She shook her head. "I don't know. I was trying to find that out when you got shot."

"Not good enough," Simon snapped.

She rounded on him, her teeth flashing. "What would you have me do? I'm telling you who is responsible. Go get Raoul! I'll find out the rest."

"How?" Ryan asked.

She swallowed. "There are people I can talk to. People who aren't addicted."

"Like the ones in the sewers? Like the guy who shot me?"

She lifted a hand in a helpless gesture. "He didn't kill you, and he was under orders." Her gaze went to Simon. "Tell your people to travel in groups. The wolves will kill them if they can."

"And let the dogs run wild? I don't think so."

"I'm trying to save lives!"

"You're doing a piss-poor job of it."

Ryan saw the impact of those words on her. She covered quickly, but the flinch told him it was a true hit. She really was trying to help, but people were still dying. "I'm giving up my brother," she said, fury in her clenched jaw and narrowed expression.

He held up his hand to stop the argument, and though his body moved closer to Frankie's, his gaze connected with his alpha. "Can you have Alyssa get whatever information she can on Raoul? Frankie and I will go talk to her people. Find her brother's stash of poison."

Simon nodded, a quick slash of his chin, but he clearly wasn't on board with trusting Frankie. "I don't want you going alone," he said but Frankie cut him off.

"I can't take him, let alone anyone else. He's a bear."

"I'm going," he said. No argument.

She tensed at his words and he reached down and grabbed her wrist. He'd meant to keep her from fleeing, but instead of gripping her in a tight hold, he ended up holding her gently while his thumb stroked up and down her wrist. He was aware of what he was doing. The pleasure it gave him to touch her was beyond anything expected for so simple a gesture.

What the hell had happened to him that he would caress an enemy wolf?

Simon was still considering his options when his cell phone buzzed. He answered it without shifting his gaze from either Frankie or Ryan, but as he talked, his expression tightened into fury.

"Yes? How many? Understood."

He thumbed off the phone and anger radiated through the room. "The wolves are scouting our territory, checking for weaknesses. Killing bears when they can."

Frankie dropped her head back against the wall. "The serum has made everyone crazy."

"Why is Emory doing this? Why poison an entire city? Why start a war with the bears?"

"It's not him. It's my brother."

Simon didn't speak, but then again, he didn't have to. Everyone in this room knew that her father did as he pleased. He was not a man to be run by his son. And yet, Frankie shook her head.

"Raoul heard about the serum. Our numbers are low since the cat-wolf war. This was a way of getting more people quickly."

"By dumping it in the water supply?"

"Yes. It activates latent shifter DNA. So people who are part wolf can turn into full werewolves."

Vic snarled out an angry retort. "And fuck the ones who go crazy? Too bad about the dead people?"

"No one knew that would happen. He started small." She gestured to the hypodermic. "Direct injection."

"They experimented on you?"

"My brother did, but my father got a taste, too. Raoul told him it strengthened shifters." She lifted her chin. "Have you seen my father hold his shift partway? That's the serum. He's stronger, but he also wants more."

Ryan was starting to understand. "He wants more people, more serum, more power."

She nodded. "He wants shifter-kind exposed. And he wants the wolves in charge." She shrugged. "He thinks we'll do a better job."

Simon snorted. "You want to run the country?"

"I don't!" she snapped. "We can barely manage our territory well, but they won't listen to me."

"So what are you going to do about it?" Ryan spoke casually, as if her answer meant little to him. But the truth was that her next words would mean everything. They would decide whether he trusted her enough to follow her lead.

"I'm taking over the pack," she said. "I'm giving you Raoul, my father's going into detox, and I'm going to make damn sure nothing like this ever happens again."

Ryan felt the truth of her words settle into his bones. He believed her. Which meant he was going to work with her—whether she liked it or not.

Chapter 9

Frankie felt her stomach twist with bitter anger. The damned bears weren't saying a thing and that infuriated her. If anyone else said they meant to take over the werewolf pack—if any *man* said it—then the bears would have shrugged and gone on with their plans. But when a woman says it, they stare at her, doubt written in every line of their confused expressions.

"Female alphas exist, you know. It's the twenty-first century and—"

"And you're not a werewolf," the bear alpha said. There was no condemnation in his tone or expression. Simply a statement of fact.

"So?"

"So isn't that a problem? Not being a full-blooded shifter."

Fortunately, the hybrid bear stiffened at the insult. "Just because we don't go totally hairy doesn't mean we can't lead." He turned to her. "The problem is that you're a hybrid *and* a girl. You're the weaker sex and though we may live in the twenty-first century, pack mentality is grounded in the Dark Ages."

Like he had to tell her? She shoved to her feet, bringing the blanket with her. Her legs were still trembling, the aftershock of the Taser making her feel weak. Damn, she really wanted a shot of the serum. Better than a triple espresso, but that way lay disaster, so she blocked it out of her mind. What she couldn't block was the way Kennedy stared at her, his gaze heavy, his expression thoughtful.

That, plus the fact that he was gloriously naked, erect, and mouthwateringly attractive to her. Stupid libido couldn't tell a bear from a wolf.

He straightened up with her, his hands ready to catch her if she wavered. He didn't touch her, which was a salve to her pride but a disappointment to certain other parts. Either way, she lifted her chin and stared all three of them down.

"Men addicted my pack to the serum, poisoned an entire city, and have gone to war with you for some idiotic reason I can't fathom. Now are you going to help me overthrow them or not?"

"Help." Kennedy's answer was quick and without reservation, which warmed her down to her toes. But it was the alpha who mattered politically, and so she focused on him.

"How long do you need?" he asked. "Emory is pushing for a conflict."

"Don't give it to him!" she retorted.

"Bears do not back down from wolves," he stated.

And right there was the problem with the entire male brain. It saw only two choices: fight or submit. "Talk. Negotiate. Stall. Anything you can while I get my people in line."

"And how are you going to do that?" the alpha pressed.

"I have allies. You get Raoul out of the way, I can stage a coup. I'm a better fighter than anyone knows, and I'm smart enough to beat my father in a dominance fight." She didn't say strong enough. Emory was more powerful physically, but she knew his fighting weaknesses. She could best him. "But it won't come to that," she stressed. "I can manage the pack while my father sits as figurehead. I've been doing it for years. But I can't do it if my brother takes me out from behind while I'm dealing with my father."

She saw doubt in all their faces but to their credit, they didn't argue with her, though the alpha pointed out her current problem.

"You're running out of time."

"Like I don't know that. My best friend was just abducted by my brother's bitch." She took a breath, hating that her gaze strayed to Kennedy. "I'll find where he's keeping the serum. I promise."

He nodded as if it were assured. "And I will help you."

"And I—" began the hybrid, but the alpha cut him off.

"You're coming with me. We're spread too thin to risk everything on a single wolf of any gender or persuasion." His gaze landed heavy on Ryan. "I do not trust her or what she's done to you."

"I know."

He dug into his pocket and handed over a hypodermic case. "This is an antidote to the poison. Dr. Lu has used it twice now in the hospital, and it seems to stop continuing damage to the brain, but it can't reverse it. Whatever damage your brain has already suffered is permanent."

Kennedy took it, his gaze troubled. "I feel fine. Better than fine."

"If that changes—"

"I'll shoot up. Promise." His lips quirked at the joke. Frankie didn't smile. She knew from experience that once a shifter started with the serum, they didn't want to stop. But after the first day, the hunger lessened. She only really craved it now when she was tried or stressed. Which meant she wanted it all the time.

Meanwhile, the alpha's phone buzzed again, and he grimaced. "We have to go," he said to the hybrid. Then he pinned her with a heavy look. "Work fast. We need leverage if you want to avoid a war."

She winced. She hated that she was now forced to give leverage to the bears. Meanwhile, the hybrid pulled some clothing out of his backpack and tossed it at Kennedy. "And get dressed. It's embarrassing to have you running around like that. People will think we're rogue cover models or something."

Kennedy looked down at himself like he just realized his nudity, but then he started pulling on the attire. Loose sweatpants, a tank top, and an extra-large pair of black Crocs. As soon as the other two left, she gestured at his erection. "That's not going to happen. You know that, right?"

He arched a brow. "I think it's pretty obvious that it is happening and will likely continue for the foreseeable future."

She shot him an I'm-not-amused look, though secretly she did think his response was kind of funny. "What I mean is that we're not going to have sex, make love, or do anything else that will make it very happy."

He shrugged. "It seems to be very happy just being around you."

She frowned, finding his words hard to believe. She was an attractive enough woman, but not someone who made guys pant. Or sprout erections without end. "It must be a side effect of the serum."

He didn't respond and wasn't that a bit of a blow to her ego? It would have been nice for him to at least acknowledge her looks. Either way, it wasn't important. She had people to see and a best friend to rescue.

"Look, you can't come with me. They'll spook for sure. You're not just a bear, you're a cop."

"We serve and protect. That includes wolves."

She shook her head. "It's not going to work."

"Make it work."

Impasse. Which meant they could stand here arguing needlessly or she could show him the truth. "Fine. Come with me, but at least stay outside. Let me talk to them on my own."

He shook his head. No words, just a flat denial.

"Why not?"

He frowned, and his expression grew troubled. "I'll give you what space I can."

She'd have to make do with that. Otherwise, her brother was going to lead them into a war and neither wolf nor bear would come out of that alive.

Fortunately, they didn't have to go far, just a couple blocks over to the apartment complex owned by her family's company. She and Kennedy walked quickly, and she noted his eyes were constantly moving. He watched, he remembered, and although he made her nervous with the way he was standing so close, he appeared completely relaxed. As if it was his right and his purpose to serve as her personal bodyguard.

They rounded the corner and Frankie saw with pride that the sidewalk had been fixed and the swing set in the back replaced. She'd had to badger her father for a week to get that taken care of. When she was in charge, there would be a large line item in the books for property upgrades, and she'd hire Hazel to regularly inspect the buildings and make recommendations.

She went to push inside the front door, but Kennedy was there before her, stepping in to make sure it was safe. She startled, oddly touched by the gesture. No one had ever done that before. Normally she was the one protecting everyone else, and his simple action threw her. Especially since he then held the door for her to enter. A protector and a gentleman? Wasn't she supposed to feel insulted that he thought she couldn't take care of herself?

She didn't. She felt cared for, and that was a very seductive feeling.

The elevators worked in the building, but she headed for the stairs. Bad crap always showed up there in the debris on the floor or a lingering smell. Plus she wanted to check that there were cases of bottled water on each floor. She'd ordered the superintendent in every complex they owned to provide cases for everyone. It was the least her family could do.

"We're heading for the sixth floor," she said.

Kennedy nodded and checked out the stairwell before he let her enter it. He did all the things she normally did, which was even more disconcerting. He slowly pushed open the door, working to be as silent as possible. He scanned the area while sniffing the air. And she immediately took up a defensive posture behind him. She was alert to anything behind or beside them while he scouted the front.

It felt like they'd been doing this for years and she stepped inside the stairwell the moment he pulled the door back for her to enter. Then they climbed with him elbowing her gently behind him as he took the lead.

She noted that the water cases were stacked right where they were supposed to be. Every floor was clean, no disasters. If it were a normal day, she'd check on any number of tenants, but they didn't have time, so she pressed ahead to the sixth floor. Then together they maneuvered down the hallway to apartment 6E.

"Just stay back," she said. "Noelle's skittish."

Kennedy arched a brow, but stepped back. Then she knocked on the door. "Noelle? It's me, Frankie. Are you in there—"

The door flung open, and Noelle eyed her like she wanted to murder her. But ten times worse was the stink of vomit that wafted out and the sound of whiny children from the back bedroom. "Now you show up," Noelle said. "After they burst through, wake up the boys, and nearly scare me to death. I'd just gotten the kids to sleep, and suddenly the goons bang on the door, and my boys are screaming and throwing up again. And everybody's looking for you."

"Noelle—" she began, but the woman held up her finger, wagging it in front of her face.

"No. You don't get to talk. It's been tag team vomit for two days. Thank God, they're keeping down the Pedialyte now, and what do those assholes do? They demand to see you, and when you weren't here, they left. Just left. Not even an apology. And they have the nerve to wrinkle their noses at the stink. Well, duh. Vomit stinks, and they're assholes."

Frankie nodded, letting Noelle burn through her fury. Fortunately, it didn't last long. The woman was so exhausted she couldn't even keep up her anger. Instead, she dropped her arm and eyed Kennedy.

"Aren't you the cop everybody hates?"

Kennedy jolted. "Um, I didn't know everyone hated me."

"Yeah. 'Cause you're a bear and you didn't do shit when you worked in robbery and all those wolves were getting targeted. What the hell are you doing here and with her?"

Frankie winced. "I keep telling you that Raoul made up that story. Raoul—"

"Didn't make that up. He just broadcast it because you were

all about how everybody should be like Detective Kennedy. He's a good cop, helps the kids, blah blah." She rolled her eyes. "If it weren't for you, nobody would have even noticed him. What do we care about a bear in the PD?" She was going to say more. The woman was definitely a talker, even when exhausted. But at that moment Harley came up and tugged on his mother's pants. Of the three-and-a-half-year-old twin boys, he was the demanding one.

Noelle sighed as she leaned down to pick him up. She groaned as she did it, and Frankie guessed Noelle's sciatica was acting up. It made her lower back ache and sometimes shoot pain down her legs. It had been a chronic problem since she'd given birth.

"My tummy hurts," Harley whined, then he added a whimper as he rubbed his eye with a fist. It wasn't a real whimper from true pain. Frankie had been around when one of the boys conked his head while roughhousing, which was often. This was an I-want-attention whine, and it worked. His mother squeezed him tight and headed into the kitchen.

"I know, baby. Those mean men woke you up, didn't they?"

Harley nodded, his expression sad. God, wasn't that just the most manipulatively adorable sight?

"Let's get you some juice, and then maybe a bath, huh? You smell awful."

The whole apartment smelled awful. Frankie trailed inside with Kennedy following, his sharp gaze missing nothing. He saw the dishes in the sink, the dirty laundry spilling out of the hamper, and the overflowing garbage can. She noted the nearly empty case of water.

"This isn't the Detroit Flu, is it?" she asked.

"Nah," Noelle said as she poured apple juice into a sippy cup one-handed. "It's the regular flu, apparently. Doc said the best thing I could do was go home and not expose the boys to the really sick people at the clinic." She handed Harley the sippy cup, and he obediently drank. Then she looked hard at Frankie. "There's been no shifting in this house. We're not drinking the water. We're just trying to get one night of uninterrupted sleep." The longing in her voice was palpable.

"Let me help with that."

The woman openly scoffed. "Don't you have more important stuff to do? Big doings at the community center?"

"This is the most important place for me to be right now." She held out her arms. "Come on, Harley. Come to Aunt Frankie."

Noelle was skeptical, but starting from the day her husband deployed overseas, she never refused help with the twins. Frankie had been a regular visitor, so Harley transferred easily to her arms. Which is when the other brother came out, his whine more genuine as he rubbed at his eyes.

"Mommy?"

"Hi, Jaxon," Frankie said.

He looked up and his eyes filled with tears. He clearly didn't want anyone but his mother.

"Right here, buddy," said Noelle as she scooped him up. One hand held him, the other felt his forehead. "Your fever's down. Do you feel better?"

The boy tucked close to his mother's neck. If ever there was a young werewolf in the making, it was this boy. His every action was puppylike and he seemed to move by scent and touch. He was the smaller twin, but he was strong and tenacious when he wanted to be. Noelle went to the refrigerator and grabbed the Pedialyte. She poured that into another sippy cup as she nuzzled her child. Meanwhile, Harley wanted attention from Frankie, and so he started patting her face to demand it.

Both women were occupied with the boys, and yet Frankie had a moment to look back at Kennedy. He stood near the door, his posture protective, but what she saw in his eyes startled her. Was that yearning there? A raw hunger that she never expected to see from the bear cop.

Until the moment he noticed her looking. At that second, his expression tightened down, his face turned sideways, and he spoke with a gruff voice.

"You're almost out of water. I'll get you another case." But he didn't move out the door. Instead, he went to the overflowing garbage can, grabbed the edges of the dark sack, and pulled it tight. Then he grabbed another trash bag from the box on the shelf and snapped it open with one flick of his wrist. "Is it okay if I get the other garbage?" he asked.

Noelle's brows went up in surprise as she gestured to the bedrooms. "Knock yourself out." Then they both watched as he went off in search of trash. A domestic bear. Weird. Except Frankie was stunned by the answering echo inside her heart. She'd spent her life managing the shifting power structure of the werewolf pack, constantly checking loyalties and underlying motivations. What she saw in Kennedy's face was a hunger for family and a need to protect and serve those he held dear.

That resonated to her core. It was her deepest need as well and the whole reason she had to take over her pack. Because her brother and her father had failed in that primary duty and she was going to right the ship by getting her brother put in jail for his crimes. But

God, how she longed to have someone help her, a man she trusted to work by her side for the same goal. She just never thought it would be a bear.

But rather than focus on what that meant, Frankie took the moment to press her friend for details on what Delphine had wanted.

"What did the goons want with me?"

The woman shrugged. "The usual. Where is she? What has she been saying? I didn't tell them anything. Mostly because I don't know anything." She narrowed her eyes. "What have you been doing?"

Frankie leaned forward, repeating what she'd been saying to every member of the pack. "Raoul is poisoning the city. That's stupid and suicidal. Revealing that shifters exist is insane, and his serum is killing us."

Noelle helped Jaxon drink from his sippy cup, but her attention remained on Frankie. "You took the stuff. Don't you like it?"

"That's how I know. It's a lie, Noelle. It made me feel all powerful, and I'm not." If only she was. She'd lock up her brother where he couldn't hurt himself or anyone else. But now it was time to put it all on the line. "Raoul has to pay for his crimes, and Father has to step down. What they've done is inexcusable."

Noelle took a moment to absorb that statement and all its ramifications. She eyed Frankie with a long, heavy stare and then slowly shook her head.

"Without them, who would run the pack?"

Frankie held her friend's gaze, letting her intention sink in. Noelle got it in the time it took her to adjust Jaxon on her hip.

"You can't lead the pack!" she friend cried, then her voice

dropped to a harsh whisper. "You'd never win the dominance fight. You've never even shifted."

"I've been winning since I was a kid."

"That's because you're the alpha's daughter. No one would dare hurt you."

Maybe. It was also because she was smart and had trained hard thanks to Hazel. "Plus, I do shift."

Noelle's eyes widened, and her expression abruptly turned joyous. "Really? When? Oh my God, you never told me. That's fantastic!"

Yeah. Well, it might not be once she saw the truth. But rather than explain, Frankie squared her shoulders and made the mental shift to her hybrid form. She looked her friend in the eye and changed. She'd had weeks to practice this, so she knew she had the smell under control, but she'd never done it in front of a true member of her pack. Someone who was a regular wolf-shifter and had no reason to respect a hybrid.

She felt her face elongate, her ears sprout fur, and her hands turn to claws. She tried to do it as slowly as possible, to give Noelle time to adjust, but the whole change was done between one breath and the next. And there she stood holding Harley while Noelle gasped and stumbled backward.

Kennedy came tearing in a second later, his fists up, and his gaze scanning everything. Frankie turned and held up a hand—er, a claw—telling him silently to stay back. He stopped and nodded, his sharp eyes landing on Noelle's horrified expression.

"She's not one of the crazy ones," he said.

"Are you sure? She's got Harley," Noelle whispered, and that hurt. It *really* hurt because even with Harley happily sipping juice in her arms, one of her closest friends didn't know her as safe. That she'd never hurt her or her child.

"I'm fine," Frankie said. "It's me." And just for emphasis, she snuggled close to Harley who hadn't reacted at all. Well, not at first. He hadn't cared that Frankie had shifted, but he was eyeing his mother closely. And in Noelle's arms, Jaxon was picking up on his mother's terror and looked ready to wail.

It was a tense situation, especially with the kids hovering on the edge of meltdown, but Kennedy ended the problem with two words. "She's safe." Then he went back into the bedroom and came out a moment later carrying another full garbage bag. "I'll take these down. Unless you want me to stay?" He was looking at Frankie as he spoke, and his steady support slid inside her heart. She didn't want it to. He was a bear, for God's sake. But it felt so good.

"No, we're fine. Right?" she asked Noelle.

Noelle's gaze hopped between the two of them. Then it landed on Harley who had finished his juice and was now getting restless. He wanted to be put down, so Frankie set him gently on the floor where he toddled off to play at parking cars in a bright toy garage.

Everyone watched the boy go, the child completely obvious to the undercurrents in the room. And just to ease the tension a bit more, Frankie shifted back to human.

"See? It's still me." She waved at Kennedy. "Thanks for helping with the garbage."

"No problem," he said as he hauled up the two large bags. His muscles bulged, and his back rippled with strength. Frankie watched as he moved, all animal grace in a hot human body. Damn the man was sizzling, and her heart—and some more intimate places—fluttered at the sight.

But then he was gone, and she turned back to Noelle who—apparently—had been watching Kennedy, too.

"I miss my husband," the woman breathed, as she fanned herself with a hand. "If nothing else, you do know how to pick the hot ones. How long have you two been dating?"

Frankie flushed. "Um, we're not…I mean, we just met. I knew him before, obviously, but—"

"Now he's looking back at you."

Frankie shrugged. "Yeah."

"And you're a hybrid."

"Yeah."

"And you're going to take over the pack?"

"Yes."

Noelle sighed as she set down Jaxon, who toddled off to play with his brother. "The pack won't accept a hybrid, Frankie. You're going to get yourself killed."

And now it was time to state her case. "Who else should run the pack? Do you want Raoul?"

The woman shuddered. "Hell, no."

"And what about my father?"

Noelle tugged her child close. "He's taken care of us. Except for this last thing with the serum, he's been a good landlord."

"Really?" Frankie challenged. "Because that's been me. I'm the one who watches the properties, helps people when they're struggling." She looked hard at Noelle. "I help when the kids are sick, not him."

Noelle nodded. "But your father told you to do it."

Is that what people thought? That everything she did was because her father told her to do it? Damn it. She should have been claiming credit every time she turned around, but she hated blowing her own horn. That's what arrogant men did when they didn't understand that there is no I in "team." Or "pack." But it was time to make the facts clear.

"My father hates that I spend so much time out here. I had to fight for the new swing set and the dog park. I got them to clean the gutters and change the hallway carpet. Hell, he wouldn't even have fixed the elevators if I hadn't told him that's a lawsuit waiting to happen."

She could see Noelle absorb the information. On some level, she must have known it was true. It's not like Emory did anything but glad-hand when there was a party and take credit for all of Frankie's work.

"I've been the force behind him for years, and you know it."

"You always said it was a family effort. That the pack—"

"Takes care of the pack." She straightened. "That's because I believe it. Raoul doesn't. And my father…" She shook her head. "He likes being in charge, but I'm the one who gets things done."

Frankie held her breath. Did Noelle see the truth? Did she look at Frankie and see just who and what she was?

Noelle shook her head. "They'll never accept a hybrid as a new alpha."

"Then you tell me, who else do you want in charge?"

There wasn't anyone, and they both knew it. Being alpha was a delicate thing. You had to take care of the pack, but quietly. You had to be diplomatic when dealing with other alphas, and yet still show strength when needed. Her father could show strength like no one else, but he'd made some really bad decisions lately thanks to Raoul. Frankie was offering a different way. And yes, she was female and a hybrid, but she could get stuff done. Hell, she'd been getting stuff done for years. She just needed the entire pack to realize it.

But she was in for trouble if she couldn't get the women on her side.

"I'm doing this," Frankie said. "And I need your help."

"No way. I don't get involved in pack politics." She wet a sponge from the sink and began to wipe down some of the mess on the counter.

"Well, it's time now. Your pack needs you." Frankie stepped closer, daring to touch her friend's arm. She pulled her around so they looked eye to eye. "I need your help. You have to talk to Brady. I need to know where the serum is held. We have to stop poisoning the city, and we have to make Raoul pay for dumping that shit into the water supply."

Noelle winced. "You're sure it was Raoul?"

"Who else could make my father do something so stupid? We don't want werewolves to come out from the shadows. I don't care how many romances are written about sexy wolves, normal people will turn on us. Especially if our first public act is to terrify a city."

"I know you're right," Noelle said, her voice plaintive. "But I don't see what I can do about it."

"Of course, you do." Frankie gently pulled the sponge from Noelle's hand and tossed it back into the sink. "You have to go talk to your sister and Brady. Find out where the stockpile of serum is located. Brady was transporting the shit, so he knows where it is. Find out and tell me. Detective Kennedy and I will take care of the rest."

"I can't leave the boys!"

"I'll stay with them."

"But—"

"We have to stop them," Frankie pressed. When Noelle didn't look convinced, Frankie turned the screws. "What happens if one of your boys drinks the tainted water accidentally? Or if, God forbid, Raoul shoots up everyone in the pack with the pure stuff?" He'd learned from her experience that it was better to drink an altered serum in water. Getting injected with the pure stuff was a million times worse.

"He wouldn't do that."

"Really? He did it to me. I woke up screaming. The pain is excruciating." She turned to look at the boys. "Do you want that for them? Because if they're like me and don't shift on schedule, then you know he'll do it to them, too."

"He wouldn't do that," Noelle repeated, but there wasn't any force behind the words. It came out more like a prayer than a belief.

"You know he would. Especially if he has time to solidify his position in the pack."

"He's already too strong."

"No," Frankie said, investing power in her words. "No, he's not. Because I'm going to take him down. But I need the location of the serum. I need you to get it from Brady. And if you won't do it for me, do it for your sons."

There it was, all laid out. But would Noelle help? Because without Noelle, Frankie was sunk.

Chapter 10

Ryan tossed the garbage in the dumpster, feeling the strength in his arms as he tossed the heavy bags away. His body was solid, eerily so given the traumas of the last week. But that was the only part of him that felt normal. His thoughts, his feelings, even his breath felt different from any other time in his life. And that worried him.

It wasn't normal for a bear to feel so protective of a wolf woman. It wasn't normal for him to think of her safety before his fellow bears, his job, or his city. He'd sworn to protect and serve all of Detroit, not just Francesca Wolf.

But what really threw him was the sight of her holding a child. She'd looked so perfect it had felt like a kick in the gut. She'd seemed beautiful, with easy strength in her body as she nuzzled the child's head. Like she could do anything she wanted with grace. But even more, he'd felt a pang that she wasn't loving *his* child. That the babe in her arms wasn't from him and her in perfect union.

He didn't even believe in perfect unions. He thought the best relationships struggled and that innate selfishness often won out over love. And yet his mind and his heart felt completely dedicated to her and their child. They didn't have a child and frankly, the odds of them ever getting together were nonexistent. He intended to make her entire family pay for what they'd done to Detroit. She might end up blameless in that, but she'd never forgive him when he arrested her father. Because he did hold the wolf alpha responsible even if Raoul was the force behind the throne.

That was the price of being a leader, especially in shifter clans. The alpha held ultimate responsibility for the pack actions, and in this case, what the wolves had done was heinous.

He left the dumpster, his senses on alert. Nothing untoward happening out here. He hurried back inside the building and headed for the cases of bottled water. An older gentleman was struggling to pick up a case, so Ryan grabbed two and followed the man to his apartment where his wife was waiting at the open door.

He knew they were wolves from their scent, and they must have known he was a bear just as easily. But though they eyed him and his police badge with suspicion, they accepted his help with grudging thanks. Even told him to be careful because this Flu was hurting everyone.

Which gave him the opening to question them, at least a little. "Isn't it the wolves who are creating this Flu?" Just how much did the normal members of the pack know about what their higher-ups were doing?

Both of them gasped in shock. "That's damn crazy," the man said. "Fact is, latest email said the bears did it."

Ryan reared back in shock. "The bears? Why? What would we gain from it?"

The wife shrugged. "What would the wolves gain?"

"So you haven't taken any of the serum or drank any of—"

"Raoul's vitamin water?" the man scoffed. "We don't hold with all that chemical nonsense. We eat local farm to table, and vegetables I've grown myself at the Wolf Urban Gardens next to the community center. Then Maisy here cooks it from scratch." His eyes narrowed in aggression. "That's right. We're vegetarian wolves, and we're doing just fine."

Ryan held up his hand in surrender. "You look like you're doing great."

"So you stop dumping shit into the water, crazy bears." He shook his head. "And if you aren't the ones doing it, then go out and find who is. Because this Flu ain't right. Things we've seen on the TV, it's bad for all of us."

"I agree."

The man snorted. "So go fix it, cop." He looked down at the case of water by his feet. "And thanks for the help." Then he shut his door firmly in Ryan's face.

Well, that had been enlightening, especially that part about an email saying the bears were the cause of the Flu. He'd have to warn Simon that the lower pack wolves clearly believed they had right on their side. Which made it all the more likely that the wolves would fight tooth and claw to defend their city.

Hell. He hefted the second case of water and headed to Noelle's apartment while texting one-handed on a burner phone Vic had given him. The need to get back to Frankie was heavy in his gut, but he also needed to solve this crime. *Someone* was poisoning Detroit—he believed it was the wolves—but he needed to get proof. And that meant pushing Frankie—

He pushed opened the door to Noelle's apartment, all his senses hyperalert. Then he felt ridiculous standing there all bristling and anxious because everything looked serene. The boys were playing with cars, Frankie worked in the kitchen making something, and Noelle...He cocked his head.

"Noelle in the shower?"

Frankie nodded. "Yup. Have a seat. I'm making dinner."

Dinner? His stomach growled in hunger, but he looked around in confusion. "I thought we were going to find your brother's cache of the serum."

Frankie looked up, her eyes flashing new grass green in the sunlight. "*We* aren't."

"I'm not letting you go alone—"

"I'm not either." She took a deep breath. "Noelle's going to talk to her sister and brother-in-law. If it works, they'll tell her, and she'll tell us." Frankie gestured to the boys. "We're on babysitting duty until she comes back."

"Babysitting?" he asked, his tone incredulous. It wasn't that he objected to it. Hell, he'd watched his niece and nephew a few times when his sister was in a jam, and he'd really enjoyed it. But the city was in crisis. How could he just sit out the problem for a few hours because—

"You want to find the serum? This is the way we do it." Frankie came around the kitchen counter to look him in the eye. "Sometimes you have to trust your friends to do their jobs. No one can do it alone. Lone wolves get picked off..." Her voice slowed down, cutting off the rest of the typical saying. But Ryan had heard it before and knew what she was covering up.

"Lone wolves get picked off by bears. That's what you meant to say, isn't it?"

She shrugged. "We're stronger together."

It was true. Especially since the bear side of the saying went "Bears get taken down by wolf packs all the time."

"Besides," she continued, "I know you feel good right now, but you've been through a lot in the last twenty-four hours. I'd feel better if you took some time to rest and regroup."

"And what about the city of Detroit?"

She snorted as she passed him her phone. It was open to a news app. "Quarantine's lifted. CDC has identified that the Detroit Flu is *not* a virus and is not contagious. It's caused by an unknown contaminant in the water. Residents are advised to drink bottled water only until the source of the problem can be eliminated."

He frowned as he scanned more news articles. "They're bringing in the National Guard to help law enforcement." He breathed out a sigh of relief at the next headline. "Looting ended. That's good."

She grinned. "The city is well on its way back to normal."

His gaze dropped heavy on her face. He didn't speak, but just watched her. She saw his expression and sobered as well.

"This is good news," she pressed.

"It will be when we find the source of the contamination and end it. Then we'll make those responsible face justice."

"I agree."

"But you still want me to sit and wait while I trust your people to do my job."

"You mean trust wolves."

He arched a brow. They both believed the wolves were responsible, so why should he trust her? She was the alpha wolf's daughter. She answered before he voiced the question.

"Don't trust wolves, then. Trust me. I want this over as much as you do."

And there was the crux of the issue. He was trusting her to do what needed to be done. He was trusting her people, her methods, even that her serum wasn't going to turn him into a drug-addicted crazy hybrid. That was a lot to ask of a bear. It was even more to ask of him because he'd been betrayed by everyone in his life including his former alpha Nanook.

"I don't trust anyone."

"Which is how you ended up in the sewer alone. Work with me, Kennedy. We're stronger together."

She had a point. And the uncomfortable truth was that he did trust her. He'd known her before as a smart woman who cared for her community and nothing in the last few hours had changed that. She'd saved his life in the sewers and probably again in Hazel's upstairs bedroom. So, he did trust her. He was just uncomfortable with the feeling.

"I've been betrayed by people who I had more reason to trust than you," he said. But to soften the words, he settled down at the kitchen table and accepted a bottled water from her.

"Who? Nanook? Can't you bears recognize a narcissistic asshole when he bites you? Nanook was always out for himself, so of course he betrayed you. That's what narcissistic assholes do."

Ryan looked away, his guts twisting at the thought. Yes, Nanook had had his faults. He was greedy and had a temper, but he was sworn to protect them and if the clan got richer, then it benefited everyone, right? That's what they told each other until the day Nanook went too far. Until he used his mind control ability to force people like Hank to obey his will. And then he'd sent four hybrids to attack Ryan because Ryan had found out he'd been selling drugs and guns.

Betrayal, and it burned that the bears had been naïve enough to think they could counter the worst of Nanook's faults. It made everyone more wary of Simon, but so far the new alpha had proven himself both capable and loyal. Everything an alpha was supposed to be.

"What about Raoul?" Ryan countered. "Can't you wolves smell a psychopath when he poisons you?"

Frankie dipped her chin at the true hit. "I did see it," she whispered. "I just didn't want to believe it. He's my little brother. I grew up protecting him."

"When did you see the truth?"

She turned aside to dump noodles into a pot of boiling water. He didn't think she would answer at first, but eventually her words came. "My older brother died two years ago in a car accident. It was awful. Hunter liked racing cars and spent every moment he could at the Pontiac track. He ran a business that let people buy experiences racing his Ferrari or Porsche. Then one day, he took his brand-new Lamborghini around the track. He was going to open it up for guests to ride, but he wanted to be sure of the car before he let people use it. He spun out of control and died on impact."

Ryan frowned. "Sometimes that happens with the most experienced drivers."

She nodded. "That's what I told myself. And then I saw Raoul celebrate." Her fingers were white on the spoon as she stirred the noodles. "It was after the funeral, after a long day of condolences and comforting his widow. I was supposed to go with my father one last time to the gravesite. He couldn't stop going there. Still visits almost daily." She took a deep breath. "But I'd forgotten my sweater in my bedroom. It had turned chilly and I wanted it." She shook her head. "I don't know if what I saw was true. I don't want to believe it."

"What did you see?"

"Raoul grinning as he played with his toolbox." She looked up. "It's a stupid thing he does, always has. He reorganizes his things obsessively. Empties out a drawer then puts everything back exactly as it was. He'd do it with his toy box as a kid, with his filing cabinet as an adult, and…"

"With his toolbox?"

"Yes. But it was his smile, you know? Something about it. About the way he was touching his tools, like he was caressing them as he remembered something." She shook her head. "I don't know for sure."

"Did you have the accident investigated?"

"Oh yeah. My father did right away, but no one could prove tampering. Not exactly. Just a few suspicions, that's all." She sighed. "But it was enough to goose my father's paranoia into high gear. He's obsessed with making the wolves stronger. He wants us feared for our power. I've tried to tell him our greatest strength is in our community, but he's so angry. He wants everyone to know about shifters and about the wolves most of all."

"You're building a good case against your father. You know that, right?"

She looked up at him. "The thing is, my father doesn't know an amino acid chain from a bicycle chain. Raoul's the one who found Dr. Oltheten and got him researching ways to make shifters stronger. He's the one who shoved that stuff in my veins."

"Raoul alone? Or him and your father?"

She didn't answer, but he could read her thoughts in her tight shoulders and her compressed lips. She'd already lost her brothers, one to a car accident, the other to his mental illness, whatever it may be. To now throw her father into that mix would destroy the last of her family. And for werewolves, family was everything.

"You have to see your father clearly," he pressed. "Emory is not someone to be led around, even by his own son."

She looked into his eyes. "You take care of Raoul. I'll handle my father."

No deal, but he didn't say that aloud. His job was to find the cache of serum and end the citywide poisoning. Whatever evidence he found would go to the DA. Since she was his only lead to the cache, he would stick to her no matter what. And whatever feelings he had for her—trust, attraction, whatever—were secondary to his mission.

So he kept silent. She wasn't stupid. She knew he was biding his time and would arrest whomever he could prove was culpable. But since their plans aligned for the moment, neither wanted to push the issue. They worked in companionable silence, her in the kitchen as she finished the meal, and him down on the floor with the boys since Harley had started to get fussy and wanted a playmate. And then a few minutes later, Noelle came out of her bedroom showered, dressed, and definitely refreshed.

Frankie let out an appreciative whistle. "Look at you, girlfriend. You look ready for a night on the town!"

Noelle snorted as she looked at her simple leggings and tunic. "You have some boring nights out, then. But you have no idea how wonderful it is to get free even for one evening."

Frankie set down the spoon. "Noelle, the longer this takes, the more people get hurt. We need the information—"

"I'll get it," she said as she grabbed a bottle of vodka off the shelf. "Me and my martinis, that is." Then she sobered as she looked to where Ryan was lying sideways on the floor next to the plastic car garage. "I want your word that you'll keep my girl out of this. She isn't responsible for what her brother did. You get Raoul, and let the wolves take care of the rest."

More conditions. Didn't Noelle know that people had to face their crimes? Wolf, bear, even normal humans—everyone was responsible for his or her own actions and no one was above the law. But rather than give the woman a lecture on civil responsibilities, he said what he could with absolute honesty.

"I don't see any reason to tie Frankie to the Detroit Flu except as another victim."

He held Noelle's gaze for as long as she cared to search his face for clues. It didn't take long, mostly because Jaxon pushed to his feet and toddled over to his mother and tugged on her leggings as he rubbed his nose on her thigh.

"Oh baby, how are you feeling?" she said as she picked him up. Then she looked at Frankie. "Do you want me to stay to help put them to bed?"

"No," Frankie and Ryan said at the exact same moment.

Which is when Noelle took a breath and handed Jaxon to Frankie. "I'll let you know as soon as I know," she said. "But it could take a while. And Brady won't get off work until two a.m."

"We'll be waiting. Call as soon as you know."

It took more time to leave than it should have. Noelle had to say goodbye to her kids who didn't want Mommy to go, but eventually she was out the door. And then it was just him and Frankie, plus the two boys. Fortunately, the kids wouldn't stay awake forever. Because if he was going to be playing house with her for the next few hours, he was going to take the time to delve deeper into the mystery of Francesca Wolf. By the time he was done, he fully expected to know all her secrets.

Chapter 11

Thank God for the twins, otherwise Frankie might be tempted to do some very inappropriate things with Detective Kennedy. He was currently melting her heart as he played cars with them. They'd given up parking the toys in the garage and were now using him as a road, rolling the cars over his washboard abs and muscled thighs. And wow, did she want to use his body as a road, too, only with her tongue, her teeth, and some very intimate parts of her body.

Was this what happened to people who were facing imminent death? Every moment, every emotion, was heightened until she thought she'd explode from the need to experience it all. She ought to be thinking of ways to survive the next few days. Now that she'd started telling people she intended to take over the pack, her brother had no reason to hold back from killing her. She was convinced the only reason he'd left her alone was because she'd been too busy helping people to mess with pack politics. She'd been keeping up the apartment complexes, built the community center, and helped whenever someone was sick or hurt or old.

But now she'd stepped into the ring and instead of planning ways to take him out first, she was thinking about things she could do with Detective Kennedy.

He caught her looking at him. His gaze was curious at first, then darkened into smoldering. She doubted the man read minds, but maybe he noticed her flushed face or her tight nipples. God, she needed to turn away. Just suppress all her lust because now was not the time or the place.

But if not now, then when? After she was dead by her brother's hand? After her father took them into a war with the bears and she got swiped by someone's deadly claws because she refused to fight?

How had the world sunk to this level of madness? How had her choices become a fight to the death for control of the pack or fight in a ridiculous war against bears who were completely innocent of the disaster her brother had created? She was dead either way, so why not embrace life while she could?

Because the situation was complicated and difficult enough without adding romance to the mix. And with a bear, no less. That's what she told herself as she started scooping casserole into a dish. She'd barely gotten halfway when one of the boys erupted in a furious scream.

"Hey, hey," Kennedy said before she could do more than spin around. "There are plenty of cars, you don't have to take the red one. That's your brother's."

Nice try, but she could already see that the boys weren't going to respond to logic. They were tired, cranky, and not in the least bit interested in sharing. Especially since the two were now grappling with each other and starting to bite.

"And we're done with the cars," he said.

She was about to intervene when Kennedy spoke, gently disentangled them from each other. Then he stood up with a boy in each arm. It was an impressive display of strength and agility given that the kids were squirming and not at all happy with the situation. And yet, he was completely calm as he jostled them into position and faced her.

"So what's the plan? Do they eat? Or maybe a bath first?" He wrinkled his nose as he held them. "They do smell kind of ripe."

"Their stomachs can't take regular food yet." She waved at the casserole. "This is for us and for Noelle when she gets back. But they can eat some animal crackers." She held up the box and pulled out a bear. "Hey, Jax. You want to eat a bear?"

She wasn't speaking metaphorically or even suggestively, but a graphic image flashed through her thoughts. And her libido answered enthusiastically. Yes, why yes she did indeed want to eat a bear. Or at least suck on one.

Her face heated at her thoughts even as Jaxon grabbed the cracker and started to gnaw on it.

"Got any wolves in there?" Kennedy asked, his voice rough and with an undercurrent of awareness.

Her gaze shot to his and he smiled, a slow, charming smile that had her melting. So yes, he was aware of her sexual thoughts. And yes, he shared them. But again, she reminded herself, this was not the time or place.

She ducked her head rather than look into his blue, blue eyes. She rooted through the box for a wolf. She found one eventually and handed it over to Harley, who wasted no time in chomping down on it.

"Darn," Kennedy said, humor in his voice. "I wanted the wolf." Then he grinned. "Well, maybe I'll find a different one."

"You cannot be flirting," she said sternly, though obviously he was. And even worse, she liked it.

"I can't?" he asked, his tone completely innocent. "And here I thought I was."

She paused and looked him in the eye. She wanted to ask him why. She wanted to know how they'd gone from enemies to playful flirting in the course of a few hours. "This roller coaster is hard to ride, you know. I don't know which end is up."

She expected him to say a cheesy, sexual thing that she could use to stomp down her libido. But instead of dismissing her, his expression sobered, and he answered honestly. "I feel the same way, you know. I don't know what direction I'm supposed to go. I just know how I feel."

"You're a bear."

"You're a wolf."

"We might be at war. There could be a notification on my phone right now telling me to kill or capture you."

He arched a brow. "Are you going to look at your phone any-time soon?"

She shook her head.

"Then I guess we're still friends." He watched as she passed over a giraffe to Jaxon and a squirrel to Harley. "And for the record, I don't go to war unless it makes sense, and there's no other way. I haven't exhausted all the possibilities yet, have you?"

"Not in the least."

"Then I guess we're agreed."

"On what?"

"That we're friends."

She let that settle into her body. The words "friends" felt good but was so much less than what she really wanted. Still, it was a start and so she nodded in agreement.

"Friends," she echoed. Then she looked at the mess on Jaxon's face from gnawed bits of animal crackers and she let out a laugh. "Friends who have to get a couple other friends into a bath." She looked at Kennedy. "So, do you mind holding them while I get the bathwater ready?"

"Not at all. Just leave the crackers. I think I'm going to need them."

She smiled and poured a small pile on the counter. And then her libido took control of her body. It was a small thing, but it was definitely something she never would have done before.

She plucked a bear out of the pile, held it long enough for Kennedy to see what she had, and then she slowly, sensuously nibbled at the cracker.

She watched his nostrils flare and heat entered his gaze. When he spoke, his voice rumbled straight down her spine into her core. "Are you flirting with me, wolf?"

She arched a brow. "Am I? I thought we already agreed we couldn't."

"That's what you said."

"Hmm," she commented as she popped the rest of the cracker into her mouth. "Well, if I said it, it must be true, right?" Then she winked at him and sauntered into the bathroom.

It took a long while to get both kids cleaned, dressed, and settled for bed. Bath time alone was a frolicking, wet adventure where they laughed a lot and everyone got soaked to the skin. Rather than risk the tap water, they put the boys in the tub and cleaned them with a few gallons of distilled water; microwaving it to heat up the water took forever. Kennedy did the smart thing by pulling off his shirt. She got to watch drops of water cling to his golden skin, slide down narrowed channels formed by his muscles, and glisten on his chest hair. She, on the other hand, kept on her tank but that and her thin bra did nothing to hide her curves and puckered nipples. She ended up changing into one of Noelle's tees, but she was bustier than her friend and the dry clothes clung almost as much as the wet.

Once the bath was done, both boys were cranky. She and Kennedy split cuddle-and-read time, each taking a child. Her book was shorter, and pretty soon, all of them were listening to the rumble of his deep voice as he read *The Berenstain Bear's Sleepy Time Book*. By the end, both boys were yawning. Easy to settle them into bed, kiss them good night, then tiptoe out. Not so easy to look at Ryan's ripped sexy body in the evening glow and resist doing all the things she was thinking about.

Not the time or place, she reminded herself. Except she couldn't remember why not, especially when he dropped down onto the couch with a contented sigh and then gestured for her to join him there.

She didn't. She went to reheat the casserole in the microwave. He watched with a hooded expression as she worked. Then he gracefully accepted a bowl when she brought it over to him.

"Beer?" she offered.

He shook his head. "Better not. Just in case."

She nodded, understanding his meaning. They didn't know when Noelle would come back or when Raoul would make his move, not to mention any one of dozens of other possibilities. So she grabbed them both lemonade and settled on the couch next to him. Next to him, but not touching. Because she was afraid if she did start touching, she wouldn't stop with just a little knee-to-knee contact.

"This is good," he said as he tucked into the food.

She smiled. "Ancient recipe found on the tuna noodle casserole box."

"No way," he said as he peered down at it. "I've followed that recipe. You added stuff."

"Yeah," she said with a laugh. "I dumped in leftover vegetables. If you want to really know what's in there, ask Noelle."

"Nah," he said as he continued to eat. "I've got more questions for you."

Uh-oh.

"Am I in trouble?" she asked, trying to keep her voice light despite the butterflies in her stomach.

"Depends on your answers." He did a mock glower, pointed his fork at her, and said with a really bad accent, "I have ways to make you talk."

"Hit me with your best shot, bear," she said with a wolfish grin.

"Okay," he said as he leaned back on the couch. "When we first got here, Noelle said I was the cop nobody liked and that's why I had to leave Robbery. She made it sound like you knew something about that." He arched a devastatingly handsome brow at her. "Do you?"

Oh shit. He'd heard that part. She looked down at her food, feeling guilt push aside lust. Truth was she'd wanted to apologize to him for a long time now. She could hardly duck the situation now that the opportunity had arisen.

"Um, yeah. About that…" She looked up to face him eye to eye. To her relief, she didn't see anger in his expression. Not even wariness. Just a patient curiosity as he waited for her answer. And since he was being so calm, she found the strength to explain. The apology would come afterward. "My father started complaining about you years ago. He didn't like that a bear was in the PD when there weren't any wolves."

He lifted his hand in a welcoming gesture. "I'd love some wolves in the PD."

She nodded. She already knew he wasn't territorial about his job, and there was room on the force for more than one type of shifter. "I started looking into you because my father never does his own research." Actually, her father had ordered her to find some dirt on the detective, but she never found any. "I learned that you'd gotten your detective badge young, there were no outbursts typical of young shifters in a violent job, and everyone generally thought you were smart, capable, and had a level head. You were the shifter poster boy, and so I told everyone I could." She felt her cheeks heat as she confessed her rookie mistake. "I thought if I talked you up, then people would look to you as an example. I even suggested some of our guys ask you for help in getting on the force."

"No one ever approached me."

"Yeah," she said slowly. "I might have been too enthusiastic in singing your praises."

He arched a brow, silently urging her to continue.

"Remember that string of burglaries in wolf territory? You were the lead detective on most of the cases." He nodded. Truthfully, she doubted he could forget them as they'd ended his career in that department. "Um, a rumor started going around that you were turning a blind eye to any crimes against wolves."

"I know," he said, his voice low. "Did you start it?"

"Not me. Raoul, I think."

"For the record, I was close to solving them."

She knew that. In fact the officer in charge said as much during the trial of the burglary ring that was shut down not long afterward. But the damage had already been done. People's first impression of Kennedy was that he was the bear who encouraged crimes against wolves. The rumor was loud enough that he couldn't do his job. Eventually, Kennedy transferred to the gang task force.

Her gaze dropped to the floor. "I should have known that Raoul would turn people against you as a way to discredit me." She swallowed. "I tried to stop it, but the more I spoke out, the worse it got." She forced herself to look into his eyes. "I've wanted to apologize for a really long time."

He kept his expression blank while her insides twisted. Would he be one of those people who never forgave? Would he explode into anger because she'd cost him his place in robbery? The longer he stayed silent, the more she wanted to apologize—again—over and over until he heard her.

"I'm really sorry," she began, but he shook his head.

"That was a hard time for me. I hadn't done anything wrong, and yet I was tossed out of robbery like a bad seed."

She winced. The things she'd heard people say about him were awful. And the more she tried to defend him, the worse it got for them both. "I was trying to help."

"No one trusted me," he said calmly. "It didn't matter what I did, the people I was trying to help assumed I was crooked." His gaze canted away as he stood up, taking his dirty dish with him. But when he reached for hers, she touched his arm.

"It wasn't your fault."

His lips twisted into a rueful smile. "Are you so sure? If I had made an effort to have better relationships with the victims, to explain what was going on and what I was doing to help, then your brother's lies wouldn't have gotten so loud so fast. That's what I learned from the whole thing. That if I don't work on establishing trust with the community, then I can't do my job."

The openness in his expression shocked her. What had happened to him was her fault, and yet he'd just acknowledged his part in the problem. It left her gaping at him as if he'd just stripped naked in front of her. No man was that forgiving or self-aware. At least no one she'd ever met before.

Meanwhile, her momentary freeze had him pulling her dirty plate out of her slack hand. And he just kept talking.

"Bad rumors happen all the time. It's part of my job to show them who the PD really is. Who I really am." He flashed her a quick smile. "I took that lesson into my work with the gangs and that's the only reason I'm so effective there. Because I let them know the real me, I let them see that they can come to me with their grievances. I'll fight for justice no matter who comes to me with what."

She knew he'd done well in the gang task force. Because of her guilt, she'd followed his career and been relieved when he'd gotten not one, but two separate commendations for his work there. "I still hate that I'm the reason you had to leave robbery."

"I love that you're the reason I learned my most valuable lesson in police work."

What could she say to that? "So...I'm forgiven?"

"You don't have anything to apologize for. You may have been the catalyst for that career change, but it wasn't your fault."

"It was Raoul's."

"And mine. For not showing people that the rumors were false."

She exhaled, feeling a huge weight roll off her shoulders. He didn't blame her for what had happened to him. And though she still felt guilty, his acceptance of what she'd done made her load so much lighter. Light enough that she crossed to him where he stood by the counter. He looked up, dishes in hand as she came close, and the openness in his blue eyes went straight to her heart.

"I'm still sorry," she said. "I didn't mean for that to happen, and I've tried to fix it ever since."

"Thank you for telling me," he said. Then he set the plates on the counter.

She wanted to say something else, but the way he looked at her tied her tongue and emptied her mind of words. He held her gaze. Then he touched her arm, sending a shockwave of heat through her body. When she didn't move away, he came in closer. Tighter. Until their breath mingled together.

He waited a moment longer. Was there a question in his eyes? She couldn't tell. She was too busy trying to think. Did she want the kiss that was coming? Of course, she did. But was it smart? Hell, no. Didn't matter. She wanted it too much to pull away.

He pressed in tight and she didn't pull away. And when he finally connected their mouths together, she melted into him. Then he angled his head, and she opened up for everything he wanted to give her.

Chapter 12

No kiss had ever felt more perfect. Her expression before he touched her was earnest and warm. Her skin when he cupped her chin was flushed with heat. And her mouth was responsive, open, and so sweet as he tasted her.

This wasn't the near mindless hunger from earlier. Then his animal had been dominant, and it had wanted her in the way of a creature who scented a good mate. This moment was held by the man who saw kindness in the woman. Even more, he saw honesty and that felt like water to a man lost in the desert.

"Stop me," he said against her lips. "If you don't want this."

He was kissing her jaw, running his teeth along the curve while he stroked down her sides to her hips. If she said no, he would force himself to pull away. He would, but God, he prayed she wanted this as much as he did.

"I do," she said.

The two most beautiful words in the English language. He ground his erection against her groin. Heat and pleasure shot upward from his organ, flooding his senses. He groaned as he did it and then let his mouth drop from her jaw to her neck. He tried to slow himself down. He wanted this to be good for her, so he distracted himself by analyzing the scents on her skin.

Lemon from the kids' soap. Salt from her body. And then there was arousal. He knew it as surely as he knew he would take her to bed and taste every single inch of her.

"This is a one-time thing, okay?" she asked, her words breathless. "No strings."

He lifted his head off her neck. It was hard, but he wanted to see her eyes when she answered.

"Isn't that usually the guy's line?"

She chuckled, but the sound was weak and not very funny. She cupped his jaw, stroking the edges of her fingernails across his five-o'clock shadow. "You're a bear. I'm a wolf—"

"So?"

"So a relationship could be challenging."

He frowned. "You don't seem like somebody who backs down from a challenge."

This time her laugh was stronger. "I'm not. But I pick my battles and I don't want to carefully consider anything right now. The twins are asleep, Noelle's got condoms in her bedside table, and I like how you feel. Do you really want me thinking deeper than that?"

No. Maybe. Yes. He frowned at her. "I liked seeing you cook dinner. I loved watching you play in the bath with the boys. And I want to suck on your breasts and be inside you when you scream out my name."

She smiled. "You want to play house with me." She grinned as she curled her leg behind his and drew him hard against her pelvis. "So do I." She rocked against him, sending bursts of pleasure flooding his system. While he was reeling from the surge of hunger in his blood, she nipped at his jaw. "I loved watching you play cars with the boys. And when you toweled them off and made them laugh? I wanted to jump you right then."

His hands slid under her shirt, spanning her trim waist, before pulling it and her bra off her. "I don't like one-night stands," he said, his rational mind losing ground as he stared at the glory of her breasts. "They're too empty."

She stilled at his statement. "Wow. That's a really evolved statement."

He forced his eyes back up to her face. "I'm a full-grown man. You want a boy toy? Look elsewhere." Despite his meaning, the words came out as a growl. Her scent was bringing out the animal in him.

"I want you," she said as her hands skated across his shoulders, creating flash fires of hunger in their wake. "But I can't promise anything more than one night."

He could tell how serious she was about that. She didn't believe they had a future and frankly, neither did he. He still intended to arrest her father, brother, and anyone else in the pack who had a hand in poisoning the city. Even if he wanted a relationship, she'd never forgive him. Which meant he could do the honorable thing and walk away, or he could give in to what they both wanted.

He wasn't that good a person. Especially as she arched back and shook out her hair. God the beauty of her body was enough to silence any doubts, though he did manage one last question.

"When you said 'one-time,' do you mean once?" He flashed her a grin. "Or just one night?"

She arched her brow, then flashed him a coy smile. "Convince me."

A challenge. That was the way to get both man and beast to rise to the occasion. So when her upper body was gloriously bare, he grabbed her by the hips and flipped her over his shoulder. She cried out in surprise but wasted no time in slipping her hands underneath the waistband of his sweatpants so she could squeeze his cheeks. It made him smile, though the extra pull on his waistband made it difficult to maneuver. Fortunately, they didn't have to go far.

Noelle's bed was three steps away. He got them there in a split second. It took longer to gently flip her onto the pile of pillows and comforter. But while she was laughing at the feel of bouncing on the bed, he curled his hands under her leggings and pulled them off in a single motion.

Naked. So gloriously naked. He let his gaze rove over all of her, seeing her pert breasts as they moved with her breath and her muscular abdominals, sleek and golden with her tan. He hadn't realized how long her legs were until now. He wanted to run his hands down the entire stretch of thigh, knee, and calf. But then his attention was caught and held by the glistening between her thighs. That was where he wanted to be. That was the scent that drew him.

"You look like you want to eat me," she said, and his gaze hopped to hers.

"I do."

She blinked and opened her mouth, but no words came out. Instead, he watched her pupils dilate as she bit her lip. Then she slowly bent a knee, drawing her leg up but not dropping it open yet.

"Is that a problem?" he asked.

She grinned. "What if that's your one shot? What if I say no afterwards to the whole deal?"

He arched a brow. "Then I'd say I didn't do a very good job." He dropped his hands down on her thighs, feeling the heat and the strength in her. "And I'd say, I'm up for the challenge."

"Prove it." Then she let her knee drop open.

He grinned. She was bold in bed, and he loved it. But instead of going straight in for his feast, he leaned forward and grabbed her wrists. Then he pulled her arms upright so she flopped back on the bed.

"Wha—?"

Her question cut off with a gasp as he put her hands on her own breasts. He massaged her, molding her fingers to pinch her nipples. When she arched with a murmur of pleasure, he grinned at her.

"Show me what you like."

She did, lifting her breasts in a way to show them off to him, and then rolling her nipples. He heard her breath speed up and her scent grew stronger. Heady enough to make his body throb with need.

His gaze held hers, though he kept watching her hands with his peripheral vision. The sight made him harder than concrete, but he also loved seeing the way her nostrils flared and her eyes held challenge. She wasn't giving herself over to him as a passive participant. She was taking ownership of her own pleasure, and that shot his to the moon.

So he held her gaze as he gently pressed her knee to the side, exposing her inner lips. They were plump and glistening, and he slid his hand up her inner thigh to start exploring her there. And all the while, he watched her play with her breasts. He heard her murmurs of delight, and he memorized every time he got her to react. The gasps were nice, but when she arched her back and offered herself to him, he nearly exploded. What he did instead was push fingers inside her, roll his thumb over her clit, and dream of the moment he could plunge into her.

But first things first. He dropped down onto his elbows and went in for a feast.

The scent of her blew his mind. Rich and fragrant, he began licking wherever the mood struck him, which meant he went everywhere. She tried to direct him, and at first he complied. As she lifted and lowered, he let her tell him silently where she wanted his attention. But as the pitch of her whimpers climbed higher, he began to tease her. A nip here, a lick there. Never enough to take her over the edge. And all the while, his fingers thrust inside her, pressed where she wanted him, and then withdrew.

Glorious.

He was just about to let her finish. A man could take only so much begging. When she abruptly grabbed hold of his hair and tugged his face up. He looked and loved what he saw. Her body flushed and open, her breasts pointed, and her lips thick and lush.

"Condom. Now."

"You sure?" he asked as he rolled his thumb over her clit.

Her inside muscles gripped his fingers like a vice, and she tugged harder on his hair.

"Don't want fingers," she said, and he liked the way she was reduced to the simplest of words. "Condom!"

Music to his ears. He stood up and shoved off his sweats. She stretched up to pull the condom out of the bedside table and ripped it open while he walked around the bed. But when he held his hand out for the latex, she shook her head.

"I'll do it," she said. Then she gripped his penis. Her hand was startling but incredibly welcome, especially when she rolled the pressure of her fingers down the shaft. The heat from just that had his balls tightening as need exploded at the base of his spine.

"Keep that up, and we'll both be disappointed," he said.

She grinned at him and leaned forward. "Just getting you ready." Then she sucked him into her mouth.

He thrust. He couldn't help it, and what she did with her tongue made him grab her shoulders to keep from toppling over. And then she was gone as she rolled the latex down.

"I'll get back to that later," she said with a grin.

Please, God, let that be true!

"Now—"

Whatever she meant to say was lost as he grabbed hold of her legs and dragged her to him on the bed. Her knees were up, her legs open, and he settled himself right at her entrance. Then he looked into her eyes.

She was grinning. She was fierce. And he'd never seen a woman look more beautiful as she wrapped her legs around him and pulled him straight inside.

Pleasure shot through his system. Heat and wet. Surrounded. And hungry for more.

But he didn't move. Not yet.

He leaned down over her. He nipped at her shoulder and then nuzzled straight beneath her ear. Then he whispered. "Hold on tight, baby. This is going to be a ride."

She gripped his shoulders, her inside muscles tightening around him. He began to thrust.

Hard slams, in and out.

His rhythm started fast, and his tempo increased. His whole

body contracted as he drove into her. She writhed beneath him, but he held her tight. And when she orgasmed, he kept going.

The burn was hot down his spine as he exploded inside her. And he still kept going.

He drilled her with every pulse. And she milked him with every thrust.

And he kept going.

Until he couldn't.

His arms gave out, his body collapsed, and still the pump kept going. He was pouring himself into her even after his strength was gone. He was so deeply embedded within her that the eruptions felt like a continuation. Like he was pushing everything he had straight into her heart.

Pulse after pulse.

And she gripped him with tiny squeezes of her own.

Glorious.

She recovered first, though her motions were weak. She kissed his brow and his cheek. She teased the tip of his nose and scraped her teeth along his lips. He opened for her and they dueled, tongue to tongue. He was the winner there, as he thrust into her mouth. A continuation of what was still happening below.

He supported his weight on his arms, but didn't have the ability to do more. Instead, he kissed her while she murmured her appreciation. Until he lifted up so they could breathe.

"I can't believe the twins didn't wake up," she said. "I feel like we hit the entire building with a sonic boom."

He grinned. Nice to know that she felt the same as he. "So," he drawled as he nuzzled into her hairline and then nipped the curve of her ear. "Did I earn another go?"

"I think you're still going," she giggled as she squeezed him down below.

He hissed as pleasure shot through his abdomen, and he pulsed again.

"Guess so," he said with a chuckle. But then he started licking her neck. "I think I saw at least four more condoms in the drawer."

She murmured something that could have been agreement. Or it might have been the wolf inside her purring.

He kept teasing her neck, exploring with increasing intent. She rolled her head to the side to give him better access. And then she chuckled.

"What's so funny?" he asked as he drew his teeth along the curve of her shoulder.

"Good news. I've got more condoms in my purse for when we use up all of Noelle's."

He straightened, and his brow arched. She met his look with an expression that challenged him to rise to the occasion. And sure enough, deep inside her, he was already thickening in reaction.

"What if that isn't enough for me?" he asked.

She sighed. "It will have to be. At some point the boys are going to wake up, and I'll need to walk."

"No, you won't," he said. "I'll take care of them."

She laughed. "Now that would be some impressive stamina."

"Challenge accepted."

Chapter 13

Had she ever felt this sated? Frankie stretched out a hand and traced the curve of Ryan's jaw, liking the rough abrasion on her fingertips. When he dropped his mouth to nip at her hand, she laughed and let him suck her pinkie finger inside his mouth.

"Why, Detective," she chuckled, "I do believe you've found the one area on my body that hasn't been thoroughly pleasured."

"Mmmmm," he said as he coiled his tongue around her finger before sucking in a thoroughly delicious way.

He played there exactly as he'd played with her nipples. And, come to think of it, he'd used a similar technique on her clit. And wow, it had been one amazing orgasm after another. She hadn't thought she'd ever find a lover who matched her endurance, but he certainly lived up to her fantasies and then some.

"I'm going to start calling you Ryan," she said. "Detective Kennedy is too much of a mouthful."

He nipped at her finger before releasing it. "Seems to me your mouth can hold a lot."

Wasn't that true? Because whoa, he was a big guy in all areas. Probably the bear genetics, but she wasn't complaining. She could have settled into sleep right then. God knows, her body needed rest, but she didn't want their interlude to end yet. And if her life was ending soon, then she wanted to wring every moment of joy out of it first.

She rolled over until they were face-to-face.

"Can I ask you a question?"

He was on his side. His face had been resting against her upper arm, but had dropped to a pillow when she moved. Now he adjusted so he could match her position.

"What do you want to know?"

He was awake, alert, and open to talking with her. That was a surprise, especially since they'd already used another condom. Any other man would be snoring now. Since he wasn't asleep, she wanted to deepen their connection. Even though she'd made it clear this was only for one night, she couldn't resist learning more about him.

"You're adopted, right?"

He nodded.

"But your parents aren't shifters, are they? Did they know anything about what you are?"

"Not a thing. They still don't like talking about, and they might not even really believe it. But I like to think it makes my mother feel better about me being a cop. Like I have an extra layer of protection because I can shift."

"It *is* an extra layer of protection."

He snorted. "Not against a bullet. And frankly, I'm better off as a man with a Kevlar vest on than I am as a bear. But it gives her comfort, and that's a good thing." Then he frowned. "Was that your question?"

"No. I've always wondered about your first shift. If you didn't know anything about anything—"

"I didn't."

"Then how exactly did that go?"

"How often have you thought about this?"

She felt her face heat. Did she confess just how much she fantasized about him? "As someone who never shifted as a teen, I have a fascination with first shift stories."

He nodded, accepting her explanation at face value. "All in all, I got really lucky. As a teenager, I was really antsy. I couldn't sit still, couldn't stop moving, always needed to be doing something. I barely slept, ate everything in sight, and needed something to occupy my mind all the time. The only place I felt a little at peace was in the woods."

"Sounds like a typical shifter teen."

"Yeah, but my parents didn't know what to do with that. And my sister was as quiet as a mouse, so she was no help. Luckily, my grandfather liked to go fishing. My dad wasn't much into it, but Grandpa loved it. He'd take me all over Michigan, and while he fished, I would prowl around."

She adjusted her position so that their legs were touching. When that wasn't enough, she entwined her legs with his. "Is that a bear thing? To go foraging in the woods?"

He teased his foot along her calf. "Wolves don't do it?"

"Not alone. We're all about group hunts. Packs of six or eight of us would go running together through the woods. All my favorite childhood memories are from doing that, before everyone started shifting, that is."

"Did they still run as wolves?"

She nodded. "Then it became more about who was the fastest, biggest, meanest wolf. Even if they wanted a straight human with them—which they didn't—it would be too dangerous. I would have gotten ripped to shreds. The only reason our teens survive is because they shift back to human when their wounds get too bad."

He nodded. "The bears do some of that as teens, but it's not important to us." He raised his arms high as if he were an attacking bear. "Roar! I'm an evil bear! Oh, look at that. It's a girl bear. Hi!" He dropped back down on the bed as he grinned at her. "I don't know if it's the human or the bear that's so hyper-sexed. The minute we scent a female, it's all about her. And girls don't usually like big, bad bears. We're too scary, even if she's a shifter, too."

"The big predators don't need to show off their strength, but take it from a girl—we notice." She stroked her knee up his thigh. "And we do appreciate it."

He grinned at her. "That's good to know." He waggled his eyebrows at her. "I've got a cabin in the UP. Come up there with me and I'll get big bad bear on you."

She laughed, and her heart beat with yearning. She couldn't imagine anything more perfect than wandering around the UP with him. Bear or human, hybrid or vanilla woman, she wanted to wander the forest with him.

But she had to live through the next few days in order to get there. And the longer Noelle stayed silent, the more likely Frankie's death became. But rather than give in to those darker thoughts, she reached out. Ryan's penis was thick and heavy where it lay against his flat belly. Not a full erection, but damn it was nice to stroke it. Large enough to hold on to, thick enough to fill her to bursting, and within easy reach.

The wolves she knew would never be this relaxed with her. Not enough to expose their belly and their organ to easy reach. Even with a lover, wolves had an ingrained guardedness. Pack culture led to a kind of hive mind at times, but instead of making intimacy more open, it had the opposite effect. Private things were guarded obsessively. Made it hard to reveal oneself even when one wanted to.

"Hey? What are you thinking?"

Her gaze hopped to his. And even though her hands were busy stroking him, his eyes were focused on her. "Nothing really. Why?"

"Your expression went sad." He stroked a finger along her cheek. "We don't have to go up to the UP if you don't want to." And with his other hand, he stilled her movements down below. "And you don't have to distract me, either."

Even if she was distracting herself?

He gently disentangled her fingers and brought them up to his mouth. "What's going on in that very scary brain of yours?"

She arched a brow. "Scary brain? What are you talking about?"

He rolled his eyes. "Maybe I haven't been stalking you for years, but I noticed you. I've never seen anyone keep as many balls in the air as you do. You were the force behind the community center. I know you managed the books for the wolves after you got your CPA license. I'm just figuring out how many people you support in wolf territory, and I know you've been trying to get a free clinic off the ground. Any one of those would be a full-time job, but you're doing all of it. Easily."

"Not easily."

"It looks it." His eyes narrowed. "Just how much does Emory take for granted?"

"A lot," she said softly, inordinately pleased that he'd noticed. Ever since she'd turned hybrid, the need to be seen for who she was burned especially bright. Like an itch under her skin that she couldn't get to. Until him. His words, his understanding, even his gaze told her that he *saw* her. And that soothed her as nothing and no one else ever had.

Oh hell. It would be so easy to fall in love with him. A wolf head over heels for a bear was bad enough—the jokes alone would be humiliating—but she intended to take over her pack. She'd never become alpha with a bear by her side. No one would follow her.

Meanwhile, he was still pressing to find out about her place in the pack. "Do the wolves know how much you do for them?"

She smiled. "The women know what I do. They're my main support and my connection to what the men are doing."

He nodded. "Smart."

"And my father takes it all for granted. Everything." She sighed. "Or maybe he sees it, but can't acknowledge it. What I do is usually reserved for the alpha female."

"Your mother isn't up to it?"

She shook her head. "My mother is in upstate New York hanging out with her friends. She only comes back for special pack events and when my father insists. It wasn't a marriage for love. They had good genetics, and I'm told they were super hot for each other once upon a time. But Mom never really wanted to be a mother. After three kids, she got her tubes tied without even telling Dad. After that, he lost interest in her."

"Because she couldn't have kids?"

"I guess. He's always been about the pack. Having strong kids to hold it together is his driving force." She sighed, the memories making her melancholy. "They made an effort with each other when we were younger but gave up after Hunter died. She moved to New York, and we don't even see her at Christmas anymore."

"Ouch." He wrinkled his nose. "My mother is all about the holidays. Decorations galore. Family dinners. She buys us ugly sweaters and makes us wear them."

She smiled, seeing the way his expression softened as he spoke. "You love it."

"No, I love her. I wouldn't dream of spoiling a holiday for her. But between you and me, the sweaters suck."

She idly caressed his jaw as she studied the minute contours of his face. Hazel had once said that if she wanted to know how a man would treat his wife, all you had to do was look at how he acted toward his mother. A kind son meant a kind husband. An angry, resentful son meant a bitter, abusive husband. It was obvious that Ryan cherished his mother, which meant his wife was in for a treat her whole life long.

Meanwhile, his thoughts were obviously elsewhere. "So your mom left and you became alpha female."

She snorted. "I wish. I never shifted as a teen, so that honor fell to my cousin's stepmother Mrs. Olivia Merriman."

"Sounds like you don't like her."

She flopped onto her back and stared up at the ceiling. "Oh, she's nice enough. Lazy and scatterbrained, but she's actually a very nice person."

"So why do people follow her?"

"Because she's a full shifter, and her husband is a badass. He tells her what to do and say, and people go along with it."

"While you do all the real work of the clan."

She winced slightly at his terminology. "We're a pack, not a clan. And I'm hoping that people remember how much I do for everyone."

"Of course, they will. You underestimate your impact."

And he underestimated pack prejudice. The most important thing for an alpha was to be a full shifter. It was a symbol of his or her strength. She wasn't and never would be. But rather than wander in that depressing direction, she rolled back to face him.

"You didn't finish your first shift story," she said. "Tell me what happened."

"Nothing all that unusual." His lips curved as he spoke, showing that it was a good memory. "Like lots of kids, I shifted in the middle of the night. A dream triggered it, I think. I was camping with my grandfather and suddenly I was this bear in a sleeping bag going crazy inside the tent. My grandfather started screaming and I was roaring. Then I got scared and ran. Ended up by the river in Gladwin State Park. There's a grizzly clan there who watches the area. Lots of Michigan shifters are drawn to the river, and so they were ready for me."

"Was it spring?" That's when new shifters tended to change, and then they went searching for their home place. Like salmon swimming to their place of birth, new shifters went to the place where their genetics began. Apparently for him, that was in Gladwin.

"Yeah. And I was damn lucky that we were camping nearby. I ended up in the river, roaring at my reflection, when some of the local shifters started talking to me. I'll never forget it. Mrs. Lansky snapped at me to remember I was a person and just get dressed." He chuckled. "I was a bear, and she was talking to me like I was a kid late for school."

"So you changed back?"

"I did. Buck naked and sitting in freezing water. She wrapped me in a blanket, gave me a Tupperware bowl of meatloaf, and then I fell asleep in their truck. I was still asleep when they found my grandfather and brought him to me. Wish I'd been awake for the conversation when they brought him up to speed. By the time I was up and searching for breakfast, he was telling me how I'd nearly given him a heart attack and my mother was never going to believe it." He cocked a brow at her. "She did, by the way, but I had to shift right in front of her."

"I'll bet that was fun." How she'd longed for the moment when she could go wolf in front of her family. It was a major achievement in any werewolf's life.

"Teenage boys do not like being naked in front of their mothers," he said sternly. But then he softened into a smile. "But yeah, except for the naked part, I did love it. My sister even screamed."

"But they accepted you?"

He hedged as his gaze canted away. "They love me. We're good like that. But they're not real comfortable with the paranormal."

"So they don't accept who you are deep inside. I'm sorry."

He shrugged. "Maybe they'll change if there are grandchildren." She heard longing in his voice. He wanted kids and a family who loved him for exactly who he was. That was something they had in common. At least he still had hope. As for her, she'd always be the disappointment in her family because she wasn't a full shifter. Meanwhile her mind skittered back over his words. She'd followed his career closely, but maybe she hadn't heard about a girlfriend.

"Do you have a woman in mind to help with that?" For all that she tried to sound casual, she hated that her voice was tight with jealousy.

His eyes widened. "You thought I'd sleep with you while dating someone else? You must really hate bears."

She felt her face heat. "No, I don't. I just haven't gotten to know one before. Certainly not like this."

He seemed to accept her words, though his expression was still stiff. "For the record, I don't have a girlfriend. I gave up on dating a couple years ago. It's hard enough finding someone who would love a cop, try explaining cop and shifter to a woman."

"I hear that," she said. "I don't date outside of the shifter community and the last time I had a date was before my brother died."

They fell into a silence and she thought they might be heading toward sleep until he stroked his hand over her arm. "Your turn. What happened with your first shift?"

She frowned, not understanding the question. "Nothing happened. I never shifted as a teen. Just many, many nights hoping and praying for something that never came."

"But it did come. You're a hybrid."

She shuddered. That was not a memory she wanted to relive. But he'd asked, and she wanted to keep this intimacy even if it was for only one night. "My brother Hunter was always supposed to be the new alpha. He was a strong shifter, smart with money, and people liked him. I would have been happy to support him."

"But then he died."

Or Raoul killed him. "Normally, the alpha mantle would go next to Raoul. He's smart and strong, but my father sees his faults. Dad would support my leadership if I was a full shifter since there's nothing to stop a she-wolf from running a pack, but I never changed." She grimaced. "I'm hoping he'll say a hybrid is good enough."

"You said you didn't choose this."

She shook her head. "Dad invited me to dinner with Raoul and they both pitched the idea to me. Inject the serum, become a full shifter. I'll admit I was interested." She sighed. "Interested, not convinced. But they didn't wait for my consent. I passed out from whatever was in my drink, and then woke up screaming."

She felt him stiffen beside her as a growl rolled through his body into hers. It was the animal in him, angry that she had been so abused. But instead of rousing the wolf in her, his fury filled her with warmth. She couldn't remember a male who had ever gotten angry on her behalf. She knew it was because she projected such an air of competence. She could handle anything, right? But the fantasy of having a man by her side to cherish and protect her—and beat the crap out of anyone who hurt her—was so tempting that she sunk into it and him. She burrowed into his side as he gripped her shoulder and she allowed his strength to support her.

Heaven.

"How bad was it?" he asked.

"Really bad. Every joint, every cell burned. Even the air felt like fire."

"Did you shift then? Into a hybrid?"

"Yes." She'd thought shifting would ease the pain, but it hadn't. She'd writhed on the floor, pouring out stink and agony. Both her brother and father had started throwing up and all the while, she'd been screaming.

"How long?" There was tension in his body from his questions. Raw fury that he held in check while he encouraged her to talk. And it helped. She was able to give him the information he wanted.

"I don't really know. It felt like eons, but I recovered faster than my brother did. He was still gagging on the stench when I managed to stand up." She grinned, sitting up. "I beat the shit out of him."

"Wish you'd killed him."

Sometimes she wished it, too. If she had, then none of this night-mare would have happened. Raoul would never have gotten her father and most of the pack addicted to the serum, he wouldn't have dumped it into the water supply and brought the city to its knees, and he sure as hell wouldn't have rounded up Hazel and started a war with the bears. But hindsight was 20/20 and even in the depth of agony, she hadn't been able to kill her brother. She wasn't entirely convinced she could do it now.

Then Ryan adjusted so they sat face-to-face. His expression was shadowed but he caressed her cheek with heat and emotion. She read anger and respect. She didn't want to think the word "love" but she felt that, too, though she had no idea if it was real or not.

"Let me kill him for you," he said. "I know he's your brother and a pack mate. You can't pull the trigger, but I can."

Overcome, she just stared at him, her mind reeling.

"I can do that for you," he said.

"Become a murderer?"

He shrugged. "I've killed before."

"In cold blood?"

He nodded, but she didn't believe it. He was all about law and order. She knew that because she'd followed his work in the gang task force. He developed relationships with kids no one else wanted to even talk to. He cooled tempers, talked about respect for oneself and others. He was not one to go out and assassinate anyone even with good reason. It's part of what made her lo—

She stopped her thoughts from that thought. It's part of what made her *like* him so much.

"When?" she pressed. "When have you killed in cold blood?"

He arched a brow. "You want me to confess my sins to you?"

"Yeah. You got a problem with that?"

"Yeah," he said. "I do. You're not my priest."

"You Catholic?"

He waved that question away. "You know what I mean."

"I do, and I don't believe you. I don't believe that you would just go out and assassinate someone. Certainly not on my say-so, but probably not even if you'd been ordered to by your captain." She blew out a heavy breath. "You just want me to hand over the problem to you. But I can't do that. I need to take care of the pack myself."

He narrowed his eyes as he studied her face. "You're too damn smart for your own good." He took a breath. "I've killed before. And people have died because of my actions. My first gang negotiation was a clusterfuck and children died." She could hear the pain in his voice and knew that his mistakes haunted him. "I've broken into crack houses and burglary rings, knowing I would kill." He trapped her chin between his thumb and forefinger, gently holding her steady as he tried to impress his next words on her. "If your brother is responsible for the Detroit Flu, I will bring him in. And if he doesn't go willingly, I will force him. And if I have to, I'll kill him."

She heard the honesty in his words, but also the restraint. He'd said *If your brother is responsible.* He wasn't just going to take her word for it. And then he continued.

"I've killed, Frankie. You haven't. Let me take this burden from you. I'll carry it responsibly."

Oh hell. So much for holding back from the word "love." Her heart squeezed tight in her chest and then fell straight into hearts and rainbows, white picket fences and babies. So many babies, all with his fierce integrity and bear-sized heart.

But even while she was reeling from her plummet into Valentine's Day, she knew this wasn't real. Good sex and a promise to take away her problems wasn't love. It might feel like it, but it wasn't. Especially since her problems were hers alone.

"You can't win a dominance fight for me. You can't take control of a werewolf pack."

"I know. But I can take out your biggest threat." He flashed her a playful smile. "If I arrest Emory and Raoul—"

"I'll handle Emory," she interrupted. "You take Raoul and let the law do what it does. Grind him up, spit him out, I don't care. But I handle the pack."

"You don't get to pick who I target. Whoever is guilty gets arrested."

"Raoul is guilty. My pack members are victims. When I'm in charge, I'll see the right people punished."

He shook his head. "You want to run the world by pack law. Drop us backward into strongmen and warlords. We have a legal system for a reason. Your pack was supposed to police its own long before the city got poisoned. It didn't. So now it's time for—"

"You? For Detective Ryan Kennedy to right the wrongs of the world?"

He straightened up. "If I can."

"*I can.* Let me fix my pack."

"It's too late. The problem is too big and has gone too far." He gripped her fingers. "The Detroit police force is sixteen hundred officers strong. Let us do our job."

Her jaw tightened in frustration. Why couldn't he just help her? "This is a shifter problem."

"I'm a shifter and a cop. And I'm trained—"

"You're a bear, Ryan. This is a wolf problem."

His fists planted in the mattress on either side of her thighs. He leaned in, his expression tight and his eyes bright with anger. "Pack problem, wolf problem, family problem. What's next? What else are you going to dredge up so that you have to face this whole thing alone? So that it's your responsibility and not your father's or Mrs. Merriman's problem? They're the alpha male and female. Just why is it that you have to walk alone, fight alone, do everything alone?" He spread his arms. "I'm right here, Frankie. I'm strong and I'm trained. Plus, I'm a cop. Why the hell won't you let me help you?"

She didn't answer. She sat there, facing him square on, and listened to his words. He had logic on his side, but she couldn't do it. He wanted her to let him control what happened to her family, to her pack, to everything she held dear. Just hand him all the evidence and let him and the justice system decide everyone's fate.

She couldn't do that. She was the daughter of the alpha wolf, and she would control what happened to whom in her pack. His job was to help her eliminate Raoul. She would deal with the rest. If that meant selecting what evidence he received, she would do it in a heartbeat.

So she gave the only answer she could. "I'm going to take over the pack and get you the evidence you need. I just need you to get Raoul out of the way while I make my move. You'll get everything you need, but I have to lead the pack first."

"And if one of his men kills you?"

Her jaw tightened. That was a very real possibility. "Then I guess I'll have to hope that you and your sixteen hundred officers can do what I couldn't."

Chapter 14

Ryan stared at the most beautiful, fierce, loyal, and *stubborn* woman he'd ever known. He saw it all the time when working with the gangs. Loyalty trumped common sense. Obligation to brothers-in-arms forced people to make stupid choices, take insane risks, and forgive the most heinous crimes. And werewolves had that particular psychosis in spades. They were all about the pack, which was indeed their greatest strength. But when the leadership went bad, it was their greatest weakness.

Frankie was trying to fix things from inside, and two months ago he would have supported her wholeheartedly. But the problem was too big and too dangerous now. It was time for law enforcement to step in. And that meant him since he was the only shifter on the police force.

But before he could say anything, before he could make the woman see reason, her phone rang, distracting them both.

She leapt on it, thumbing it on and answering with a desperate, "Noelle?" Her gaze connected with his, and she nodded. "That's great!" Her voice was happy, but her expression fell, and she tried to speak but kept getting interrupted. "I understand, but—" Her shoulders sunk. "They're fine. Why don't—" Her gaze cut to the ceiling. "I know, Noelle. Thank you. You know, we can—" She looked at her phone, then dropped it back onto the bedside table. "She hung up."

He arched a brow in query and she gave him the bullet points.

"Brady will show us where the serum is held, but not until he gets some sleep. He's wiped out, plus Noelle and her sister are drunk." She held up her hands in defeat. "I tried to find a way around, but she was barely coherent. We'll just have to wait. He'll come over here when he's ready."

"Do we know when that will be?"

She shook her head. "We just have to wait."

Not his favorite words, but he understood patience. Sometimes it was all he had. So he nodded, but before he could say anything, Harley toddled into the room rubbing his eyes.

"Where's Mommy?" he asked, his voice high and tight.

Noelle scrambled sideways and quickly dragged on an oversized shirt. Ryan moved equally quickly as he hauled on his sweatpants. Meanwhile, Jaxon joined his brother in the doorway. "Mommy?"

Ryan finished with his pants and scooped up both boys, one in each arm. "Mommy's not here right now, but I am. What say we—"

The two started crying as if they'd timed it together. Wails in stereo, straight into both ears. Ryan winced as he tried to comfort them, but it didn't work. It was the middle of the night and the kids wanted their mother.

"Come on, Jaxon," Noelle tried as she pulled the child out of Ryan's arm. "Don't cry. I'm here."

That left Ryan able to support Harley with both arms as the kid squirmed and worked himself up into a major fit. "Hey, buddy, why the fuss?" he tried as he started heading to the boys' room. The kid wailed even louder.

Meanwhile, Frankie took the opposite approach. She sat down on Noelle's bed and murmured something to Jaxon. He quieted quickly as he nuzzled into her neck. Ryan frowned at her, wondering how she'd done that when Harley was screaming like he was being tortured. Fortunately, she had the answer. In the pause where Harley had to take a breath, she spoke up loud enough for the both to hear.

"Harley, do you want to lie down here with me and your brother? We can rest right in Mommy's bed until she comes home."

The kid pulled it together in a split second. He nodded tearfully and reached out to her. Well hell. Ryan carried the boy to the bed where Frankie had stretched out with Jaxon snuggling her on her left. Harley went to her right, curling into her side as if she were his whole world. Which left Ryan standing there in shock as the boys settled down.

Meanwhile, she flashed him a rueful smile. "Noelle says they do this to her every night. They wake up and won't be quiet until they can sleep with her like this."

He nodded, seeing everything he craved spread out before him: a woman and children, all snuggled together on a bed. As he watched, he saw the stress of their argument melt from Frankie's body. She dropped kisses on both boys' head then extended her legs and exhaled with a sigh. He tucked them in, gently pulling the blanket over all three bodies.

"Do you need anything?" he whispered.

She shook her head, her eyelids already drooping. Then just as he was about to leave, she called out to him. "It's a big bed. There's room if you want to join us."

"Do you want me to?"

Her eyes opened, and she gave him a tired smile. "It's up to you, bear. Do you join the puppy pile here? Or sleep alone in the next room? It's all a matter of choice."

Prudence told him to keep his distance. Setting aside their earlier argument, he was still a bear, and she was a wolf. No sane person entered a cross-breed relationship without careful thought. And yet, no part of him wanted to go slow. He wanted her and them.

So he climbed into bed. He had to lift Jaxon and resettle the boy. He worried he was upsetting things needlessly, but a moment later, the child flopped over and dropped his head onto Ryan's arm. It was sweet and allowed him to stretch out his hand to stroke Frankie's shoulder.

"This okay?" he asked.

"Mmmm," she answered. Her eyes were closed, Harley had started sucking his thumb, and everything was quiet outside.

He didn't think he'd fall asleep. And frankly, he worried that if he did, he'd have a nightmare and wake everyone up. But he didn't want to leave, and so he resolved to stay awake and just bask in the feel of warm, innocent bodies sleeping next to him.

He basked. And soon, he slept.

* * *

Ryan woke with a jolt at the sound of keys turning in the front door lock. He was out of bed and heading to face the intruder before he fully cracked his eyes. Unfortunately, his movement woke the boys who leapt up and started calling out.

"Mommy?"

"Is it Mommy?"

He held out his hands to block them from coming out of the bedroom, but by that point the door pushed open. It was Noelle looking happy, but with dark sunglasses covering her eyes.

"Mommy!" both boys cried in unison. He could see her wince, even behind the dark glasses, but her smile was genuine as she squatted down.

"Shhh, boys," she said as they rushed into her arms. "Geez, you'd think I'd been gone for a month."

"Nah. More like a week," Frankie said as she stepped out from behind Ryan. She was fully dressed, though her hair was an adorable mess. She waved as another man stepped into the doorway behind Noelle. He was large, the muscles in his forearms bulged, and Ryan recognized him immediately.

It was the man who had shot him in the sewers.

"Hey, Brady," Frankie said.

"Hey," the man's rumbling voice answered. And though he seemed casual enough, his gaze was trained on Ryan and his stance was that of a man who was ready for a fight.

"Did you two have any breakfast?" Frankie asked. If she were aware of the tension mounting between the two men, she gave no indication of it.

Neither did Noelle as she groaned, "Not after what I drank last night."

Frankie chuckled, a warm, happy sound. "I'll bet." Then she crossed into the kitchen. "Ryan, be a doll and start making the coffee. I need some caffeine."

Ryan turned toward her without taking his eyes off Brady. Meanwhile, Frankie kept talking.

"And while he's doing that, Brady, would you please tell Ryan that you're sorry you shot him? That you were under orders then, but it isn't going to happen again."

Brady shifted uncomfortably where he stood. "Still under orders," he muttered.

Frankie stepped out from behind the counter.

"Really?" she challenged, as she got straight in Brady's face. "Since when do you take Raoul's orders?"

His gaze dropped hard and heavy onto Frankie, and Ryan had to stop himself from moving to protect her. This was a dominance fight right in front of children. If Frankie couldn't win this, then she wasn't going to win over any of the wolves. Fortunately, Noelle wasn't stupid and immediately ushered her kids to their bedroom.

"Time to get dressed," she said firmly, as she shot Frankie and Brady a worried look.

Meanwhile, Brady was squaring off with Frankie. "It wasn't Raoul's order," he said.

Frankie cocked her head. "You sure about that?"

Brady frowned, and his expression tightened. "Yes," he said quietly. "I'm sure." He ducked his head as he looked her in the eye. "You're asking a lot here," he said.

"Really?" she challenged again. "I'm asking you to think for yourself. Hopping up the pack on serum is insane. It isn't 'vitamin water' and you know it. You also know going to war against the bears is stupid. Hell, everything about that serum in wrong. So, you tell me, is it asking a lot for you to stand up for what's right? To stop poisoning a city in trouble? To not risk your life on—"

"Okay, okay," Brady said, holding up his hand. "I already said I'd show you where the shit is." He glanced uneasily over her shoulder at where Ryan stood ready to fight if Frankie needed him. "Just don't ask me to be friends with him."

Not a problem. At least it wasn't for Ryan, but apparently it was for Frankie who exploded into motion. While Brady had been looking at Ryan, she slammed a hand hard into the middle of his chest. His breath exploded out of him as he fell backward against the wall. His eyes widened, and his mouth curved into a snarl.

Ryan took a single step forward. He was ready to rip the guy's face off for that snarl, but Frankie was there going nose to nose with the bigger man.

"Do you think this is a game?" she snapped. "You shot the man twice, and he hasn't killed you. And do you know why?"

A rumble started low in Brady's chest, but Frankie cut it off with a hand to the man's throat. Ryan couldn't believe it. What man or wolf would let a smaller female do that to him? But Brady allowed it, though the fire in the man's eyes said how much he hated it.

"Answer me!" Frankie snapped.

"Why?" said Brady, the word more like a low bark than spoken language.

"Because I told him not to."

That wasn't true. He wasn't killing the man because they needed the guy and because he didn't kill people unless he had to. What was true was that he wasn't *arresting* Brady. That's what he did to men who shot him, and the only reason he was holding off was because Frankie wanted to do this her way. And for the moment, he was letting her. If she failed, then the guy would show them the serum while in handcuffs.

Meanwhile, Frankie wasn't done. She had her hand on Brady's throat while she asked her last question. "Who do you follow?"

His answer was gratifyingly quick. "You," he said, and again the word came out as a bark.

Frankie eased back on his throat. "Do you know what you have to do now?" she asked.

He ducked his head, and when he lifted it, he turned to Ryan. "I'm sorry I shot you. I was under orders, but I'm not now." He lifted his chin. "As long as Frankie's okay with you, then I'm okay."

Huh. Pack leadership handled with finesse. Bears didn't mix it up often, but when they did it was big and bloody. Frankie had just established dominance over the very big werewolf without so much as sharpening a fingernail. She used logic and force of personality. And it worked. Ryan relaxed his shoulders. "Will you show us where the serum is being kept? And how it gets into the water system?"

Brady nodded. "Soon as you're ready. It's best if we go there. It's hard to find on a map."

"Anybody defending it?"

He nodded, and his gaze cut to Frankie. "Jer and Paul, but they shouldn't be there now."

She blew out a breath. "If they are, I'll take care of them."

Like hell she would. The cops would take care of them, but that was a fight for a later moment. Especially as Noelle stuck her head out of the boys' bedroom. "All good out here?"

Frankie spun on her heel with a grin. "Yup. All good." She headed back to the kitchen, and with her back to Brady she waggled her eyebrows at Ryan. "It's all under control."

He snorted. She was way too happy with how easily Brady had bowed to her wishes. Especially since the guy had come over here with his decision already made. What was she going to do with someone who wasn't already on her side? Did she really think they'd all submit from just her tone of voice?

He opened his mouth to ask her that very question. Something to temper her cockiness, but she cut him off.

"You going to call your cop buddies in on this or not?" she asked.

"I am. Stupid to go in without backup."

"That's what I thought." She glanced at Brady. "Give Ryan the details. We roll as soon as the coffeemaker finishes."

Chapter 15

Frankie had all sorts of guesses about where the storage place would be. Abandoned warehouse, secluded self-storage pod, high-tech bunker. Never in a million years would she have guessed it was the back of a Chinese restaurant deep in bear territory. But on closer inspection, she saw the logic. The sewer access was close and in a dark alley. Two very smelly dumpsters hid the entrance and the immigrant owners of the franchise were not ones to ask questions. And most important, if the location was discovered, it could all be blamed on the bears.

"It's just a small room with shelving units," Brady was saying as he tugged on his Kevlar vest on the way to the alley. "We have a key to the back of the restaurant and then a code to punch into the pad that unlocks the side door."

"And the restaurant owners?" Ryan asked.

"Never seen 'em. We go during off-hours."

Frankie wrinkled her nose at the ripe smells coming from the dumpsters, her own vest feeling hot and tight. Ryan hadn't wanted her here for this part, but she pulled the alpha card. It was her right to be here with her pack mate and so Ryan had given in with a tight-lipped nod.

"Where are the guards?" she asked.

"If we're moving the stuff, they're just behind the dumpsters. But the restaurant's open. Shouldn't be anybody around."

Ryan nodded, then spoke into a walkie-talkie. He'd been coordinating with the police during the entire ride over. Right now, he was telling them to hang back while they went in with Brady. Twenty minutes ago, he'd been dancing word circles as he tried to explain to his boss why he'd been secretly searching for the serum when he was supposedly out on sick leave.

Frankie knew the answer: He'd been following up on shifter leads, but that wasn't exactly something he could say to his captain. Easier to claim he'd been home hunched over a toilet like half of the police force. He even dredged up a realistic-sounding cough to support it. But then a tip had come in from one of his gang contacts, he'd told his captain, and so he was following up.

Fortunately, his captain had bought it. Or maybe he was too grateful for a lead to question things more deeply. And so now the three of them were walking cautiously down the alleyway while Ryan thumbed off his phone.

"We've got an audience, so no shifter stuff," he said in a low voice.

Frankie nodded. She'd been fighting as a normal human against wolves her entire life. Fortunately, Brady was right and there weren't any guards. Better still, it was early for the lunch crowd, so Ryan had been able to quietly usher the staff out the front door to talk with a grim-faced officer. And now they were slipping in the back while Brady indicated a keypad beside a door.

"Time to go in?" Brady asked.

"Yeah," Frankie said right as Ryan called out, "Wait!"

Both froze while Ryan stepped back outside. She heard him rooting around in the dumpster before he came back with a busted selfie stick, which he extended with a quick pull.

"There's no facial recognition or anything, right?"

Brady nodded. "Just the code."

"Then stand back. I'll do it."

Brady shrugged and backed away. Ryan hadn't even let Frankie come fully into the building. She stood outside, holding open the door while he used the selfie stick to key in the numbers Brady gave him.

"Paranoid much?" Frankie muttered. She didn't see any reason to expect a trap. Brady had been going in and out of here for weeks.

"I'm a cop, and I'm alive. So yeah, I'm paranoid."

She knew better than to argue with the experienced professional, so she held the door while Ryan carefully punched in numbers.

Time seemed to slow as he awkwardly maneuvered the selfie stick, and Frankie couldn't shake a sense of unreality. It was midmorning on a beautiful day, and she was about bust into a serum stash with the cops. She felt like she was on a TV show complete with a hot cop in a Kevlar vest right in front of her. Ryan was everything a TV hero ought to be: confident, alert, and sexy as hell with his bulging biceps and quiet authority. If she weren't about to betray her brother and her pack, then this would be really exciting. Instead, she gnawed on her lower lip and tried not to be sick from nerves and the smells from the nearest dumpster.

Fortunately, it would be over soon. A few more seconds and—

Boom!

She was looking right at the keypad as the explosion happened. She saw the burst of color, but it didn't register in her brain. Neither did the fact that she was thrown backward, off the door. It wasn't powerful enough to land her in the dumpster, but she'd definitely been knocked back. Brady, too, as he stumbled beside her. But what about Ryan?

Ryan!

The sound hit her brain next. The boom and the muffled silence afterward. It had happened simultaneous with the explosion, of course, but her mind was just now processing it. And her vision was stabilizing as the dust started to clear.

"Ryan!" she screamed.

Then she saw him, plastered against the side of the hallway, his face red but not bloody. He was staring at her, his gaze wide and his mouth open in shock. She straightened, as much as her rubbery legs allowed her to and headed for him.

He acknowledged her with a relieved breath, then abruptly started bellowing into the walkie-talkie. Her ears were still ringing, but she could process his words.

"We're fine! Stand down!" His gaze shifted then, cutting hard to the blown doorway. She saw the same gaping hole and—much worse—the charred remains of the selfie stick. She didn't know a whole lot about explosives, but she could see that the blast had centered behind the keypad and had been designed to blow up whoever was entering a code.

Score one for paranoia. If Ryan hadn't been using a selfie stick, he would've been the charred mark against the wall. Or Brady would have been.

She looked over to her pack mate who was standing with

openmouthed shock. She reached out to touch his arm and he flinched away from her, but then steadied. His expression told her everything he was thinking. That Ryan had just saved his life. That Raoul had tried to kill him. And that this whole situation was getting incredibly real.

Meanwhile, she watched as Ryan squared his shoulders and moved through the busted door. Damn it, she couldn't let him go in there alone. No matter what her asshole brother had put in there, she was not going to let Ryan face it by himself. So she pushed her shaky legs to move and made it to his side in a few nervous steps. But then she stopped right next to Ryan as she took in the space.

Just as Brady had said, there were racks of jugs containing the serum. Enough to poison the city for years to come, and she shuddered at the thought. Then she turned to a small table with a corkboard above it and a sign-in sheet below. On the corkboard was a map with a big red line showing the pathway to where they were dumping the serum into the water supply. But it was the sign-in sheet that caught and held her attention.

On it were names along with a place to log cases put in storage and cases emptied into the water. But a quick scan told her none of her pack mates' names was on it. Instead, she saw neat rows of names she recognized as members of the Griz.

Nanook—the former Griz alpha—was in a bold scrawl. Simon's name came later, along with a date that tracked to when he'd become the new head. She saw the names Vic and Hank and had only a vague idea who they were. But a final name popped up as if it were highlighted.

Ryan Kennedy.

She reached out and grabbed the clipboard, pulling off the loose pages. She was about to fold them into her vest when Ryan grabbed her elbow.

"What are you doing?"

"This is bullshit."

He nodded. "I know that."

"Your cops are coming in." She lifted up the pages. "These are a distraction. The Griz didn't do this, but if they see this, you're in for a shitload of trouble." She could hear people coming and so she quickly shoved them into her jacket. But he just as quickly dragged them out of her hand.

"Do you seriously think we're that stupid?" he demanded as he dropped the pages back on the table. "That's a plant."

She rolled her eyes. "Well, duh. But it's also going to wrap you up in bullshit for days." She reached for the pages again, but he stopped her.

"It's evidence, Frankie. And you don't get to hide it."

She blew out a breath. "I'm trying to help."

"I know. But this isn't the way."

"It's a lie—" she began, but he cut her off.

"I haven't checked for more bombs," he said loudly as he looked over her shoulder. "But I think it was just on the door."

She turned to see the same officer who had handed her the Kevlar vest. He had a hard jaw, cold eyes, and a square face that was grim as he looked at the jugs on the shelves.

"I've already called the bomb squad."

A little late, but she understood the need. Meanwhile, the guy studied the map on the corkboard. "Fuckers," he grumbled. And then he saw the pages she pulled off the clipboard. It took two seconds for his eyes to leap back to Ryan. "You've got an enemy."

Ryan nodded grimly.

"And a friend," she said firmly. She needed him to know that she was on his side no matter what. Wolf or bear made no difference. This was a lie and she would not have him pay the price for her brother's machinations.

Ryan's expression softened as he looked at her. He opened his mouth to say something, but was cut off as his walkie-talkie blared. Something about the bomb squad coming in and that they were all idiots for standing inside the room before it had been cleared. He grimaced, and he gestured for her to go out the door. She went, but she longed to reach back and nab the pages. Even though the other cop obviously knew it was a forgery, it would still taint Ryan's investigation. He'd be thrown off the case and unable to arrest Raoul. Which put that much more pressure on her to deal with the situation herself.

She stepped out into the sunshine, her gaze quickly scanning the area for Brady. She had some questions she wanted to ask him, starting with why hadn't he told them about the map and sign-in sheet. Except that when she got all the way out into the alley, he wasn't there.

Hell. He'd run, probably terrified since the bomb had been meant for him. She hadn't ordered him to stick around, and that was her mistake. And worse, part of her worried that he'd been playing her and was now off to report to Raoul that he'd managed to wrap Ryan up in hours of red tape. She didn't want to think that of Brady, but she'd be a fool not to consider the possibility. Either way, Brady was not going to help her anymore.

Her allies were dwindling by the second. Hazel was trapped at the community center, Noelle had done what she could, Brady had skipped, and now Ryan was going to be caught in police procedure for who knew how long. Which put her right back where she always knew she'd be.

The cops had the serum, so Detroit was safe. Now it was her turn to settle things among the wolves. She'd wanted Raoul out of the picture while she confronted her father, but it didn't look like that was going to happen. At least not anytime soon. And every minute she waited was time for her brother to gain more control. She had to act now even though her brother was still free to cause trouble. Not a fun scenario, but she didn't see any other options. She didn't want to abandon Ryan, but if she stayed here, she'd get caught up in the police investigation and who knew how many hours of interrogation. She had to go now.

She chose her moment carefully. She waited until the bomb squad came out of the room and there was maximum confusion with some people reporting, others heading in to gather evidence. It helped that the ambulance they'd called had arrived. Paramedics pulled her out of the main throng to check her out. She followed them until she was out of Ryan's line of sight, and then she ducked away.

Chapter 16

Ryan drained the last of his stale coffee and tried not to wish it was something else. The serum in his blood had burned off sometime during the last four hours of interrogation, and now he was fighting the shakes as the addiction kicked in. His mouth was dry, his head was pounding, and he wanted, wanted, wanted anything that would make it end.

Damn the woman for injecting that shit into his veins. And yet he couldn't really blame her if the other option had been death. Still, the need was stripping him raw just when he needed to keep it together.

He was sitting in the interrogation room of the precinct that covered the grizzly territory. He knew most of the guys here, but those weren't the ones who had grilled him for the last four hours. No, he'd been under the spotlight of the stars of the Detroit PD, the ones handpicked to catch the villains who had poisoned the city. They didn't know him from the lowest drug dealer on the street, and they'd treated him with equal disdain.

In their defense, they didn't seem to think he'd been the one who'd poisoned the city. But he was named on that damned sign-in page, so he was involved somehow, and they wanted to know why. He gave them everything he could, including Raoul Wolf. He just didn't speak about people changing into animals. Or that he'd slept with one of the lead suspects.

Then the door opened, and his captain walked in. Ah, shit. Ryan had watched the man talk to suspects. He had a way of cutting a person open so that his or her secrets were exposed. He did not relish being on the receiving end of one of Captain Abraham's interrogations.

He sighed and looked up. "Ready to cut me loose?" he asked. It was a vain hope, but he had to give it a shot.

The older man smiled as if Ryan had just made a joke and then passed him a water bottle. "You look like shit."

"It's the coffee."

"Don't think so." His eyes narrowed as he studied Ryan. He'd been Ryan's mentor since the day he'd stepped into the gang department, and Ryan hated lying to the man who had taught him the ropes and showed him just how to gain people's trust. It was by talking honestly, heart to heart with people. And that's what he did now. "You on something?"

Ryan nodded. "Drank the water. It's made me..." He shrugged. "Reckless, I think."

"You were the one warning us about the water. How'd you forget?"

He sighed. He'd gone over this with the other guys. "I figured out about the water afterwards." He wiped his hand across his forehead and was ashamed at the sweat that had beaded there. "This is withdrawal."

"Are you in a relationship with Frankie Wolf?"

Hell if he knew. Had last night been a one-time moment of playing house? Or a prelude to something more? "What does she say?"

"Nothing. We haven't found her yet."

Ryan controlled his reaction. He knew she'd skipped from the crime scene, but he'd held out a silly hope that she'd come back. She'd declared to one and all that she was his "friend" inside the storage room. But then when he needed her to corroborate his statement, she was in the wind. She'd abandoned him, and damn his heart for hurting from that. She'd never made any promises to him. Her loyalty was to her pack and he was a bear.

And yet her disappearance cut him deeply. She'd declared them friends and then bailed.

She was probably confronting her brother. Or at least trying to stop her father from going to war with the Griz. But both of those paths were suicide without backup. He could have helped her, but she hadn't stuck around long enough to see that.

Meanwhile, Captain Abraham held up his phone and read off the screen. "The Wolves aren't a gang in the traditional sense. They're a powerful family trying to build a community. Francesca is the force behind those efforts. Emory is the glad-handing mayor, and Raoul the quiet nerd. She is the power behind the throne and our efforts should focus on her." Captain Abraham looked up from his phone. "Remember when you wrote that?"

Ryan nodded. It was part of his report on the shifter "gangs" in Detroit, though no one in the department knew they were shifters.

"Were you seeing her then?"

"No."

"But you tracked her, watched her, knew what she was up to."

"That was my job."

"And you do throw yourself a hundred percent into your job," he drawled.

Ryan didn't like his captain's tone, nor did he appreciate the sleazy inference the man was making. He hadn't written that report because of some relationship with Frankie. He'd done it because it was the truth. And because he was the only one on the force who could track the shifters in Detroit and who knew exactly what each species was up to. It had nothing to do with a relationship then or now.

"I'm just trying to find the asshole responsible for the Detroit Flu."

Abraham nodded, his expression compassionate. But when he spoke, his words were anything but kind. Still, his tone was gentle, and that made it a hundred times worse.

"Interesting that you say 'asshole' in the singular. Like one person could have pulled off poisoning an entire city."

It was possible given werewolf pack structure. He just hadn't figured out if it was Emory or Raoul who was the ultimate culprit.

"Want to know what I think happened?" Abraham asked. Ryan didn't, but he was about to hear anyway. "I think you were getting close to figuring things out. I think you took sick time in order to do some private investigating, and that led you to Frankie Wolf."

"She came to me," he said. In fact, she'd saved his life.

"I'll just bet she did. She probably spun this whole damsel-in-distress tale and how she needs your help to expose Raoul."

Ryan lifted his chin. "Frankie's the opposite of a damsel in distress." If anything, she was too damned independent for her own good.

His captain kept going as if he hadn't spoken. "She's pretty, she's been doing good things in the neighborhood, so you believed her."

"I do believe her."

"But you're not stupid. You're not just going to take her word for it. You need evidence. So she takes you to that storage facility where your name is written on everything. Then she disappears, leaving you neatly tied up here and out of her hair."

Was it possible? He was a good judge of character, but his captain spun a convincing picture. Especially since he knew wolves were devious, political creatures. But Frankie wasn't like that. "She wanted to hide the paper with my name on it. She knows it was a lie."

He snorted. "She also knows you'd never hide evidence even if it lined you up for the electric chair."

Ryan didn't answer. Instead, he grabbed the water bottle and started chugging. He felt weak and antsy at the same time, and he didn't like where this discussion was going.

"She drug you before or after you slept together?"

He choked, sputtering as he gaped at his superior.

"You didn't accidentally drink any of the water. It got poured into you or shot straight into your veins. Do you know who did it?"

Of course, he did. But Frankie had been saving his life.

"You're smarter than the average junkie. You don't addict that fast. She couldn't control you with the drug, so she went for sex, for damsel in distress, for any one of the many ways Mata Haris trick us dumb men."

"She's not some devious female spy."

"No, but she is a princess in an organized crime family."

He bolted upright at that. "They're not organized crime. Their businesses and their money are legit." He planted his hands on the table as he leaned forward. "We both saw the report on their financials. They're clean."

"Not if they poisoned Detroit. Not if they've declared some sort of territory war against the Griz and mean to go killing people in the streets."

Ryan swallowed. That was true, and that was exactly why he'd gotten involved to help Frankie. And yet here he was, tied up with the police and absolutely unable to do anything but sit and feel useless. And doubt every decision he'd made in the last twenty-four hours.

Captain Abraham leaned back in his chair. "What's the one rule of all gangs?"

Ryan didn't answer. He didn't want to follow this line of thought.

"Come on. First thing I taught you when you came onto my task force."

"Don't involve the cops."

Abraham smiled. "That's right. Do everything you can—lie, cheat, steal…" He leaned forward. "Poison or seduce. Anything you can to keep the cops out of it. The gangs take care of the gangs, and they'll do anything to keep the cops away."

Ryan gripped his half-empty bottle and tried to get hold of his emotions. It was hard. The addiction was riding him, making him sweat and ache all at once. And the captain's logic was eating at his confidence, throwing everything that had happened into a bad light. Had he been played? He sure as hell had been abandoned, and that carried so many emotional echoes that it was hard to think beyond it.

"She came to me. She involved me. Why would she do that if she wanted me out of the way?"

"Did she? Or did you stumble onto her and she had to cover?"

He arched a brow and Ryan felt his face heat. Damn it, she'd come on him being shot and had saved his life. But he couldn't say that because then he'd have to explain how he took two slugs to the chest and there was no sign of it now. And still the man kept hitting him with logic.

"Maybe she's the best of a bad lot. Maybe she's trying to do good here, but everything she's done has been to get you out of their business. And look, she succeeded. You're burned out from the drug, you're trapped here getting interrogated, and when she could be right beside you adding her voice to yours, she's gone. And that Brady guy, too."

Was it true? God, he couldn't think straight right now. Not when he was fighting the sweats and had had nothing to eat all day except bad coffee.

Even so, he pulled it together. He lifted his chin and gave the facts to his boss as clearly as he could manage.

"I'll tell you who was organized crime. Nanook of the Griz. And I took him down, didn't I?" Not exactly the truth, but Simon had ordered him to take the credit for it. "The bastard's dead, and we got all the pieces to take out three other drug and gun operations."

Abraham nodded. "You did damn good work—"

"And now there's another crime going on, and the Griz are the target. I know for a fact that they didn't poison Detroit, but some- one sure as hell wants it to look like they did." He pushed out of his chair. "You say they want me out of the fight? Don't give them what they want. Let me finish what I started. Let me find the proof. If it's Frankie or Raoul or the whole damn pack, then I'll arrest them all. I swear it."

They stared at one another for a long minute. Ryan let the force of his drive burn through his entire body as he stood there vibrating with the need to see this through. Captain Abraham leaned back in his chair and studied him. His expression was thoughtful without giving anything away.

"You're going to do that all by yourself? Detective Lone Wolf taking down the baddies."

Ryan winced at the phrase. "You know as well as I do that sometimes it comes down to one man." Or wolf. Or bear.

"Sometimes," his boss agreed. "But you've shot your wad this time, Kennedy." He grimaced as he stood up. "She outplayed you. It happens. You're out of this fight, but the rest of us aren't. Let us finish what you started. We'll make sure that justice is served." He cocked his head to one side. "That is our job, too, you know."

"Captain—" he began, but Abraham shook his head.

"Go home. Get some sleep. That's an order."

Ryan waited, knowing there was more. Eventually, Abraham sighed.

"You're on desk duty pending an investigation. This is big stuff, Kennedy. An entire city was poisoned, lots of people died. Everything has to be by the book, and that means you stay out of it."

"And what if I'm the only one who can keep this from escalating into an all-out war?"

"Then I'd say you were thinking like them. You think it's just you when you're actually part of a larger team, and I'm not talking about the police. I mean the justice system. I mean the National Guard who are helping us out. I mean the whole damn city of Detroit that has stopped rioting and is finally starting to pull together. So pull together, already. Work with us, not against us."

"So let me work—"

"You've given your best shot. Now it's time for you to rest and recover. That's teamwork." He wrapped a thick arm around Ryan's neck and squeezed. "Have a little faith in your team."

What was he supposed to say to that? Captain Abraham was right. He either worked within the system or outside it. And he was no lone wolf, rogue agent, or vigilante to take the law into his own hands. So what if the system didn't need him right now? That meant he could take a breather and sort through his feelings for Frankie. Then after all the dust settled—and he could think again without hungering for more serum—he could decide what to do next.

That would be a good plan if it weren't for one simple fact. He was the only shifter cop in Detroit. The only representative of the legal system who could stop a shifter war. And if he found out that Frankie was Mata Hari in the process, then that would make his feelings real damn clear.

But he couldn't say any of that to his captain.

"Okay," he said, doing his best to look compliant. "I need some food anyway."

"How about you start with a shower?" the captain said as he opened the interrogation room door. He waved over a waiting officer. "Simpson, give Kennedy a ride home, will you? And pick up a pizza on the way. My treat. And stay a while, just to be sure he eats it."

The young officer stepped forward quickly and accepted a twenty-dollar bill from the captain. His expression was an innocent grin, but all three of them knew the truth. Officer Simpson was Ryan's babysitter. He'd drive Ryan home, feed him pizza, and keep Ryan locked inside until told otherwise.

Five minutes passed as they called in the pizza order then got in a squad car. Ryan responded politely to everything the young man said, agreeing to the escort and the pizza with as much good grace as he could fake. Once inside his home, he showered, then ate while Simpson kept up a running commentary on the Tigers' chances this season. Turns out the kid was a huge baseball fan and as pleasant a babysitter as could possibly be managed.

He really didn't like drugging the guy's soda with the ketamine he kept on hand just in case a twitchy gang member visited him at home. And he sure as hell was going to pay for that later. But he was the only one who had a prayer of stopping a grizzly-wolf war.

So he knocked out the very young Officer Simpson and left to get some answers.

Chapter 17

The late afternoon sunshine was pleasant on Ryan's back as he walked away from his apartment building. He'd gone to the right out of habit, but a block away, he had to make a decision. Where exactly was he headed?

His first instinct was to find Frankie, but she was either hiding out or at the wolf community center trying to talk to her father. Everything she'd done so far was to get her brother out of the way, so he doubted she'd go head to head against Raoul. She would have done it already if that were an option.

If she was hiding out, he'd never find her. If she was at werewolf central, then he'd be a fool to walk in blind. He needed more intel and backup before he tried that. So he hauled out his phone and dialed up the Griz. Alyssa answered on the second ring.

"Ryan, are you all right? I've been following the police chatter. I'm going to kick that bitch's ass for abandoning you."

It was gratifying to hear someone else get angry on his behalf, and yet he couldn't stop himself from defending Frankie. "She thinks she can stop the wolves on her own."

"And how's that working out?" Alyssa grumbled. "We're suiting up to meet with Emory Wolf right now. Supposed to be a 'talk sense before there's a war' thing, but I think something else is going on. It would be good to have some police backup."

"Text me the address, I'll go there now. But I'm solo out here. Officially, I'm at home recovering from the Flu before desk duty in the morning."

"Got it. Damn bitch."

"She couldn't have saved me from desk duty. All she would have accomplished was getting herself locked up, too. If she's putting pressure on the canine side, then that's a good thing." At least that was one perspective. The other was that she'd been playing him from the beginning.

But damn it, no matter what his head said, his gut told him something completely different. His instincts said she was on the level but in way over her head. Anybody who was willing to poison an entire city wasn't going to hold back when it came to hurting his own sister. Or daughter. Ryan just had to do his job and hope that she was able to do hers. Though the restraint twisted up his guts.

Ryan caught a taxi and was pleased to see signs of the city coming back to life. Cars were on the road, storefronts were open for business, and no one looked like they were about to riot. Lots of people were still out with the Flu thanks to the tainted water, but no more poison was being dumped into the supply. It would take a few days, but the crisis would pass and the city would go on stronger than ever. He took a great deal of comfort from that. The bears and wolves might be about to annihilate each other, but the city would survive.

The meeting was being held in an old ceramic tile factory on the edge of wolf territory. He'd arrived nearly an hour before the appointed time, but nobody liked showing up to these things without first scoping the place out. Until the others got here, that would be Ryan's job.

He started with a slow lope around the whole area, checking out the block of deserted businesses near the closed factory. He was back in his own clothes now, which meant easy-tear sweatpants and tee. It was still too early for him to go grizzly again, but thanks to the serum Frankie had injected him with, he felt closer to the magic than usual. Like he could shift now if he really had to, but it would be at a heavy cost to his body. His badge still hung around his neck, but underneath his shirt so it wasn't so obvious.

Nothing unusual as far as he could see. At least until he got to the loading dock at the back of the factory. He could smell the wolves long before he got there. They were supposed to meet on the opposite side of the factory, but clearly, the wolves were up to something. He texted Alyssa with a quick update, then crept forward as inconspicuously as he could given that it was an open stretch of concrete, potholes, and the occasional dandelion. Fortunately, the wolves weren't paying any attention to him.

"This is an insult! Where the hell are they?" It was Emory Wolf's voice, though more jittery than usual for the normally unflappable alpha.

"Bears aren't smart enough to tell time," one of his men joked, and a few others chuckled in response. It took a moment of digging through hazy memories, but eventually Ryan remembered the asshole's name. It was Wade, the guy who'd drawn a gun on Hazel.

Meanwhile, Emory was clearly pissed off. "Do they want to start a war?" he asked no one in particular. "They're taunting us."

Well that was weird. Wolf clearly thought the meeting was now and at a different location than agreed upon. Which meant someone was screwing with Emory because Alyssa never got this kind of detail wrong.

Ryan eased forward, steeling himself to explain the situation. But he didn't like stepping in blind, especially since he knew Emory never went anywhere without a full contingent of eight bodyguards. He counted only four, which meant there were four more lurking around somewhere.

"Maybe you should text Raoul and tell him that the bears didn't show. That they want war," Wade suggested.

Emory turned on the man with an irritated swirl of his elegant suit jacket. "I'll tell Raoul what he needs to know when he needs to know it. I'm going to call that prick Simon. At least he's more rational than Nanook ever was." He pulled out his phone, but apparently had to concentrate. He was a big man and his phone was small or he was too hopped up on serum to focus well on the tiny screen. His head was bowed in concentration when the attack started.

Two of the men eased behind Emory and raised their hands. Sunlight flashed on brass knuckles outfitted with large metal claws. Damn it, whatever wounds they inflicted would look like they came from bear claws.

"Duck!" Ryan yelled as loud as he could. Then he ran full tilt for the wolf alpha.

Fortunately, Emory had a wolf's reaction time. He'd leapt two feet away by the time Ryan's shout finished echoing in the space. Not so fortunate was that he jumped straight into the sneering Wade who had his own set of brass knuckles.

Ryan had the benefit of surprise. He jumped the two guys who'd been about to rip through Emory, but they were both big men with brass claws and superhuman strength. Ryan fought quickly and with a steady hand, but it was a losing battle. He could handle two to one, but as soon as he knocked the closest one on his ass, another stepped into the fray. Not to mention the growls of actual wolves coming from somewhere close by. It would be seconds now until they attacked. And even though Emory was fighting like a demon against Wade and another attacker, he had the same number problem that Ryan did.

It was the same as when Nanook had the hybrids attack him. The sweat, the smell of blood, and the steady, growing ache in muscles that were already well past tired. How many life-or-death fights had he faced in the last week alone? This time added a flash of metal, bright and deadly. He blocked one of the bastards, but pain burst through as metal cut into his forearm. He adjusted just as another blow tore into his shoulder.

Pain. So much pain. He was going to die now.

The knowledge almost felt welcome. Ever since Nanook set the hybrids on him a week ago, Ryan had felt like death was stalking him. He was going to die violently, if not under the hybrids, then in the sewer. And if not there, then now against souped-up werewolves who were staging some kind of pack coup.

He dug deep, searching for an escape. He ducked and pivoted, he watched his opponents and tried to keep track of new threats. And he fought with precision, power in his punches like never before, speed that hadn't been there two days ago. A dozen times he thought he was too slow to dodge a strike only to hear the whistle of the brass claws slip past him. He closed in with one werewolf, managing to grab its head and twist hard when he shouldn't have had the speed or the strength. The wolf went down while Ryan spun to take on the next.

He felt the energy of a shift hovering close, but he was in sneakers. It would only take a second to toe them off before shifting, but he didn't have that kind of time. He could just bust through them, but he knew from experience that it still would foul his footing for some very important seconds. So he stayed as he was and fought as he'd never done before. But even that strength wasn't bottomless. He started to flag, his breath coming in harsh gasps. He took a hit on his side and felt the hot slick of his blood. Out of the corner of his eye, he saw Emory go down. The alpha had taken out two of his attackers, one man and one wolf, neither of which was Wade. Ryan had finished off three—two men and one wolf. But that left three more somewhere, still alive and lethal.

Damn it! He wasn't going to make it. And now Frankie would have no one to back her against her brother. No one to tell her that her father had been betrayed by his own men. And no one to hold her when she sobbed out her grief.

That was unacceptable. He had to survive if only to help her through her pain.

Then something hit him from behind. Claws? A bullet? Who the hell knew? But the force of it threw him forward. He landed on the wolf coming for his throat, startling them both as he rolled to the side. But he was on his back then, his belly exposed and—

Gunshots. Several in rapid fire.

He saw the wolf shudder from the impact. The only reason Ryan hadn't been hit yet was because he was on the ground already. But that wouldn't last. He had to get up. He had to move away while the wolves were distracted.

He rolled to his stomach and crawled. His leg wasn't working right. Neither was either one of his arms. Still, he dragged himself a foot, maybe two. But in the end, he realized he'd failed. Not only himself this time, but Frankie, too. The thought stole the last of his strength. Not in an ebb of power. Not in the way of a slowly dimming light.

He went dark, like a candle finally guttering out.

Chapter 18

Frankie slipped inside the community center doing her best to be inconspicuous. It wasn't going to work. Her brother had spies everywhere and someone would spot her soon, but she had to find her father. He was the only one who could end this without bloodshed.

She'd spent the better part of the day visiting each of her supporters inside the pack. Every single one of them—Noelle included—had been rounded up and taken to the community center "for their own protection." A few had gotten off a message to her via social media, but most of them simply weren't home. But she saw them now, isolated into a small group near the nurses' office.

Hazel was there, unconscious on a cot. Noelle played with her boys nearby, her expression haunted. They were guarded by one of her brother's thugs who wore a pistol on his hip and looked menacing next to the barrier sign, which read "Infected Area. Stay Back."

That was total bullshit. The only thing they were infected with was common sense and her friendship. But at least they weren't being hurt, just turned into pariahs. She sighed as she looked around and wondered how to find her father. He never missed an opportunity to glad-hand, so he ought to be obvious as he worked the room, telling everyone how he was making sure they were safe during this crisis. She'd intended to talk to him in the middle of the pack, lay out her case, and pray that her father and the rest of the pack saw what was happening.

But she couldn't do that if her father wasn't here. Which made her wonder exactly what had happened to the man. Had Raoul locked him up? Did her brother have so much power that he could imprison the alpha without consequences? If so, then she'd waited too long to make her move. He was in control, which meant she'd have to directly challenge him in a dominance fight. And there was little hope that she could survive that.

She slipped along the side of the room, moving casually through the chaos as she studied those present. Most of the pack was here in small clusters sharing food, watching kids, or sleeping on cots. A couple wolves prowled the edges of the building, both loyal to her brother. How Raoul was keeping everyone here was a mystery. The citywide quarantine was lifted. Detroit was returning to normal. She needed more information—

"There you are! I was so worried!"

She turned at the sound of her brother's voice. She heard the false sincerity in his words and wondered if it had always been there or if she'd just now started noticing it. Either way, she lifted her chin and steeled herself for a confrontation.

"Raoul, you look very dapper." Wavy dark hair, heavy horn-rimmed glasses, and a silver pinstriped suit all combined to cut an almost regal figure. Her brother had always gone for the geeky look—mostly because he was a geek—but Delphine's influence had him tripped out in the latest *GQ* fashions. And speaking of the bitch, she paced beside her man as a full wolf in spandex leggings. She looked ridiculous, but anyone who sneered would get an up close look at her sharp canines. Frankie didn't sneer, but she also didn't give the woman any attention. That was the best way to annoy her.

He brushed her compliment aside. "Where have you been? It's childish of you to disappear like that with everything that's going on. We've been worried sick."

"I've been checking on our people, Raoul. It's what a true leader does."

He reared back, his brows arched. "A true leader protects the pack, Frankie. That's what I've been doing, and you made it harder by running around and hiding from us. This isn't a game."

She bit back her hard retort. It wouldn't help anyone if she got into a childish spat with her brother. Instead, she focused on the business of the pack. "Why have you trapped our people here? What threat are you protecting them from?"

He gaped at her. "From the bears, you fool. They've declared war."

"No, they haven't. You have."

He rolled his eyes. "If you would check in regularly instead of pursuing your own amusement, then you'd know that they have."

"How—"

"They poisoned the city! If that's not an attack, then I don't know what is!"

His words were loud and all around them, pack members nodded in agreement. "The bears didn't do that. You're the one who—"

"The police found the proof today!" he cried, his voice booming across the space. "They raided a storage area filled with the poison. It was in the back of a Chinese restaurant deep in grizzly territory."

Hell. He was up to date. And he was pulling the pack around to his point of view. She needed to contradict his lies right now or everyone would blithely go along with her brother. "They didn't do this," she said, trying to keep her voice even and calm. "They're the ones who told us not to drink the water."

"I told everyone to avoid the tap! And Father."

She shook her head, stunned that people were still nodding at such obvious lies. "You created the serum, Raoul. You had Brady and our pack dump it in the water."

He huffed out a frustrated breath. "Why do you say such things? I created a vitamin for our people." He turned to the room at large. "Didn't it make you feel strong? Didn't you like how it made you healthy and vibrant?"

"It's an addictive drug—"

"Because of the bears' tainted water. But that was their plan all along. Weaken us so that they can take over."

Oh God, he was twisting everything to make it the Griz's fault, and the pack was buying it. They just couldn't accept that one of their own would knowingly poison them. And who could blame them? He'd injected the shit straight into her veins and she still struggled to believe he'd done it.

"The Griz don't want to take over. You're the one pushing for war."

"They are trying to exterminate us! But thanks to my vitamins, we're stronger than ever. We'll punish them for hurting us and the city we love." All around them, people were clapping as they got caught up in Raoul's enthusiasm. He turned to her. "So sister, are you with us or against us? Are you one of the pack, Frankie? Or a bear lover?"

She winced at his phrasing since it was true. She was well on her way to being a bear-lover and that would not play well with the pack. "I have spent my whole life supporting the pack, and everyone knows it. I built this center for us."

"Yes," Raoul said gently. "You helped Father a lot with that. A pretty face always gooses the fund-raising."

She was a hell of a lot more than a pretty face, but his supporters took their cue from him. They looked like they wanted to pat her on the head and send her off to play with dolls. So she looked away from the men to see the women. Surely, they knew her worth. They remembered the times she'd babysat their kids, fought for improvements in the neighborhood, made sure the walk to and from school was safe.

But when she looked to the women, they weren't saying anything to help her. Some flashed her a brief smile, but most were occupied with their children who were getting stir crazy in this confined place. Some were taking care of food, others helped with diaper changes, toddler fights, or reading to sick kids. And wasn't that the problem in a nutshell? Even in this day and age, the men still had time for politics while the women—many of them working professionals—spent all their spare time managing food or the kids. They might remember when she lent a hand, but they certainly didn't have time to support her in the middle of pack politics. They just wanted to get home and get back to a normal routine.

"Where is Father?" she said. She was losing the public opinion battle, so she had to focus now on their father. He certainly saw some of Raoul's faults, assuming he wasn't too addicted to the serum to hear reason. If she could convince her father to publicly throw his support to her, then she'd have enough power to end the madness.

"He's trying to get the bears to see reason." He rolled his eyes. "Personally, I think it's a waste of time. They're stupid and aggressive."

"Don't be ridiculous," she snapped. "The bears are as logical and sane as—"

"Your pal Detective Kennedy?" he interrupted. "The one who didn't give a shit about our wolves getting robbed? It wasn't until I got involved that the crimes stopped."

She stiffened. "You didn't do a thing!" She'd been the one who followed the case, who reported…Oh hell. Raoul had been there when she reported all the details to her father. He would know everything about the case and be able to twist it.

"While you were strutting around fund-raising, I was working with Detective Bell. I helped him find the thieves—"

"He never once mentioned you," she interrupted. "He said that Detective Kennedy did all the work in solving the case."

Raoul snorted. "If he did, then why didn't Kennedy arrest the thieves? That didn't happen until he was off the case."

Damn it, when did he get this good at twisting words around? She gritted her teeth and headed for the exit. "I'll take this up with Father. You go ahead and strut around making yourself look important while I—"

"I'll tell you one thing the bears did," he interrupted, his voice loud. "They helped bring shifters out into the sunlight."

Frankie spun around. Here it was. The main purpose of everything Raoul had done. "People are dying, Raoul. And shifters need to stay in the shadows."

"Why?" he challenged. "Look, I'm not saying what the Griz did was right—"

"They didn't do it!"

"But have you seen the YouTube videos? People are recording the shifts. We're getting video. It won't be long now—"

"Until magic is exposed? And how well has that worked in the past? Are you asking for a volcanic eruption? An earthquake to rip apart the city?"

Raoul stared at her in pity. "You don't understand science or magic. It's not your fault you're not as smart as I am."

Had he really just said that? "You have got to be kidding—"

"Magic isn't alive any more than static electricity or gravity." His smile was condescending. "Come out of the Dark Ages, sister dear. Magic isn't some demon or God. It's just a force that we didn't understand." He turned to everyone and held out his hands. "Imagine if we began to study magic like we do electricity or cold fusion. We're magical creatures. Imagine the power we could harness if we only stopped hiding. If we stopped pretending we didn't exist. Isn't it time we came out into the open?"

"There are more of them than there are of us. You want our children rounded up and studied in some lab?" She hated bringing the kids into this, but that was one of her biggest fears. It was every mother's fear. Hell, hadn't that happened just a few miles away in Gladwin? Some asshole had grabbed the teens just before they shifted and started experimenting on them.

"Of course not!" Raoul cried, looking indignant. "That's why we need to get strong! That's why we need my serum to fight for our children! So they can stand in the light as they really are. Werewolves! Proud and strong!"

Oh hell. The men were really loving that. Especially the ones already hopped up on Raoul's serum.

"And what if you're wrong?" she pressed. "What if everyone for the last few millennia had it right? That magic fights back. It doesn't want to be found."

He sighed. "Only children believe such foolishness."

She shook her head. "This is not for you to decide. This is something all the alphas must decide together."

He chuckled low and sweet, and for the first time, she saw true evil in her brother's eyes. "I didn't decide this," he said. "The Griz did. I'm just playing the hand that was dealt." He spread his hands open as if it was the most natural thing in the world to poison a city then use it to expose shifters to the world. God, did no one else see what he was doing?

"Raoul, think!" she pleaded. "This is not smart."

"Oh sister, don't play with the big boys when you're not equally equipped." And then, just in case no one understood that he was making fun of her inability to shift, he curled his fingers into Delphine's ruff while she jumped forward and growled. The wolf bitch looked magnificent if one ignored the spandex. Thick lush fur, sharp teeth, and a powerful jaw. And didn't Raoul look like every guy's fantasy—a sophisticated man restraining a powerful wolf as if it were nothing at all.

She almost did it then. She almost shifted into her hybrid state and went to town on Delphine. But this wasn't the time to reveal her true nature. It wouldn't win her any favors, and she couldn't be sure she'd win in a fight against a full wolf. This was an argument for her father. He was the alpha, at least for the moment.

So she turned her back on her brother and his bitch. Her gaze caught on Noelle's as she moved, and she saw the woman's sympathy in her expression. But there was nothing her friend could do.

Nothing either of them could do but hope that Frankie could make her father see reason.

Frankie headed toward the exit, only to be stopped short as the community center's doors burst wide open and Wade ran in no longer brandishing his gun and looking like a badass. Wade was covered in blood, and his face looked ashen. Worse, she could smell the blood clearly and knew before he spoke exactly whose it was.

"They've got him!" Wade bellowed. "They got Emory Wolf!"

Horror and a cold fear froze Frankie from the inside out. She struggled to take a breath for a moment, much less ask any one of the questions burning through her brain. Her brother, however, had no such restraint. He reacted immediately, almost as if he knew this was coming.

"Tell me everything," he ordered. "What exactly happened?"

Wade swallowed and reported to Raoul. "We went to the warehouse, just like they wanted. You know. For the meeting."

"Did you go early? To check everything out first?"

"We did everything exactly like you said." Wade's eyes were wide and terrified, but he kept talking, emphasizing the wrong words. "Everything. Exactly. Just like…" He choked off his words, but Frankie knew what was missing.

Like you said. As in, exactly the way Raoul had instructed. Meanwhile, her brother held out a calming hand.

"There's no need to fear." He took a deep breath. "Where's the body? Let me see it."

Frankie's head snapped up. Wade had said "they got him" not that their father was dead. But obviously her brother was following a different script. When she turned her horrified gaze on him, she saw him flush. He knew he'd made a mistake. But then his eyes narrowed, and he advanced on Wade.

"Who has him?"

"The bears," Wade said with a gulp. "They took him."

"You abandoned your alpha?" Raoul bellowed. "You left him there to die—"

"I had to! I had to get back here to report!" Wade babbled. "You had to know what happened and there were bears everywhere. Everywhere!"

Raoul reacted with a speed that shocked even her. Worse, he was precise as he swiped across Wade's throat. He didn't use claws. Years ago, he'd made brass knuckles with sharp claws attached so that it looked like he killed as a werewolf when it was actually a man with a very human tool. He'd told her then that it impressed weak minds, making them think he could hold a shift partway. If they didn't know he had the brass claws, it would look like he swiped across someone's throat with his wolf claws while the rest of his body remained human.

It did its job quickly now. One swipe of his hand and Wade's throat erupted with blood. He grabbed his neck, trying to staunch the flow. Frankie leapt forward, too, instinctively trying to stop a pack mate from dying. But also because they needed him to tell the truth. No matter what he'd said, Frankie knew that the bears hadn't attacked her father. She'd met Simon. He was not a man to start a war casually.

She covered Wade's hands with her own, but it was too late. Blood was spurting faster than anyone could stop, and he quickly collapsed.

"No," she moaned as she saw the life drain out of his face. Wade was a prick, to be sure, but he didn't deserve to die like this, and certainly not by his own pack mate's hand. Her gaze shot up to her brother's. "How could you?" she breathed. She invested all her shock and horror in those three words. Not just because he'd killed their cousin, but because he'd orchestrated all of this. The attack on her father—probably by his own men—and blaming it on the Griz while he took control. She saw it all so clearly, and when she looked in her brother's eyes, she saw confirmation. His expression went from a wide-eyed shock at what he'd just done, to regret and a flash of panic.

But then his expression locked down. She could only read it because she'd spent her life caring for her brother, protecting him when he was picked on by the other boys, even playing with him when no one else could abide his tantrums. She'd made a study of his expressions growing up, and now she saw absolute confirmation of her fears. And a dogged determination to follow his plan.

"Any man who betrays the alpha deserves to die," he said coldly.

"No," she said. "That's not how it works. The pack protects each other."

He curled his lips. "We're wolves, silly girl. The weakest one among us is cut from the pack."

"We're humans, too," she said loudly. "Evolved humans who don't kill out of pique or fear." She stood, her hands dripping with Wade's blood. Her brother didn't realize it yet, but he'd erred badly in killing Wade in front of the pack. All around them men and women recoiled, never having seen violent death before. Parents were clutching their kids and everyone was backing up, their hands over their mouths to cover the smell. She was shaking from the horror of it, but she was the daughter of an alpha, and she would not give in to weakness when the pack most needed her clarity. "Raoul, look around you. This is not the way to power."

She watched his eyes dart around and she could tell he saw the same thing she did. The pack had turned against him, at least for the moment. And so, she pressed her advantage.

"I've been with you since you were a baby. I've held your hand, changed your diapers, and cheered the loudest when you excelled at school. I understand that you're trying to make us stronger. You want us so powerful that no one can touch us." In truth, he wanted himself to be so powerful no barbs could touch him, no insult could wound him. More than anything, her brother wanted to feel safe, and so she tried to give him that safety in a different way. "I understood when you injected me with your serum. I was angry, but I knew you were trying to make me and the pack stronger. But Raoul, this is not the way. Violence only makes people more afraid, more likely to lash out." She held up her hands. "Think about it. You're stronger than you've ever been before, but are you less afraid? Or more?"

She knew the answer to that. In his heart, her brother was a chemist. He'd pursued the serum as a way to make him and everyone else in the pack stronger. She didn't know how he'd gone from injecting it straight into people's veins to dumping it lock, stock, and barrel in the water supply, but she would bet he hadn't intended a citywide disaster. She smiled reassuringly at him.

"We can figure this out, Raoul. You and me, together. Just like when I tried to help you with your chemistry homework and was awful at it. But we always found a way through, remember? We just had to work together."

He wavered. She could tell by the way his expression shifted to a younger look. Suddenly, he was more like the confused and angry teen she remembered. The one who often turned to her when the world got to be too much for him. She held out her hand and he started to reach back, just like he had when they were kids.

Success…almost.

She hadn't counted on the other female in his life. Delphine had never given up anything in her life, not once she considered it hers. And she had a nearly psychic ability to sense when things were not going her way.

She'd been standing beside Raoul in her wolf form, clearly following the shifting currents in the room. Just as Raoul began to reach for Frankie's hand, she shifted back to human. She surged forward, stumbling slightly as she found her human feet right between Frankie and her brother. And there she stood, panting and flushed, wearing only her spandex leggings while her magnificent breasts swung free. And suddenly all eyes were on her.

"Don't do it!" she gasped as she turned to Raoul. "Frankie's been lying to you. She's been lying to us all!"

"I'm the only one who hasn't been lying!" Frankie snapped, anger getting the better of her tongue. But no one was listening to her. Not with Delphine's breasts bobbing in full view.

"I was waiting to bring this up with the alpha. I didn't want to air the shame right in front of everyone." She rounded on Frankie. "But you leave me no choice. I know you've been consorting with the bears. How could you betray your own sire to them? It's disgusting."

"What are you talking about?"

"We all know about your fascination with Detective Kennedy." Her voice took on a singsong quality. "He's the best shifter among us. We should all be more like Detective Kennedy." Her voice dropped to an accusing register. "The grizzly Kennedy."

"He's a cop. He helps—"

"He helps himself." She curled her lip. "And you apparently. Go ahead. Tell them all who you were sleeping with last night."

"What?"

"Did you set Emory up? Did your pillow talk with the bear ensure your own sire's death?"

"What the hell are you talking about?" The question was all bluster. Somehow Delphine knew that she'd spent the night with Ryan. Maybe she smelled the man on her or maybe she had spies watching Noelle's apartment. Either way, just about anyone in the pack could go to Noelle's apartment and smell them both there. Even if Frankie talked her way out of this, the attention would then shift to Noelle who was completely innocent.

"You're sleeping with a bear," Delphine pressed. When Frankie didn't immediately deny it, she turned to the pack at large. "The Griz have declared war on us. They've attacked our alpha and poisoned our city. And now we find out how. Francesca Wolf has been a mole inside our own pack. She's betrayed us to the bears!"

"That's not true!" Frankie cried. "You all know me! I've been spent my entire life helping you, working for the pack." She scanned their faces. Maybe at a different time they would have believed her. Maybe if they hadn't just seen a man murdered before their eyes, they would have had room to put aside their fear and think clearly. But that wasn't what was going on. And right now, every single pair of eyes looked at her with doubt. They didn't know who to believe. Which meant she had to get her brother back on her side. So she appealed to him. "Raoul, why would I do that?"

She looked into his eyes and pleaded with him silently to remember all the things she'd done for him, all the ways she'd nurtured not just him, but the entire pack. Yet two seconds later, she saw that Raoul remembered something else entirely.

"Because you've always wanted to lead the pack. You told father that I wasn't good enough. That I would be a disaster in charge."

A sick dismay flooded her system. Raoul knew what she'd said to their father. The conversation had happened in private, but she'd guessed that Raoul would learn of it. He was smart, and he'd spent a good deal of his childhood learning about interesting electronic devices like bugs for eavesdropping. He probably had listening devices all over wolf territory. Hell, he might even have been surveilling Noelle's apartment. Who knew what paranoia Delphine had fostered in him?

"Raoul," Frankie said softly. "I would never hurt you."

"But you did," Delphine said, her words cold. "You cut him out. Your own brother. You never saw his worth." She sidled up to Raoul, making sure her breasts bounced in his view. "But I see what he's worth. I love him."

Frankie didn't think her brother was dumb enough to be taken in by a pair of magnificent boobs, but apparently she was wrong. He looked down at Delphine's face and his eyes softened. Was he in love? With a shallow, social-climbing bitch just because she flashed her tits? Apparently so, because without even lifting his gaze from Delphine, he called out to the pack at large.

"Restrain my sister. We'll lock her up downstairs while we make the Griz pay for what they've done to our alpha."

"Raoul, no!" Frankie cried. "The Griz didn't do this."

He turned to her and smiled. It wasn't the look of a man besotted by a conniving woman. And it certainly wasn't the lost little boy she remembered from her childhood. This was all Raoul, supremely confident in his choices and gleeful even. "Didn't they?" he mocked. "I think they did. And I think you were in cahoots with them." He arched a brow. "And I think I'm the only wolf who can lead us out of this mess you've created."

She'd seen it before. She'd even told herself that her brother was not the little boy she remembered, but she'd never really believed it. Not in her heart of hearts. Not until this very moment when she realized just how much she'd been holding on to a boy who maybe never was. Raoul's expression told her everything she'd suspected but was afraid to believe. That he had orchestrated everything. That he had cold-bloodedly planned their father's attack and to oust her from the pack in shame. Maybe he'd planned this from back when Hunter had died.

But the gloves were off now. He'd just shown her his true self, and she had to look to her own survival. No more trying to reach him. It had been a long shot anyway. Which meant she couldn't allow herself to be grabbed or put in the restraining cells in the basement. She had to get to her father.

Emory was the only one who could stop Raoul and save the pack. And so she turned to run. She knew it made her look guilty as hell. She knew that she was abandoning Noelle and Hazel and all her friends, but she couldn't help them if she was locked up or worse. She spun on her heel and took off.

Except Raoul had more friends than she thought. Aggressive ones hopped up on the serum.

She dodged the first, put an elbow to the face of the next and spun around him. But it wasn't going to be enough. Not with the werewolves leaping toward her, all with murder in their eyes. The only way to survive this was to go full out, and that meant full monster.

God, she didn't want to do it this way, but she'd run out of options. She had to fight free. She waited until just the right moment. They were coming at her from all sides. Fortunately, the families and the kids had already scrambled out of the way. She wouldn't hurt any innocents. Still it ached to attack her own pack mates like this.

They were almost on her, the wolves leaping at her from left and right. So she let fly with the monster change complete with killer BO. It was a defensive mechanism unique to hybrids like her who were neither fully human nor fully wolf, but something in between. When a human caught a whiff of the stench, they started to gag. But wolves with their much more sensitive noses immediately spun away. It was instinct, pure and simple. Anything that smelled this bad had to be poisonous and no creature wanted to bite down on that.

With the wolves out of the way, she just had to dodge the gagging humans. A couple hardy souls made a stab at blocking the doors. She was impressed that they had kept focused on their task despite the urge to retch, but she couldn't let them stop her. Thanks to Hazel's training, they were no match for her, and soon she was out the door.

But once free of the community center where was she to go? Only one place. She had to find Ryan. She'd been a fool to think she could manage this alone. This problem had grown bigger than one person inside a pack could fix. Which meant she needed him and all the help he could bring.

But how was she going to find him? She had to call the Griz and pray that they still trusted her enough to talk.

Chapter 19

Pain swamped Ryan's consciousness with every breath. At first, he hadn't even realized the connection, only the steady ebb and flow of agony. But with awareness came patterns. A knife blade at his ribs, sawing at his concentration.

He also isolated a sound and a warm grip on his hand. He focused on that small heat, absorbing the comfort it brought him.

"It was my brother Raoul," she was saying, her voice choked with tears. "No one else makes brass knuckles like that. He's trying to make it look like a bear attack."

Frankie.

"Yeah, we got that." Simon's voice was hard. "Why the fuck would he attack your father?"

"To become alpha. And he wants a war with you."

"And why haven't you stopped this? That's what you promised, isn't it? You begged me to delay so you could take care of things internally. Does this look like it's been taken care of?"

"I didn't think he'd attack our father!" Frankie said. "I

didn't think it was possible. Wolves can't go against their alpha."

"Apparently, wolves can," Simon growled.

"It's the serum. I should have seen it before. Brady defied a direct order in the sewers. Everyone's more aggressive while on it." She sighed. "Even I never contemplated taking over the pack until I became a hybrid."

"Not your fault," Ryan said, his voice rusty as pain burned through every word. But he didn't stop. "Everyone waits too long to get help."

"Ryan!" she cried out, and she gripped his hand tighter.

"You're awake," Simon said, and there was relief in his tone. "Can you shift?"

He couldn't even open his eyes. But he did have the strength to squeeze Frankie's hand. And damn, the pain from speaking was burying him.

"Ryan? It's Frankie."

Yes, he knew.

"You're hurt pretty bad, but it'll heal if you shift. Can you do it?"

Of course, he could. He reached for the energy state. He pictured himself as a grizzly and tried to slide into it. But the pain burned through him, fracturing his focus. Worse, his mind kept replaying everything that had happened the last two times he'd shifted. Torn apart by Nanook's hybrids. Shot in the sewer. Didn't matter, he told himself firmly. But the moment he reached for the energy state, pain shredded his intention.

Then another voice intruded. A female's voice with the authority of a doctor. Must be Hank's woman, Dr. Lu from the CDC. "I've got to give him some painkillers. He's in so much pain, there's no way he can concentrate."

"If you drug him, he can't focus enough to shift." Simon spoke logically, as usual.

"He needs rest. Look at him. Do you really think he has the energy? Even without the pain, he's exhausted."

"Doctor—" Simon began, but Frankie interrupted them both.

"Just ask him what he wants."

Smart woman. It was one of the reasons he liked her so much. But it was hard to think, even harder to speak. Still, he forced it out because Frankie believed he could. "No drugs."

"Detective Kennedy," the doctor was saying. "There is no point in macho heroics. You've done your job—"

Had he?

"—now you need to recover."

"Emory... Wolf?"

"Alive, thanks to you." Simon again. "Do you remember what happened?"

Ah hell. He didn't want to remember. In truth, he was trying hard to not remember getting gutted. Again. But he knew his duty, so he forced himself to report what he could. Scoping out the warehouse. Emory attacked. The fight. He used short sentences. Clear words. He nearly passed out before he was done, but he made it. And once he'd finished, Simon took up the tale.

"We got there at the end. Alyssa shot the ones on you."

Alyssa could shoot the wings off a gnat. Thank God she was on their side.

"Then we carried you both here for the doc to patch you up."

His voice dropped to a deeper register. "You'd feel a lot better if you just shift."

He knew that. He wanted that. But he couldn't grab hold of the process. What was wrong with him?

Then there was a commotion nearby and another voice, this one deep and familiar. Hank. The quiet Zen master who could kick major ass when needed. He spoke to Simon, but everyone heard. "Raoul sent a message. Did it old school on parchment, written in blood, wrapped around a rock, and thrown at our door."

"Charming," the doctor drawled.

"Message says, 'Return Emory and the traitor Francesca.'"

"Not much of a negotiator, is he?" Simon answered. Then when no one responded, he sighed. "Anything else?"

"Just a time and place for the exchange. Dawn. A park on the edge of wolf territory."

"He'll attack here first," Frankie said. "Sometime tonight."

"Isn't he worried about the cops?" Simon asked.

She sighed. "He wants to expose shifters to the world."

Silence. Then Simon spoke with an incredulous tone: "Just how crazy is your brother?"

Ryan felt her grip go painfully tight, but when she spoke, her voice was flat. "I don't even recognize him anymore."

"Hopped up on his own poison?" That was from the doctor, condemnation in every syllable.

"I don't know. Maybe." Frankie's voice dropped into resignation. "Probably."

"Didn't anyone tell him that drugs are bad?" Simon asked. It was a rhetorical question that no one bothered to answer. And then Ryan felt a grip on his shoulder. "Do whatever you need to do, Ryan."

Thanks. Assuming he could figure out what that was.

He heard several people leave, but Frankie wasn't one of them. He kept a grip on her hand and felt her drop her forehead to his arm.

"I should have listened to you," she said. "I was stupid to think I could handle this on my own."

He wanted to stroke her hair. He needed to open his eyes and look at her, but speaking with Simon had drained him. It was all he could do to just lie there and touch her. She seemed to understand. Or maybe she needed to talk to him. Either way, she stayed and started whispering to him. Simple things at first. He dozed to the sweet sound. But eventually, her words took on different meaning, and he roused to listen more clearly.

"We're alone now. Dad's in the next room recovering, and everyone else has gone to prepare. We're in the upper floor of your headquarters. It's kind of nice. Not exactly the mansion my parents have, but comfortable upstairs and useful downstairs. Who'd have guessed that bears were more practical than wolves?"

Anybody. It was well known that wolves like to put on a show. Every wolf alpha in a major city had a mansion, whereas the bears just liked a cozy, protected den.

"Growing up, I was the daughter of an alpha. They told me there was nothing I couldn't do. I just had to work hard enough." She snorted. "What a load of crap. I've never worked harder in my life and I'm still out here and called a traitor."

"What happened to pulling together as a pack?"

She looked up when he spoke. He'd managed to finally open his eyes because he was pulled to look at her face. He wanted to see the emotions there, to catch the shift of grass-green eyes and the sweet curve of her mouth.

"The pack is only as strong as its weakest link." Her lips quirked in a bitter twist. "I guess I'm the weak one here."

"Or your brother."

She shook her head. "He's the leader over there now. That means he's the strongest."

He focused, lifting his hand to stroke across her tear-streaked face. "I was told to protect my family."

"And you have."

"My family didn't protect me. My parents can't even say the word 'shifter.' Nanook tried to kill me. And even the cops I work with day in and day out don't know what I really am." He wiped at her wet cheek. "I say we throw out all those stupid sayings and start making some of our own."

Her mouth curved into a smile. "Like what?"

"How about, I've got your back, if you've got mine."

She tilted her head, nuzzling her cheek deeper into his palm. "Do you?"

"Tried to."

"Yeah, my bad." She glanced across his shoulder to the hallway where—he guessed—she could see her father through the open doorway. "You protected my father anyway."

"I still serve and protect. What I'm looking for is my family."

She arched a brow. "The Griz don't support you?"

"Not one went up against Nanook when he tried to kill me. He might have been holding them back. I don't know."

"But you don't trust them now."

"Simon and Alyssa are new. They seem okay. Vic, too. But I've been going it alone since Nanook betrayed me." And where had that gotten him? Nearly dead in a sewer. Nearly dead at an abandoned factory. "Going solo isn't working for either of us."

She nodded but if anything, her expression turned even more sober. "Why do you trust me?"

Good question. There were obvious reasons why he shouldn't. She was a wolf and she'd bailed on him at the storage area. But he'd understood why and would probably have done the same if he were she. She'd saved his life in the sewer and tried to protect him at Hazel's home. That counted for something, but it wasn't enough to explain why his instincts kept pushing him to trust her.

"Remember when I told you about roaming the woods? When I was a teenager?"

She nodded. "While your grandfather fished."

"I was amped up from shifter hormones, but something about the place centered me. Life was chaos, or at least it felt that way, but the smell of the pine and the whisper of leaves made me feel stronger. Like the storm was outside instead of inside. And I could deal with that."

"I get that." She pressed her lips to his palm in a quick kiss. Then she pulled back enough to explain. "It's what a good pack feels like. No matter what's happening in your life, there's that solid center inside." She blew out a breath. "I haven't felt that since turning hybrid."

"Because your brother started taking over the pack?"

Her gaze turned thoughtful. "Maybe. I just assumed it was because I'd changed into a monster."

He smiled. "You're no monster." Then he took a deep breath, letting her scent settle into his lungs. "No one who smells so good could be evil."

She snorted. "I need a shower. I went full hybrid to escape the community center, stink and all."

He frowned. "Were you hurt?"

"Only my pride." Then her expression turned confused. "Do you seriously like the smell?"

He smiled. "I do. Could that be because you injected me with the stuff?"

"Maybe. Or maybe you're just weird."

Maybe. He let his gaze linger on her face and he fell into the emotions that swirled inside him whenever he thought of her. "It feels like you're my woods. When you're around, the problems are external, not internal."

Her eyes widened in surprise and she went statue still, but in the end, her lips softened. "You know that doesn't make logical sense, right."

"I know."

"Yeah. And…" She blew out a breath. "I feel the same way about you."

Warmth flooded his body at her words along with a healthy dose of surprise. "I need to shift," he said. "I need to get healthy, so I can kiss you."

She grinned. "I'm okay with that."

Yeah, so was he. Except when he reached for the change magic, it wasn't there. "I can't do it."

"Why not?"

He hadn't the foggiest idea. "Could it be the serum?"

"It makes you stronger. Even after one dose, you should be able to shift more often, not less."

"Even after it wears off?"

"Yeah."

He grimaced. That eliminated a physical problem as the cause. Which meant his problem was all mental. He could have guessed that.

"Except for my night with you, I haven't slept since Nanook attacked me." He would have shrugged, but knew his side would punish him for the movement. "If you don't count when I was unconscious."

"What happens when you try to sleep?"

He tried not to remember even as he spoke. "My thigh gets shredded, two slugs hit me in the chest, and Nanook laughs."

She shuddered. "That's some grade-A trauma you got going there."

His lips quirked. Trust Frankie to put it bluntly. "Guess so."

"It's a wonder you're not in the corner drooling on yourself."

He arched a brow. "I kind of am, aren't I?"

She tilted her head as she inspected him. "No drool, so you're okay there."

"Good to know."

Her face softened as she stroked his good shoulder. "I am so sorry for leaving you to face the police alone. I shouldn't have bailed. We could have helped each other."

"At least you know it now."

She nodded. "But I don't think your magic does."

He frowned. "What?"

"Think about it. Everyone you trust has betrayed you. And then you find the one person who makes you feel like you're centered again, and what do I do? I bail."

"I understand why."

"Maybe on a conscious level, but what about underneath where the magic comes from? At this point, your magic has got to think that the world is a terrible place and it'd be way better if you just stayed in bed where it's safe."

He couldn't argue with that. Hell, his conscious mind thought that too. But he had a duty to the people of Detroit, promises to the Griz, and a bone-deep need to stop the coming violence between the wolves and the bears. Up until now, he'd always relied on that moral center—the knowledge of duty and responsibility—to guide him even when the rest of the world seemed to think lies were the norm. Now he wondered if that was enough. All those responsibilities didn't really feel like they gave anything back to him. And right now, he was running on empty.

She stroked a finger across his brow, gently smoothing away the frown he hadn't even known was there. "You seem to be thinking a whole lot of stuff right now. Care to share?"

"I can't argue with what you're saying. I just don't know how to fix it."

"Your subconscious needs to feel safe again."

He snorted. "Great. How?"

"Do I look like a therapist to you? I haven't a clue. But I'm willing to sit here and talk it out with you if you want. Will that help?"

It couldn't hurt. And looking into her soft green eyes, he believed it would help. A lot. "I don't know where to begin."

"Start anywhere. Let me listen."

So he did. He talked backward in time, starting with Nanook, but ended by relaying how his parents had reacted when he'd told them he was a shifter. Back in Noelle's bedroom, he'd told Frankie it was a fun experience, that he'd loved showing his parents that magic existed and making his sister scream. He hadn't told her about the rest because he didn't like to think of the negatives. When he'd first said the words to his parents—not shown them—his father had stared at him like he was insane and his mother had shaken her head, no. As if he'd shared a cancer diagnosis or something. They fought the knowledge even after he shifted right in front of them.

They were good people, and he loved them, but they struggled to accept what he was. It made them uncomfortable on a gut level, and he didn't want to force them into a place they couldn't go.

It hurt. Deep down, it really hurt, and this was the first time he'd told anyone about it.

She listened to him. And though they held hands at the beginning, eventually she stretched out in the bed beside him. Her body pressed intimately close to his, but she kept her head braced on the palm of her hand as he talked. Every once in a while, she would tell him a similar story from her childhood, but mostly she listened as she held him. And when the pain seemed to pour out with every word, she wrapped her arm around his torso and pressed her lips to his cheek.

He felt the wet of her tears, but didn't acknowledge them. Especially since they might have been his own. His throat gave out more than once, but he sipped water and soon fell into talking again. She brought that out in him. Words, feelings, things he hadn't acknowledged even in the privacy of his own thoughts. They spilled out to her, and she absorbed them as if she couldn't get enough.

At one point, Hank's mantra slipped through his thoughts. *The greatest mastery is a mind that lets go.* He'd been trying with very little success. Until now. Now he saw that he had to let go by giving it to someone else. To share the pain and the burden so that it could finally dissipate.

He gave it to her. He told her everything until his throat shut down and his words failed. He closed his mouth and his eyes. He settled his cheek on her head, and he held her just as tightly as she held him.

And together, they slept.

Chapter 20

Frankie woke with a start, the feel of her pack mates in her head. Normally that would reassure her, but this time, she felt their aggression, knew they were angry, and all of them were very close.

"Easy. You're safe." Ryan's words rumbled through his body into hers. He was lying flat on his back and she was wrapped around him.

"My pack is near," she said. "And they're pissed."

She started to get out of bed. She had to go downstairs and warn—

"We know," he said as he tightened his hand on her shoulder. She could have broken his hold, but didn't want him to strain his injury.

"How? I just started feeling them."

Ryan's expression eased into a smile as he held up his phone in his free hand. "Simon just texted me. Told me to keep my ass in bed or he'd personally kick it back up here and he can't afford the distraction." He arched a brow. "Yours, too, by the way. Nothing you can do but make it worse."

Unfortunately, that was probably true. Still, the need to go burned in her. From the feel of them, her pack was hopped up on the serum and ready to eat bear. Literally. "You don't know what you're up against."

"Simon knows. He's got surveillance cams and nonlethal surprises. Plus, the police on speed dial."

She frowned. "You'd bring cops into shifter business?"

He arched a brow, not even bothering to respond, and she felt her face heat. Of course he'd bring cops into their business. He was a cop.

"Look, the bears aren't doing anything but hanging out and respecting your brother's wish to talk in the morning. If he wants to attack us unprovoked, then he can explain to the police why he's creeping through the streets with cherry bombs and rabid wolves."

"They'll say it's because you bears poisoned the city."

"And the cops will say, they already suspect us, and that vigilante justice is a crime."

She winced and looked out the window at the dark night. She couldn't see anything. Just a haze of light over the city streets and the shadows of nearby buildings. First thing her brother would have done is kill the electricity to the block. "How come the lights are still on in here?" She could see the red numbers from a clock on the nightstand. 2:48 a.m.

"Building has its own generator." He arched a brow. "Got a black bear security expert and a grizzly bear electrician." He tilted his head. "Don't you wolves have people?"

She nodded. "My brother loves electronic toys." God only knew what elaborate stuff he'd set up around the mansion and the community center. She'd been involved in every aspect of the construction process, but Raoul had added all sorts of special stuff at night. At the time, she'd thought it a good idea. Now she wondered if he'd doctored the water pipes so he could easily dose the pack with serum. Not to mention what he could have done to the electricity, the air vents, and she had no idea what else.

Before she could comment, floodlights kicked on all around the neighborhood. What had been dim or shadowed a second ago, now stood out in stark relief. And inside, she felt the collective surprise ripple through her pack. As best she could make out, they were coming from all sides, intending to surround the bears as they stormed the former hardware store. But with the sudden flood of lights, they all seemed to pause.

"Can you send them a message?" Ryan asked. "Through the pack link?"

She shook her head. "It's not a verbal thing. We get each other's emotions and sometimes a general sense of direction. No words."

"Then there's nothing you can do." He said it as a statement, and she wanted to argue. She was an alpha's daughter. She ought to do something, but what? Usually she would send support vibes through the link, but she didn't support what they were doing. "Go away" would likely inflame things. At best, she should stay quiet and pretend she wasn't even here. Few people in the pack could get a directional sense from the pack link, but those who could would know she was sitting here with the bears.

She sighed and dropped her head on his shoulder, feeling frustration eat at her. The drive to do something—anything—to save the ones she loved from disaster churned like acid in her gut.

"Simon won't hurt them unless he has to."

She tried to take comfort in that. Maybe the pack would get

spooked by the floodlights and turn around. Except the moment she thought the words, she felt the wolves stir. Anger surged quickly followed by defiance. It was a madness she hadn't felt from her people ever. Normally the pack link calmed and soothed, but this link stirred to violence, and she felt her own blood surge with the connection.

Worse, she felt a single, strong vibration through the link. A dark mind pushing the rest to madness.

Raoul. What the hell was wrong with her brother? Why would he push the pack to madness? Unless he was already there, and he was just bringing everyone else along with him.

"He's going to get them killed." People she'd known all her life, pack mates who were good people, though maybe not very discerning when it came to complicated issues. They didn't know how to think logically, to separate emotions from passionate words to look at the sense of things. She'd tried to reason with them, but they moved with the crowd without thought or discretion.

She bit her lip, beating her brain for something—anything—that she could do to stop them. They had to *think*. But she could already tell from the link that there wasn't a soul among them who would listen to reason now. Not with Raoul stirring them up.

She pushed up from Ryan, breaking the restraint of his arm with an impatient growl. "I have to stop them."

"You know you can't."

"I have to try. It's what an alpha does." She said the words with conviction, knowing that it was the first time she'd called herself an alpha. Not just the daughter of one, but a leader of a werewolf pack. It didn't matter that her pack wasn't following her right now. She was an alpha inside.

He pushed up on his elbow, wincing as it pulled at his side. When the pain built to excruciating, he flopped back down and looked at her. "You have to *think*. They're not, but you can."

She went to the hallway and looked into her father's room. He was resting peacefully, the shallow lift and fall of his chest the only indication he was alive. She thought about waking him, but the doctor had told her the longer he slept, the better. If he hadn't woken from the mental turmoil of the pack outside their window, then he wasn't strong enough to do anything even if she could manage to rouse him. He had to rest, which meant it was up to her to do...what?

She paced back into Ryan's bedroom, crossing to the window to stare down. She saw the naked street, empty of everything except a few parked cars. She felt her people out there, hovering on the edge, slinking through the shadows as they hugged the buildings.

"You've talked to them already," Ryan pressed. "You've told them everything they need to know."

"Yes," she acknowledged. Then she bit out the word in fury. "Yes!" Why wouldn't they listen?

"So you've given them all the information, but they're choosing Raoul anyway."

She dropped her head against the cool windowpane. They were right there on the edge of her awareness. So close. So bitter. Was that Raoul? Or was that seething resentment inside everyone?

"They're going to die."

"Maybe. Maybe not. But you can't stop them from making bad decisions."

She spun around, her agitation making her voice sharp. "I'm an alpha. I may be just a hybrid, but I've always taken care of the pack. Everything I've done is for their good."

"You are not God. And you wouldn't want to take away people's free will anyway."

She threw up her hands. "This is not a philosophical debate. Raoul is going to get them killed!"

He just looked at her, his blue eyes practically luminous in the floodlights. She read compassion in his expression, and an implacable steadiness in his eyes. Firm, calm, and cold. Like a steel blade honed to a razor's edge.

"There is nothing you can do," he said.

"Stop saying that!" There had to be something.

He sighed. "You've done everything you can. Now it's up to them to choose."

"But they're choosing wrong!" she huffed.

"And that's their right."

He was right. She *knew* he was right, but God she hated it. To the depths of her soul, she despised what her brother had done. Somehow, he'd subverted the pack, put her on the outside when all she wanted was to help them. It was her right to serve and protect the pack, and yes, she felt the irony in those words. Ryan's job was to serve and protect all of Detroit, and she'd fought him every step of the way.

Pack business. Shifter politics. Hell. And now she felt just as he did. Sitting outside when the very people he was spending his life trying to help cut him out, ignored him, or worse, hated him for doing his job.

"How do you stand it?" she whispered. "You're on the gang task force. You work with kids. How do you make them listen?"

He lifted his hand in a vague gesture before letting it drop. Then he sighed. "Same way you have. I talk and talk. I reason, I plead. I even apply pressure when I can. But in the end…"

"You have to let them choose."

"You know a teenager who isn't hell-bent on deciding things for him or herself?"

No. She sighed and crossed back to the bed. Nothing was happening out there right now. Her people had the place surrounded, but they hadn't yet stepped into the light. And thankfully, Simon wasn't pushing things but sat waiting for the pack to decide what it wanted to do.

"I hate this." Her body twitched as she looked at the door. She almost went straight for it because, come hell or high water, she needed to be with her pack. But that was stupid, and she knew it. They'd chosen Raoul. All she could do was inflame matters—and emotions—even more.

So she sat and entwined her fingers with Ryan. "How'd you get so wise?"

"I work with teenagers. It's the only way to keep sane."

"But the stakes are so high. A wrong choice—"

"Gets people killed. Yeah, I know. And the bystanders are the worst casualties. They haunt me at night."

Yet one more reason why he couldn't sleep. The hollow note in his voice pulled at her. Especially since it was an echo of the pain she felt now. If the pack chose to fight, there would be casualties on both sides. Bear, wolf, human bystander. She'd remember every one and feel the loss until the day she died.

"How many bystanders?" she asked. "How many souls haunt you, Ryan?"

"After three years working in gangs? Seven. Two were just at the wrong place at the wrong time. Five were too young to have a chance to think on their own. They were just used by the people who said they'd protect them."

She touched the worry lines on his face, smoothing them gently with her thumb. "You can't hold on to them. It wasn't your fault."

"You can't go out there. You've done everything you can."

She looked at his face and saw the pain etched in every line. He wasn't hiding his feelings from her. Right now, he was showing her the path she was on. He was letting her see the pain that came from not letting go of what you couldn't control. It was eating him alive, and she was a few hours away from that exact same place.

"I'll make you a deal," she said softly. "I'll stay right here, right now, if you forgive me for not knowing how to do better. I've failed to convince my own people to see reason."

"You can't convince people who won't listen. What is happening is not your fault."

She nodded, knowing it was true. "So am I forgiven?"

He smiled. "Of course."

"Then you have to forgive yourself, too. I don't know what happened to those seven people, but I know you did everything you could."

He blew out a breath as he looked away. "You don't know the mistakes I've made."

"And you don't know how I might have stopped it weeks or maybe months ago." She leaned forward. "Did you forgive me for skipping out at the restaurant?"

His gaze cut to hers. "You know I did."

"Then why don't you deserve the same respect?" She stroked his very rigid jaw. "Tell you what, I forgive you for not being a super-human God who can control teenagers bent on destruction."

His lips curved at that, and she felt the tightness in his jaw ease. "And I forgive you for loving your brother so much that you forgave him for the unforgiveable, and you still love him despite him leading your people into madness."

Her chest squeezed at that. The grip was so tight and so painful that tears sprang to her eyes. He had pegged her straight on. He understood exactly where her mistakes were and the error she was still making. She hoped that somewhere, somehow Raoul would turn away from the darkness. And if he did, then the pack could find the right path. But so far, it wasn't happening. And she couldn't forgive herself for allowing him to drag the pack into insanity.

But apparently Ryan could. He could forgive her and, in that moment, she felt the guilt ease. If nothing else, the burden was now shared with him, and she felt so much better for it.

"Thank you," she whispered.

"Thank you," he echoed. And in those two words, she heard the same relief that she felt. The same whisper of surprise and awe that echoed in her soul because they had helped each other. And together, they breathed out their pain. A moment later, she dropped forward until they were forehead to forehead.

"I wish you were better," she said. "I'd really like to make love with you right now."

The words hadn't even finished. Their sound still hovered in the air when she felt the tingle.

Magic. Shifting.

She jumped back. Grizzlies needed a lot more room on the bed than an injured man. She saw the golden light and felt the abrupt coolness in the air. Ryan was a vague shape of grizzly mixed with the lines of a man.

He shimmered there on the bed, the glow neither man nor bear but part of both. And best of all, as she watched, his bandages lost traction on his skin and floated down to the bed. She held her breath, watching, and then the glow contracted. It pulled together into one body, one man, whole and complete.

And he was grinning.

Chapter 21

The man was radiant when he smiled, and it wasn't just his blond hair and blue-eyed good looks. There was a lightness in his being that softened the angles of his body, eased his hard jaw, and made his lips kissable instead of tightly pressed. After the confessions of the last few hours, it was beautiful to see him happy. Even better, she'd been the one to bring it out in him.

He tugged her close and she fell willingly into his arms. "You're so beautiful," he said.

She smiled. "I was just thinking the same thing about you."

His hands flowed down her back and shivers made her arch in response. "I want to go slow," he said, "but I want you so bad right now."

She teased her lips along the seam of his. "Want some wine to go with that cheesy line?"

"Nope," he said. "Just you." Then he flipped her over on the bed and straddled her.

She slid her arms over his shoulders and into his hair. "Are you really okay? I mean physically and emotionally. No aches? No pains?"

She thought he'd come back with another corny line, but he paused as he thought about her question. He took a deep breath and she felt his lungs expand and his groin thicken against her.

"Body's fine," he said with a grin. "And you feel great."

"What about the rest?"

He arched a brow. "Am I still messed up in the head? No more than you are." He glanced out the window. "There's a whole world of trouble out there. But you and I are in here, and we can't do anything about out there."

"So gather ye rosebuds while ye may?" she asked, quoting her favorite high school English poem.

He shrugged in a why not gesture. "You wanted to make love to me, and I want to give you so many orgasms you pass out and forget all about everything else. You okay with that?"

She jerked her chin at the nightstand. "I still got condoms in my purse."

"Thank God."

"You'll have to get off me if you want me to grab them."

"In a minute," he said. Then he began licking her lips, tasting her mouth and her face in a way she recognized though had never experienced before. It was an animal thing, this exploration with tongue and teeth. Wolves did it, but only with their closest friends and always in wolf form.

She arched her head back, exposing her neck to him. Throat, belly, even her groin was his. Sure, he'd had her back in Noelle's apartment, but that had been a thing of the body. This was deeper, more intimate. And with every brush of his tongue, she felt herself relax into his attention.

He pressed kisses into her neck and she felt her heartbeat flutter.

She held onto his shoulders, squeezing as he tasted her pulse point and purred against the underside of her jaw.

"I want my legs free," she whispered. Her feet had caught on the cotton sheet as he'd flipped her over. She wanted to grip him with her knees and scrape her toes along his calves.

He responded quickly, leaping off her with gratifying speed. He pulled the sheet completely off the bed, freeing her legs to move as she wanted. But he didn't stop there. He tugged at her T-shirt and she sat up so he could strip it away. She unhooked her bra while he headed for her hips. She didn't hesitate to lift for him, and a moment later she was free of all restraint. No sheet, no clothing, no doubts.

"Kiss me," she said. "Everywhere."

"Planned to," he said.

"No. Like a bear. Like one with his mate."

He paused, and his nostrils flared. No doubt he took in her scent, the musk of hunger and of something more. His hands clenched at his sides then released. She could tell he was aroused by what she said. His eyes burned bright and his organ pulsed thick and hungry before her. But he didn't move.

"You want me to pretend we're bound together?"

"It's possible, isn't it? Between wolf and bear?" Cross-species mating wasn't unheard of, but it wasn't exactly common. Every single one claimed to be a love match. No reason to buck the animal demands for anything short of love.

"Of course, it's possible." He swallowed. "But are you ready for that? Or is this us playing house again?"

Was this pretend? She wanted him desperately. She was wet with lust. He also eased an ache inside her. He had from the very beginning.

"What do you want?" she asked.

He didn't answer. He held her gaze though, as he crossed to the nightstand. He found her condoms quickly enough, and she watched as he put one on with sure and steady hands. Then he spoke, and she heard a tremor beneath his words that betrayed his need.

"I can't think clearly when I'm this hungry for you." He crossed to the edge of the bed, drawing her down it with a quick tug on her thighs. She was open for him, her musky scent thick in the air. "So how about this? The first O is for fun." He grinned. "Just to take the edge off."

"And the second?" Because she guessed that with him, there was always going to be a second.

"That's when we'll get real."

It was already real for her. She knew it deep in her bones. She was in love with him. He believed in her, he centered her, and most of all, he saw her. Exactly as she was, faults and all. But she couldn't forget that she was on borrowed time. That at some point her brother and the pack he controlled would come for her, and she wasn't likely to survive. So what harm could it do if she allowed herself to commit to a man now? To bond with a bear who had shared his burdens with her even as he eased hers. Why not make it real for now? Just so long as she didn't tell him how deeply she was in love with him. Just so long as he didn't tumble as far into bonding as she was with him. She didn't have a future, but he did. And she wouldn't steal that from him.

"Okay," she said. "First one just to take the edge off."

He grinned as he leaned forward. He pulled her legs up and spread her knees, inhaling deeply as he did. He settled right where she was most open to him. Pelvis to pelvis, penis to opening. Then he pressed his lips to hers.

"Well," he hedged. "Maybe a little tasting." He licked her lips and her mouth. He nuzzled into her hairline and ran his teeth along her cheek and the curve of her ear. His breath was hot and sweet, and she smelled his scent as hungry as her own.

When her breath grew ragged just from the scent of him, she clutched at his shoulders. He was tugging on her earlobe, the nip of his teeth as erotic as the stroke of his tongue. And then he thrust.

She'd been ready for it. Hell, she'd been dying for it, but even so the rhythm wasn't what she expected. It felt like he had tried to hold back, but couldn't. Need overpowered him, so that when he thrust, both of them were surprised. But she was so wet, he slid right in and moaned in delight at the stretch. He was big, and she wanted so badly for him to fill her.

She heard the shudder in his breath or maybe she felt it move between both their bodies. But either way, he moaned low into her ear. A deep vibration that echoed down her spine and straight to her womb.

"Don't stop," she whispered.

"Can't," he panted, though he wasn't moving below. And yet she felt him, thick and hard. A pulse deep inside her. Not orgasm, but the prelude. "Trying. To. Last."

"Next time," she whispered as she squeezed him tightly. His inhale cut off on a startled gasp.

He thrust again. The movement was more jerky than smooth, but she loved it all the more for his break in concentration.

And then it was like he couldn't stop. He drove into her hard and the impact on her clit made her see stars.

Again, he slammed against her. He had his rhythm now, hard and increasingly fast. She matched it, wrapping her legs around his hips.

She arched as he impaled her. She threw back her head and rode him as if she were on top. She wasn't, but he lifted her with every impact and her breath caught every single time.

She gripped his shoulders as he pushed a thumb down between them.

He didn't need to do it. She was already at the edge. But at his next thrust, the pad of his thumb bore down onto her clit, and she crested right over with a cry. He joined her a split second later, his whole body pulsing into hers.

She felt his release, and she greeted every throb with happiness. As if they really were bonded. As if their children were a foregone conclusion. As if they had a glorious future stretched out before them, and she felt it everywhere. Their shimmering life together, and she embraced it with every part of her. She held it strong to her heart just as she held him when he collapsed on top of her. And she kept her eyes closed so that she could see it all so clearly for a moment longer. So that she felt perfect union with him for a moment longer.

A—

He exhaled close to her ear, his breath hot, nipping her erotically with his teeth.

Moment—

She held him tight, but he eased to the side. He was trying to keep his weight off her. Considerate of him, but she didn't want to be spared. She wanted to hold him.

Longer…

She felt the magic hovering, just on the edge but not quite locking in. She knew instinctively what it was: a magical bond between shifters that created mated pairs. She'd never heard of it happening between cross-species though, and maybe that was why it didn't land. Bear and wolf didn't mix, not even in magic.

Her mouth opened on a frustrated cry. She wanted that connection with him. And when she looked into his eyes, she saw indecision there. Did he feel the same thing, too? Did he know what had almost happened?

Maybe. Because he pressed his lips to her neck. A kiss. A lick. Then he spoke, his words low and barely audible even though his mouth was right next to her ear.

"I had to wait until the edge was off. I had to hold it back until we weren't so desperate."

"I'm not—"

"Shhh. Just listen."

She quieted. Her entire body stilled. She didn't breathe, and she wasn't even sure her heart was beating. Every part of her strained to hear him, but he didn't speak right away. Instead, he pulled back far enough to look into her eyes.

"I feel like you're my home," he said. "Like you could be everything to me." Then he grimaced. "You *are* everything. It's already happened, Frankie."

Her eyes widened as he spoke. Her heart lurched inside her chest, and her breath seemed to burn.

"What I'm saying," he continued, "is that this is more than playing house to me. It could be love. The forever, bonding kind of love."

Her hands tightened on his shoulders, squeezing just to be sure that he was real. "It didn't lock in," she whispered. "Did you feel that? We didn't—"

"I don't care about magical bonds, Frankie. It's you. It's me. I'm all in."

Her breath caught. She couldn't be dreaming this. He was committing to her. A bear promising himself to a wolf. And the magic of that was enough for her.

"Me, too," she said. "All in."

She expected his expression to lighten then, to burst into the kind of joy she felt bubbling inside her. And it did, though not nearly as fully as hers. Instead, he drew his body back from her. Not far. He still pressed her down into the mattress. She still felt him thick and alive inside her. But she also sensed him drawing back.

"Frankie," he whispered.

"Yes?"

"Don't betray me." She heard the meaning in his words. They were both an order and a plea. After everything he'd been through, he couldn't be hurt again. Not by her. Not after he'd just become so vulnerable to her.

"I won't," she answered. "I swear it."

And she did. With every cell in her body, every aspect of her soul, she promised not to hurt him. She'd never turn on him, she'd never turn away even though he was a bear and she was a wolf. In that moment, he became her pack, and she shuddered at the implication of that. But she also welcomed it. Lost no longer, outcast no more. He had called her his home, and now he was hers.

Suddenly she was pushing him over. She didn't let him fall out of her as she straddled him, pinning his shoulders and his hips to the mattress. His eyes widened, but he didn't comment. Especially when she began to lick him.

She did everything a wolf did with her mate. She tasted his skin, she bit gently at his throat. She nuzzled into his belly. The position forced them to separate and she helped him clean up as well. And then she licked his thighs and his hips. She inhaled his musk deep into her lungs, and she licked his organ. He was thick and hard as she took him deep into her mouth. She thought she'd finish him off that way, but he didn't let her.

Well, not exactly.

He lifted her off the mattress and twisted her around. She pulled off him to support herself on her elbows while he began to taste her in the way of a bear. Broad flat licks, rumbling nuzzles, and suction in surprising ways, special places.

She moaned her delight with every caress. And as she allowed him to touch every part of her—including her vulnerable belly—he settled deeper into her soul. One pair, one pack. They claimed each other, and when orgasm hit, they did it together.

Joy pulsed from her to him and back.

Together.

And maybe it went just a bit further.

Her eyes shot open in shock. Maybe it went *a lot* further.

Chapter 22

Ryan felt her stiffen, moving from orgasm to languid to suddenly anxious way too fast for him to follow. He was still boneless from his own release, reveling in the scent of her all over his face and body, not to mention his position between her thighs. But when she tightened—in a bad way—and started to roll off him, he gathered his scattered wits and tightened his grip on her thighs.

"Frankie?"

"I think…" He heard her swallow and pulled back far enough to see her face. "I think I just did something…um…unusual."

He waggled his eyebrows. "I hope so."

She flushed and shook her head. "No…I mean, yes of course. But…um…" She was obviously struggling to pull her wits together. That made him feel a little better, but it also showed him the importance of what had just happened. Whatever that was…

He took a deep breath and gathered his thoughts. He also adjusted their positions on the bed so that they now sat facing each other. She pressed her hand to her mouth and her eyes lost their focus. It didn't take him long to guess that she was feeling her pack link.

His gaze slid to the window where everything was as it had appeared before. Floodlights on in an empty street. No attack, at least not that he could see. No werewolves or bears mixing it up. When he listened, he couldn't hear anything unusual either.

So he waited with increasing impatience as Frankie continued to stare blindly into space. Fortunately, she soon took a breath and focused on him, but she didn't speak.

"What happened?" he prompted.

"I think I just told my entire pack what we were doing."

He blinked and tried not to gape at her. "Uh, why would you do that?"

She sighed and looked away. "Do bears have an alpha link?"

"You mean a psychic connection with everyone else in the clan?" She nodded.

"Not generally. Nanook had something like that, but it's rare. We all thought it was because he was part polar bear."

"It's an alpha trait in wolves. Everyone in the pack feels the connection, but the alpha can broadcast. Usually it's just emotions, sometimes it's commands, but that's rare. Either way, it's what makes the alpha so hard to unseat. Once he takes control of a pack, the other members are compelled to fall in line on a subliminal level."

He nodded as if he understood what she'd done. He glanced out the bedroom door—startled to realize that they'd just made love with the thing wide open—to see her father still sleeping unaware of everything. "Your father's not awake, so you broadcast?"

She shook her head. "I shouldn't be able to do it at all. I mean,

I'm good, but I'm not a full shifter. I can feel the pack, but I've never broadcast."

"Until just a few moments ago?"

She nodded, her eyes wide.

"So...um...just what exactly did you tell them?"

She opened her mouth, but no sound came out. Her hands in her lap tightened, entwining her fingers together into a clenched knot. He covered them with his own, using his calm to settle her. Except, of course, he wasn't fully calm. The last thing they needed was for the wolves to realize that Frankie was sexually involved with a bear. That would cement her as a traitor to the pack.

"I shouldn't have been able to do that," she said. "I mean, it's not like the pack link is flooded with orgasms all the time, even if the alpha is getting it on."

He swallowed. "You broadcast your orgasm?"

She shrugged, her blush burning hot on her skin. "Maybe they just got happy, loving feelings."

"And...um...how did everyone react? Can you tell?"

"Yeah. They're...um...confused." Her gaze wandered out to the street. "They were all 'I hate bears, I hate Frankie.'"

"And then you flooded them with an orgasm?" He couldn't help it, humor laced his tone. Fortunately, she caught the ridiculousness of what had happened. Her lips curved, and she ducked her head in embarrassment.

"I think so, yeah. Now they're just milling around, wondering what to do." She looked out the window. "It's hard to go kill people if you're stuck in afterglow."

Now his smile turned into a grin. Trust Frankie to find a new way to avert a war. "So can you broadcast at them again? Something like, 'Bears are the good guys'?"

She closed her eyes and apparently tried to send the message. Ryan received it loud and clear. Not in words, but in a sudden flush of feeling that went: *Bears were friends. He liked the bears.* It probably helped that he was already part of the bear clan, but that wasn't what surprised him.

"Should I be getting that message?" he asked. "I'm not part of your pack."

She opened her eyes, and when she spoke, her voice was filled with happiness. "Yes, you are. You are my pack."

Okay, so that was new. A bear in a wolf pack. He kind of liked the idea, assuming she and he were the only two members. But apparently everyone else was included in that link and that wasn't nearly as nice. He shifted uncomfortably on the bed, and this time she was the one who squeezed his hands.

"Can you feel me?"

He knew she meant psychically, and so he tried to narrow his focus down. To feel—

Her!

She was warm and solid, like a bright pillar of strength. He could settle himself inside her light and feel the power of their link. It was wonderful, and it shook him to his core. No one and nothing had ever been this deep inside him before. What if she betrayed him? What if she went bad? But her light was so bright, so strong that he couldn't believe she'd do it. Not just because she was a good person, but because they were so linked together it would be like betraying herself.

"I feel you," she whispered. "It's like I can sink into your presence." Her eyes shone. "You're wonderful."

He swallowed. "So are you." But who else was on this link? He tried to feel around for anyone else, but all he felt was her. "Is anyone else…here?" He was just getting comfortable with trusting her. The idea that suddenly her entire pack could touch him mentally was terrifying.

"Not like you. And not…" She shook her head. "I can barely feel them." She shrugged. "You swamp everything."

Was that good or bad? What exactly did this mean?

She took a deep breath. "I think it's us together. *We* broadcast that orgasm. *We* have the alpha power." She frowned trying to understand the details. "I can send to you, but I don't think I can get anyone else. Maybe we have to do it together?"

His eyes widened. "Send that 'bears are friends' message together?"

She shrugged in an I-have-no-idea gesture. A moment later, they entwined their fingers and tried to send it. Ryan felt a little ridiculous shooting out a mental thought, but Frankie seemed to be completely at ease with the idea. So he tried…and came up empty.

"All I get is you," he said.

"Yeah, me, too."

"Maybe we have to be…um…revved up to do it?"

They stared at each other. His mind was filled with questions that he wasn't even sure he could phrase. And while he struggled with his thoughts, a distant sound cut through the night air. It was faint, but he knew it intimately.

Sirens. Multiple ones headed this way. The police were coming, and he and Frankie turned to look out the window. It wouldn't be long now until the building across the street started reflecting red and blue strobe lights.

"Frankie," he said, "what do you want to do?" She had to take the lead here. He could barely fathom what had happened, though from the look on her face, she was equally baffled.

"Don't freak out, okay? I'll figure this out."

He wasn't the one freaking, so maybe she was talking to herself. But he didn't like the way she said that *she'd* figure it out, not *they*. He didn't have a chance to respond as her cell phone suddenly buzzed. She leapt to get it, her motions jerky and obviously keyed up. She was still naked and he wanted to appreciate the view. He did appreciate it, but he also heard how she answered the phone with a panicked, "Hello?"

If she'd wanted to, she could have kept him from hearing the other person on the line by pressing the phone tight to her ear. She didn't. He heard the first squeak of a cry—Noelle—and crowded close to her as she returned to the bed and tilted the phone so they both could hear.

"Oh my God, girlfriend, tell me that was you!"

"Noelle?"

"That was you. I know it was you. No one else feels so...so...I don't know. Powerful woman."

"Um, what exactly did I send?"

"It was like a rush of love. I mean fated in the stars kind of love. I've heard about this kind of thing before but never thought it would blast through the pack like it did. I mean, everyone felt it. You should see the look on some of the guys' faces. They don't know what to think."

"Oh shit..." Frankie murmured.

"Don't say, 'oh shit'! It was wonderful! And it completely took the wind out of your brother's sails. We could hear him screaming in the other room. 'Attack! Attack!' but my guess is that nobody listened. I really hate that my husband is overseas. I want some of that loving right now."

"So Raoul isn't out at the bears? He's still back at the community center?"

"Yeah, in one of the back offices. I was really worried when a bunch of the men left an hour ago, though I was relieved, too. They were the meanest ones. Good for us, not so good for you because I was sure they were going after you."

"They were supposed to attack the bears."

"So did they?"

Ryan crossed to look out the window. He could see the flashing lights of three different squad cars, but no werewolves. Only cops who were leaning on their cars while Simon and Alyssa talked to someone in a National Guard uniform. He looked back at Frankie and shook his head.

"No attack," she said into the phone. "That's a good thing. The bears were not going to roll over quietly. It would have been ugly."

"Well, it was ugly here. Kids crying, mothers cranky, and the men looking edgy and mean. A couple teenagers got into a fistfight, and the wolves were snapping at everyone just to scare them. And then you happened. It was a miracle. Everyone looked shocked, but the little kids settled down. The women went mellow, and the men got embarrassed. And everyone is asking, who's the new alpha? Like I didn't already know, so I sweet-talked our guard and got my phone."

"Did you tell them it was me?"

"I didn't say a word, but all the women could guess. It certainly got everyone's attention."

"Noelle, I…um…I didn't do that on purpose."

"Well, pretend like you did." Her drawl was laced with humor. "You wanted to be alpha. So come over here and cement your position."

Frankie nodded as if that was expected, but when she looked at Ryan, he saw an edge of panic in her eyes. "Um, yeah," she said. "No time like the present, I suppose."

"Look, you've got the alpha power. Just blast everyone with a 'stay put' message. Say you're coming to sort things out." Then when Frankie didn't respond, Noelle sighed, and her voice dropped to a whisper. "You can send the message, right?"

Frankie looked at Ryan and shook her head, but the message was obviously just for him since she said something different into the phone. "Why don't you tell them I'm coming? Tell them it's time to talk common sense."

He could hear Noelle blowing out a heavy breath. "I can spread that message around, but you've got a plan, right? How about your father? Is he really dead?" Noelle's voice broke a bit on the question.

"He's not dead, but he's unconscious. Raoul's guys messed him up bad."

"Right. So it's up to you."

"Yeah, and don't worry. I've got a plan."

"Okay. But hurry. Afterglow doesn't last long with these guys."

"As soon as I can." Frankie thumbed off the phone, dropped it in her lap, and looked at Ryan.

"You don't have a plan," he said. More a statement than a question. She shook her head slowly.

"And you can't do the alpha thing again."

Again, she shook her head. Then she took a deep breath, gave him a quick, very abrupt kiss, and started to get dressed.

"What are you doing?" He knew the answer before she said it.

"I'm going over there."

He nodded and started grabbing clothes for himself. Fortunately, the Griz kept lots of XXXL sweats around for just this kind of thing.

"You're going to confront your brother." It wasn't a question, but she nodded anyway. A shallow dip of her chin. "A dominance fight." He swallowed. "Can you win that?"

He was watching her closely and so he knew that she didn't answer by even the smallest movement. She'd locked down everything—thoughts, feelings, even panic—under a stoic mask of determination.

He touched her arm, pulling her gently so that they faced each other. "We'll fight this together."

"Dominance fights are one on one. You can't help." Her voice was tight, and he read despair in her face. "I'll have to kill my brother."

After everything Raoul had done, she still wanted to save him. His heart swelled in pride for her fierce love. Especially since he'd just become part of her family. "We need a different option," he said.

She nodded slowly, and he felt her rigid mask soften. He felt *her* soften. "Okay, so that's the plan."

"What?"

"To figure out a plan on the way there."

Chapter 23

Frankie had butterflies in her stomach and knots in her neck, shoulders, and back. She had her phone in her pocket right next to their entire plan: a hypodermic needle with the anti-serum. Dr. Cecilia Lu had made it clear that it wouldn't reverse any brain damage, but it did noticeably decrease aggression. So the plan was to get close enough to her brother to inject him. If nothing else, it would ease off his push to drive the pack into war and hopefully allow her to reach the sweet boy he'd once been.

Not much of a plan as those things went, but it was all she had. Plus Ryan at her back and the Griz waiting nearby. The cops were aware in a general sense and on standby if things turned ugly. That was the best she could hope for as she turned the corner to head to the front door of the community center.

"Frankie—" Ryan said, his voice low.

"You can't talk me out of this," she interrupted. "Anyway, it's too late to turn around now." They'd been spotted by the wolf stretched across the front step.

"I was going to say that I've got your back. No matter what."

Her step hitched and she winced at her own stupidity. Of course, he was going to say something supportive. That was who he was. He served and protected, and right now that meant he stood behind her when she knew he really wanted to be in front shielding her from her own kind. But this was a wolf matter and a bear could only make it worse. Unless, of course, he was quiet, smart, and waited for her signal to go all grizzly. "Um, yeah. Thanks."

Talk about a lame response. That wasn't even remotely what she wanted to say. She ought to be saying that she felt him deep inside. He was a calm presence that gave her hope for a future that—a day ago—had seemed impossible. That right now it was taking everything in her not to grab his hand and run away. It didn't have to be far. Hell, they could get lost in Chicago and live happily ever after. That was only a short five-hour drive. And most of all, she wanted to say the words that she'd been holding back for a while now.

I love you.

She hadn't said it and neither had he, but that's what she felt for him. But how could she say that to him when she might very well die in the next few minutes? The odds of her winning in a straight fight against her brother were slim to none. Then again, how could she not say it? It might be her very last chance.

And then she ran out of time. That's what happened when she dithered. The wolf guarding the front door raised its hackles and growled menacingly.

"Get out of the way, Stark," she snapped. That wasn't the wolf's real name, but he'd started styling himself after the brilliant super-hero when he'd gotten a B in high school chemistry. "I'm here to put an end to this nonsense."

The wolf didn't move, just bared his teeth. To his credit, the threat wasn't aimed at her but at Ryan. Didn't matter. She lost her temper with the kid.

"Your mom knows you're having unprotected sex. She said if you get an STD, you're enlisting so the government pays for your health care. And if one of the girls gets pregnant, then your ass is getting a job. In fact, she asked me to write down a list of the ugliest, dirtiest jobs I could think of." Frankie grinned. "I told her the government is always looking for more sewage grunts. Gave her a few names to call."

Wolves don't get pale, at least not that can be seen. They show fear in the tremors along their fur and stiffness in the tail. Right now, Stark's tail stood out rigid as stone. The kid was terrified, probably because he knew his mother didn't make idle threats.

He jumped off the steps with gratifying speed.

She moved past him and put her hand on the center's door, but she didn't push through. Instead, she took a moment to find that place inside her where Ryan held strong. She found it quickly, but just to make sure, she glanced behind her to where he stood with quiet power. His blue eyes were clear, and his blond hair was a soft yellow under the streetlights. He smiled at her with a slow, sweet curve of his mouth.

Right there was the image she wanted of him. One to hold on to in her mind for as long as she lived. Even if it was for only a few more minutes. She returned his smile, wishing she could put all the words she'd never said into her one expression. Then she opened the doors.

The place was unsettled. Given that it was barely four a.m., it should have been quiet. But most of her brother's men had come back and were milling around disturbing kids and parents alike. Raoul was in a back room, and his angry voice beat the air of even this huge space. She couldn't make out the words, but the growling tone was obvious enough.

But first things first. She looked to the "quarantined" section of the room to check on her friends. Sure enough, Noelle was there, giving her a grinning thumbs-up. Even Hazel was awake, waving her bandaged arm then clenching her hands in a get-fierce gesture. Frankie headed there, hoping to get a word in before the trouble started.

She was at the edge of the quarantined area when her brother came storming out of the back room. One of the sentries must have told him she was here. His face was flushed, and his men flanked him on either side. And then there was Delphine, back in her wolf form and spandex pants. She bared her sharp white teeth the moment she came into view, and even Frankie had a moment of envy for her rich brown fur. If nothing else, the woman had good hair.

Thinking of the hypodermic in her pocket, Frankie extended her arms out to hug her brother. He'd never been a touchy-feely kind of kid, but maybe things had changed. He had a girlfriend now, after all.

No such luck. He drew back from her with an appalled look on his face. "You are not welcome here, Frankie," he said darkly. Then he glanced at Ryan. "And his presence is a declaration of war."

Frankie let her arms drop to her sides. "I thought one of your demands was that they turn me over to you."

He acknowledged the point with a dip of his chin. "Is that what you're doing?" he asked as he turned to Ryan. "Are you turning her in to me?"

Frankie tensed. If Ryan responded to the jibe, it would make her look weak. He had to keep silent and let her be the power. She opened her mouth to forestall any of his comments, but she needn't have worried. Instead of responding, Ryan simply turned to smile at a nearby child who was whimpering in his mother's arms.

It was perfect. Not only had he shown himself to be friendly, but he'd completely dismissed her brother as unimportant. And if there was anything her brother hated, it was being ignored.

She watched Raoul's neck flush, but she didn't give him a chance to speak. "What makes you think you have the right to make any demands or speak for the pack?" she asked. She held up her hands. "Our alpha isn't dead. You aren't the beta. And yet you stand there and declare war as if you think our lives are your toy soldiers. We aren't. And we certainly aren't going to war on your say-so."

"We don't have a beta because they killed him!" Raoul snarled.

"Derek was killed when he attacked an innocent CDC doctor in front of her mate. If you ask me, he got what he deserved for being so stupid."

Raoul shook his head. "Why are you spreading lies?"

"Why did you poison the city? Why do you want war?" She made an expansive gesture. "Are their lives nothing to you?"

His lip curled as he looked around. "You have no voice here. You can't even shift."

She watched his words impact the people around them. As one, the onlookers winced. It wasn't fair or right, but full shifters had a stronger voice.

"I can shift," she said loudly. "And I speak to the pack with an alpha voice."

"Alpha voice!" he scoffed loudly. "That was disgusting. How dare you share your filthy relations with a bear over our link?"

She hated that her skin heated at his words. What she'd done—and shared—was neither filthy nor intentional. "I stopped the pack from following your stupid orders. Do you think the bears were defenseless? And the National Guard was on the way. Our people would have been slaughtered."

"You have no faith in us. You've abandoned everything that makes you a wolf."

She held her tongue, biting back an angry curse. This kind of back-and-forth spat helped no one. Worse, the antagonism keyed everyone up, and not in a good way. She had to end this now, which meant it was time for desperate action. She fingered the hypodermic in her pocket and judged the distance. She needed to slam it into his neck, but she'd have to get past his guards first.

She knew Ryan was ready to leap into action, but would that be enough? Didn't matter. She'd have to risk it. So she said the cruelest thing she could think of. She felt sick to her stomach as she spoke, but it was the only way to push Raoul into attacking her.

"No, Raoul, I have no faith in you. You've backstabbed your friends, poisoned those who love you, and betrayed the pack at every turn. Everyone knows it. And for those who don't, I have pr—" She was going to say proof, but she didn't get the chance.

He leapt for her as he screamed, "Lies!"

She was ready for the attack, so it was easy to flow with his lunge. A smooth move to twist into his leap so he fell past her. At the same time, she hauled the hypodermic out of her pocket, popped the cap, and slammed it down on his neck. He roared as the plunger sank home, but she had her knee in his back to keep him down.

Done. Now she just had to wait until he simmered down.

It was only then that she realized things were happening all around them. She'd been completely focused on Raoul, but suddenly she noticed that she was not being dragged off him by his henchmen. That's because Ryan had stepped into the breach. While she'd been injecting Raoul, he'd blocked or punched out four others.

Pretty impressive for a guy who hadn't even gone grizzly.

And then there was Hazel. She'd apparently leapt the quarantine barrier at just the right time. As Delphine lunged to attack, Hazel had landed feetfirst on the wolf's hard snout. Wolf and woman had gone down in a tumble with Hazel coming out on top. Frankie caught enough of the fight to see Hazel deliver three blows to Delphine's face, hard impacts from her good hand.

"That's for my arm," Hazel said as she punched. "That's for your ugly clothes. And that's because you're a bitch."

Delphine's wolf eyes rolled back into her head. Unconscious.

Great, but that was only the nearest of her brother's allies. Raoul had a lot more men around, and they'd been spoiling for a fight. As Frankie quickly scanned the crowd, she counted a half dozen moving forward. Most of them had been patrolling on the edge of the room, but now they stalked her. Hazel adjusted her stance, preparing to fend them off. Ryan flanked her on the opposite side. But then rescue came from an unexpected place.

"Stay back!" Raoul called out as he dug the needle from his neck. "There's no point in fighting within the pack."

Frankie exhaled, the relief in her body making her weak. Her little brother was back. There was no other explanation for his sudden change in heart. "Raoul," she breathed, and there was joy in her voice. Except he didn't look at her with kindness. What she saw on his face was pity, and that knocked the wind straight out of her sails.

"What was in this?" he asked, as he held the hypodermic.

"It's from the CDC. It counteracts the aggression that comes from taking your serum."

He rolled sideways, dislodging her knee. She didn't fight him. He appeared completely rational. And as he sat up, he tossed the needle onto a nearby table. "I haven't taken any of that. Don't need it." He pushed up to stand before her. "I'm a full wolf-shifter with a big brain and an implacable will. Why would I need anything to push me to fight for the wolves every way I know how?"

She stared at him. She saw no lessening of the darkness inside him. He stared at her with hate, and when he looked at the pack around them, he spoke calmly, clearly, and with enough alpha power in his voice to resonate through the pack link.

"I fight for the wolves against the bears who killed our beta. I fight for the wolves who are low in number and need new blood. I fight for the wolves who have been hiding in the shadows but now need to come out into the light of day. Did I give you vitamin serum? Yes. And you feel better for it! Did I declare war on the bears? Yes! We will not let them stop us! And when my own sister turns on us, I will deal mercifully with her out of the love we share for our father."

Oh God. Oh no. He sounded completely rational, and her entire plan had hinged on the fact that he was addicted to his own serum. But if that wasn't so, then his madness was completely his own. The horror of that squeezed her chest. And yet, she couldn't give in to that pain. She had to fight for sanity.

"You attacked our father," she cried. "We have the proof."

"Lies!"

"You poisoned an entire city!" She looked around. "How many of you had friends who got sick? Businesses who suffered because the city shut down?"

"A temporary setback," Raoul said loudly. "When werewolves take their rightful place—"

"The normals will hunt us, capture us, and kill us. Bad enough that he incites a war with bears, how will he protect your children when *billions* of frightened normal people come? He terrorized an entire city." She looked around, her heart in her throat. These were people she'd known all her life. How could they not see what he was doing? In the end, she held up her hands. "The pack has to choose. He incites war. I give you love. He sits in a lab and tinkers with chemicals. I help with your children, give support in times of need, and created a safe community center in which to gather. The pack has to choose. Hatred or a happily ever after?"

She thought the answer would be obvious. Who wouldn't want a happily ever after? But as she studied their faces, she realized most of the pack didn't think the way she did. Which meant she was doomed.

Chapter 24

Ryan looked around the room and felt his breath freeze. This wasn't going well, and he'd worked with enough teenagers to know why. No one was listening to the words. They'd long since made up their minds. Some wanted Raoul and his promises to make werewolves the most powerful people around. Others wanted Frankie and to live their lives without all this conflict. And everyone was getting angry, which was like piling dynamite on top of smoldering coals.

"You have to show them," he said. He stepped into Frankie's line of sight and spoke loud enough for everyone to hear. "They have to feel the difference."

"I did that," she said.

He nodded. "And you have to do it again. Now."

He saw the panic enter her gaze. He knew what she was thinking. That she'd done it in a moment of orgasmic bliss, which was a far cry from broadcasting as an alpha on command. But she wanted to take control of her pack and this was the only way. She had to do it or her brother would win. And if that happened, then they would likely have to fight their way out of here. Or die trying.

"Ryan—" she began, fear echoing in his name.

He smiled at her and held out his hand. "I'm here. Let me help you. This doesn't have to be done alone."

She looked at his hand and then at the people around them. He saw the tension in her body, the twitch in her hand, and the way her eyes looked everywhere but at him.

Refused.

His heart sunk and his body froze. She wasn't going to do it. She wasn't going to claim him or their relationship to her pack. She'd said he was her pack, and he'd told her she was his home. But just like every other time he'd thought he'd found home, it turned out to be a lie.

The reasons for her betrayal piled up in his head. She was a wolf, he was a bear. This was pack politics, not love. They'd just met and while he was falling in love, she was just having great sex.

God, the pain of it made him feel as if he were cut in half and left bleeding right there in front of everyone. His hand dropped to his side and he drew back from her. But he couldn't go far because then she wouldn't have anyone to watch her back.

But who would watch his? Where could he go where he was safe and loved? Obviously not—

"We got you," Hazel said loudly as she stepped across Delphine's unconscious wolf body to stand in front of Frankie.

Noelle crossed to protect Frankie's back. "Do what you need to do. Nobody will touch you."

And then two more women stepped up to circle Frankie...

No, actually they were surrounding *both* Frankie and Ryan. He was in the safe center. And as soon as Frankie felt like they wouldn't be attacked, she nodded her thanks to her friends and reached out for Ryan.

It threw him, this sudden openness on Frankie's face as she looked at him. He was still deep in the litany of betrayal in his head. She was just like Nanook and his so-called friends on the police force. Turning their backs when things got rough. She didn't really love him. How could she when even his parents weren't so sure about him?

And yet she stood there with her eyes wide and her hand stretched out to him. He couldn't quite process it.

"I need to be open to do this," she said. "And I can't watch for attacks at the same time."

There it was. The verbal proof that she hadn't been rejecting him at all. And yet, his body couldn't catch up.

"Ryan?" she said, confusion flitting across her expression, and no wonder. He'd just offered himself to her and now was contracted away.

"What do you need?" he asked without touching her. She'd know if he touched her. She'd realize he was afraid to open himself to her again. Even though he'd been wrong, the pain of betrayal still ate at him. God, it hurt, and she hadn't even done it. And now she needed him, and he was holding back because he was afraid. *Damn it—*

"I love you," she said. "I should have said it before, but I'm saying it now. Whatever happens, I love you."

He felt the resonance in her words. Even if that was just the vibration of her alpha voice, his heart responded. Warmth pulsed through his body, melting his panic. His mind stopped its litany of betrayal and was shocked into seeing something completely different. It saw a wolf declaring her love to a bear right in the middle of her pack. And she was doing it during a dominance fight. She was declaring to all around her that this was who she was, and then letting them choose.

It was the bravest thing he'd ever seen. And if she could do that, then he could face down his own demon. She hadn't betrayed him, and he needed to trust her.

"I love you, too," he said, and he reached for her hand.

Click. Bonding magic locked in place. He felt it like a shift in the order of the world. There wasn't even a sound, just an internal shift as the two of them became a bonded pair. Bear and wolf, alpha mates, while in front of the entire pack.

Her eyes widened, but she didn't speak. Neither did he. He was feeling too much for words, and he felt the echo of her surprise and her love as their palms connected. She gripped his hand and smiled. And a moment later, she stretched her other hand out to him, so he could clasp that, too. They stood face to face, hands held and hearts open.

She loved him, and he loved her. They were home together, each other's safe harbor. Bonded mates, and the beauty of that pulsed back and forth between them. It grew stronger in his heart, swelling with each beat. Strong. Solid. Safe.

When he thought he would burst from the power of it, she let her gaze move outward. She looked first at Hazel's back and Noelle's side. She did a slow circle, looking at each member of the pack in turn. He followed with her, knowing that where she loved, he would as well.

And as he did, his heart expanded. He offered himself as a safe home to her pack. He would protect and serve them. And—to his surprise—he saw them accept his offering. He knew it was carried on the force of her love, but he didn't care. They welcomed him with varying degrees of surprise and suspicion. But even so, they accepted him as her mate, as her shelter, and as her love.

At least most of them did.

It took a while for her to turn full circle, and he had to release one of her hands to let her do it. But when she completed her turn, her gaze landed solidly on her brother. Ryan thought this would be the hardest for her, but the depth of her love for her brother stunned them all. He felt it well up in the room. A pure, sweet love that accepted him and cherished him as part of her pack. Even with everything Raoul had done to betray everyone, she still loved him.

He watched Raoul's eyes widen in shock, but he held himself back. His hands were clenched, and his jaw worked though no sound came out.

"I'm not blind to our problems, Raoul," Frankie said. "But we have to start from love first." She held out her hand to him, just as she'd done to Ryan. But here was the problem with this pack openness. It required a measure of vulnerability on both sides.

In order to receive it, Raoul would have to become open to it, expose his inner heart to everyone in the pack. Ryan could see that the man wasn't going there. Raoul couldn't. And while Frankie opened her hand and her heart to her brother, Raoul teetered and fell on the opposite side.

He landed in hate and fear. Maybe the two emotions were the same thing.

Noelle was closest to Raoul, but her eyes were on a pair of bristling wolves near the wall. When Raoul roared his defiance, she was caught off guard, jolting sideways in surprise. That gave Ryan the space to save her life.

He leapt forward to protect her and was met with Raoul's open jaws. The prick had gone wolf and was of a damned impressive size and strength. Ryan's only hope was to go grizzly or lose an arm. But when he reached for the power, it wasn't there. He might be a healthy human, but his magical tank was empty from all the shifting he'd done. Which meant—

Frankie shoved him aside. She was in full hybrid mode, both wolf and woman as she saved Ryan and protected Noelle. She rolled with her brother's attack, dropping him into the center of her circle without suffering any damage. But Raoul wasn't staying down. He scrambled on the wood floor but was able to gain purchase as he spun back and attacked.

Ryan tensed to intervene, but a cry to his right showed him that Raoul wasn't the only werewolf too afraid to open up to what Frankie was offering. Some of Raoul's men were attacking as well, and Noelle was not trained in hand-to-wolf combat.

He wanted with every part of him to protect Frankie, but he knew she had to face her brother alone. It was the only way for her to establish dominance over the pack. Plus, he had complete faith that she could hold her own. She might not defeat Raoul, but it wasn't going to be a quick fight and Noelle needed the protection now. So Ryan engaged the wolves coming at them. Two medium-sized ones with speed behind their assault.

He pulled Noelle out of their path and timed his own attack for the exact moment they sprang past. To the other side, he heard Hazel chuckle, apparently pleased with whatever attack she was handling. And then there was no more time for thought. Just duck and punch, kick and haul ass. Most of the bystanders scrambled away while a few closed in to help.

It was just like before. In the sewers and the loading dock. The sweat, the adrenaline, the blood. Only this time something else stood with him. A shimmering pool of strength inside his soul.

Frankie was with him, and suddenly, everything was different. He was still tired, but his heart and his head were at peace. Whatever came from outside, inside he was at home with Frankie. And since he was no longer fighting himself, he had more power to use in the fight. He countered claws, bites, and a couple very human fists. But this time the good guys had the advantage of numbers. It would be over soon.

He knocked the nearest wolf out while Noelle fouled the footing of the other one. He heard a yelp behind him, but didn't know if it was Raoul or the one fighting Hazel. He spun, intending to deliver a knockout blow to the remaining wolf's temple, his fist raised—

Freeze!

The message was blasted psychically throughout the room, but if there was any doubt, a loud voice followed next.

"Stop!"

He recognized the voice immediately. Hard to forget Emory Wolf's command tone. It was enough to pause Ryan's fist, but it had a dramatic effect on the wolves. They all dropped to the ground and gave some sign of submission, human and canine alike. Even Ryan tilted his head to the side, exposing his throat in an instinctive act, though it was only a slight tilt. Emory wasn't his alpha, and so the impact was significantly lessened.

That gave him the strength to straighten up to his full height and study the situation. First and most important, Frankie had Raoul on the ground, her hand on his neck and her knee in his back. Her arms were bloody, but Ryan didn't see any wounds on her body, meaning the blood was likely Raoul's. Behind Frankie, Hazel straightened up as well. She wasn't a shifter, so her head wasn't canted to the side like everyone else's, but she wasn't fighting either. No need since everyone who'd come at her was stretched out on the floor, most of them as unconscious as Delphine.

He quickly scanned the rest of the room. Nobody moved. Everyone who could was looking at Emory, who was leaning heavily on Simon's arm. And behind Simon was Alyssa, Vic, and…now there was a surprise. It was Brady, the wolf he thought had skipped the city but had apparently been around enough to bring help when the shit had hit the fan. And then stepping around the lot of them was—hell—Captain Abraham.

Ryan's gaze shot straight to Frankie, but she was ahead of him. She'd already reverted to her human form. Everyone else was either fully human or fully canine. That meant no shifter exposure to his very vanilla boss.

Meanwhile, Frankie looked at her father. "Dad? You're looking better."

Was he? To Ryan's eyes he looked frail. The man had been a force within the shifter community, but now he leaned heavily on Simon as he gazed around the community center. At least his physical wounds were healed. He'd probably woken enough to shift. But some vital aspect of him had weakened considerably. Still, his words carried loud enough into the silence.

"Is this what we've come to?" he asked. "Brother against sister, men against women, wolves attacking our own?" His gaze went to his two children. "How did this happen?"

Simon answered, his voice carrying throughout the room. "It's the shit in the water. It makes us all angry."

Emory looked to his son. "I thought it made us all strong."

Ryan winced. That was as much of a confession as his captain would need for a temporary arrest.

Meanwhile, Frankie stepped back from her brother. "Does this look like strength, Dad? We're destroying ourselves and hurting everyone else in the process." She looked down at her brother who was slowly gaining his feet. Or rather pushing to his four paws. He was still in his wolf form and was not about to get arrested for his crimes.

Emory shook his head. "What was I thinking?" he murmured.

Which is when Ryan understood what had happened. Frankie, too, because she spoke it out loud. "They gave you the antidote. You're thinking clearly now."

Her father nodded as he looked around the room. "I renounce leadership of the pack. I failed you all."

Frankie took a sharp step forward. "No!" she cried. "It was Raoul and the serum."

Emory spoke slowly, his words having a double meaning. "I'm not above the law," he said, meaning both human and shifter law. He or Raoul had broken both, and as alpha, Emory was ultimately responsible.

"You didn't know what you were doing," Frankie said, her voice breaking. She knew, as did everyone else here, that her father was going to take the blame for poisoning the city of Detroit. And the humans were not going to be kind.

"I didn't know that my son would attack me, either. That he sent his men—"

Whatever else Emory was going to say was never uttered. Instead his eyes went wide with horror as Raoul sprang forward, teeth and claws bared. Emory was too weak to react fast enough, and though Simon tried to step in between, he didn't have the angle. Everyone else was either too far away or was caught flat-footed.

Emory went down beneath his son's assault.

Gunshots rang out, rapid and strong. Frankie screamed, "No!" and Ryan leapt forward to try and hold back his captain, but it was too late. Captain Abraham had pulled his weapon and gotten off three shots.

Raoul was dead, his wolf body bleeding from multiple wounds. Simon dropped down beside Emory, shoving the wolf aside to look beneath. But it was too late there, as well. Emory's throat was gone, and his eyes stared blankly ahead.

Raoul had just killed his own father. Ryan didn't know if it was an act of rage or mercy. Emory surely would have spent the rest of his life in prison. Either way, they were both dead now. Meanwhile, his captain was staring around in shock.

"What the hell is wrong with you people?" Captain Abraham bellowed. "Why would you bring wolves to a community center? God, they're even dressed up like people."

No one answered. No one except Frankie who cried out, the pain of her loss reverberating through the room. Ryan grabbed her before she collapsed in grief. Simon grabbed the captain's gun, yanking it free with a shifter's strength. And then the others started to react. Children cried, parents murmured, and everyone did whatever they could to keep the situation contained. But Ryan's focus narrowed to his mate's.

"I've got you," he murmured as he held her tight. "I'm here. I've got you."

Frankie gripped him, and her whole body shuddered from the force of her sobs.

He stayed with her then. He held her tight through the endless cleanup of the bodies, the interviews from the police, and the inevitable dispersal of her pack back to their own lives. Nicole helped, as did Hazel, but so many questions were directed at her. Why did Raoul do this? How could you mate with a bear? What's going to happen to the pack? How can we survive this?

She answered those she could; dismissed those she couldn't. He ran interference with the police all while refusing to leave her side. Eventually it was done. The police interrogations were over, the pack had gone to their homes, and he was left with her.

They went to her apartment next to the community center. They dropped onto the bed and settled into the safe harbor of each other's arms. And just before sleep claimed them, he whispered the truth into her ear.

"I love you."

"'Love' feels like too small a word for what I feel for you," she answered.

He knew exactly what she meant.

Chapter 25

Cleanup always took longer than expected. Frankie thought Raoul's serum and the Detroit Flu were the roughest part of the past year, but actually, it was the aftermath. The city had not been kind once the news went public that Raoul and Emory Wolf were responsible. Frankie had turned over everything she could find to the police and the entire pack had tried to disappear into anonymity under the onslaught. And no one spoke again of trying to reveal werewolves to the general public.

Shifters were back in the shadows, and that was a good thing.

The public part of the nightmare had ended within a few months, but the investigation from other shifter alphas had taken much longer. In this, the werewolves had come together, supporting Frankie in taking over the pack and declaring in one voice that she had fought her brother and father from the very beginning. Even better, no one had fought her when she declared Ryan her beta. In truth, she and Ryan were co-leading because they had complementary strengths. But since she was the wolf, he let her claim the alpha title while he took beta. He didn't care about titles anyway.

And now it was spring. The time when the newest shifters burst into their animal forms and went looking for the wildest spot along the River Rouge. Frankie walked along the edge of it, breathing the spring air and appreciating the shoots of green that waved in the early morning sunshine.

"I did good here," she said to no one in particular. Her first act as alpha of the Detroit Wolves had been to establish a regular patrol of this stretch of the park. She wanted it safe for all the shifter young to come here and get their animal on. It was something every shifter could get behind, and even the humans liked it when the park was safe. Thanks to Ryan's help, the Griz and two new shifter cops were part of the rotation.

To her right, she saw the grass near the water move. She smiled, knowing what was coming, and she held out the cup of coffee she carried. Ryan crept out from behind a tall patch of wildflowers and volunteer trees. Technically, they were all weeds, but they looked pretty nonetheless, and he looked ruggedly handsome as he shook leaves out of his hair. Good sleep, good sex, and a good life did that to a guy. He looked as healthy as a...a grizzly bear.

"Everything okay?" he asked.

"Shouldn't I be asking you that?" she teased as she helped him brush some dirt off his jeans.

"All good. A new cougar-shifter came through around three a.m. A girl and she was all, *I love the water, I hate the water, no, I love the water!*"

She smiled. "You like seeing the new shifters in spring."

Ryan took a grateful pull on his coffee. "Yeah, although cats are weird. Bears just shuffle around and roar."

"Wolves love the water. We can hardly get our teens out of it." That had been last week's problem when two new teen wolves had started playing in the river and refused to leave despite the presence of family, cops, and one city official. She'd managed to smooth things over even though the wolves were hated by most of the population. They were still called a "disreputable gang" by most journalists, but at least she could walk the streets without someone spitting at her.

And now she was settled as alpha of the werewolves. Ryan was her beta even though he was a bear, and every one of the wolves in her care had broken their addiction to the serum. Better yet, Frankie had given the secret wolf research facility over to Dr. Cecilia Lu to use for shifter research. The woman wanted to dig deep into a few shifter-only illnesses. There would even be a small clinic on site and shifter doctors were relocating offices to the space. Detroit would finally get a medical facility for shifters, and that was a boon to all of their kind throughout the Midwest.

"What's going on in that head of yours?" Ryan asked, his tone teasing. He'd been stunned by the depth and variety of programs she'd planned for the moment she became alpha. "I am not taking another shift in the day care," he said. "Not without a lot more coffee."

She smiled at him, her heart so full. It was time to tell him the real reason she'd met him at dawn by the River Rouge.

"What about caring for your own kids? You up for that?"

He'd been about to take another sip, but at her words, he slowly pulled the cup away. "Don't know of any kids," he said. "But I'll always be happy to take care of my own spawn." He was teasing when he called his kids spawn. She could tell by the intensity in his eyes that he wanted children with a fierce, quiet need. It was all part of making his own home with each other and their offspring.

Fortunately, she wanted it just as badly.

"I'm going to hold you to that," she said with a smile. "Because in about eight and a half months—"

Her words were cut off by his whoop of joy. Then she was laughing as he picked her up and spun her around. She wrapped her arms tight around him, dropping her forehead to his as he slowed their spin.

"So I take it you're happy?" she asked.

"Thrilled. You?"

"Ecstatic."

He grinned as he gently set her down. "So we're both happy, but…um…how did this happen?"

She shrugged. "Magic? Broken condom? Hell, if I know."

His eyes widened. They both knew that strong shifter kids were usually surprise pregnancies. What made this crazier was that she and Ryan were different species. Their children ought to be normal humans without enough DNA to manifest either bear or wolf. But stranger things had happened when magic got involved, and she'd be happy no matter what.

Meanwhile he was touching her face, stroking along her jaw line and looking at her like she held the sun and the moon in her hands. She leaned in to kiss him, only to be startled as he sank away from her. She pulled back in surprise then realized he was going down on one knee. And while her mouth dropped open in shock, he pulled a ring box from his pocket.

"I meant to take you out to dinner tonight and do something

special afterward. But I can't think of a better moment—or place—to do this."

He grabbed her hand in his, but she noticed he couldn't resist stroking across her belly first. "Francesca Wolf, you're already my home, my alpha, and my love. Will you do me the greatest honor of becoming my wife? And the mother of my children?"

Happiness welled up inside her, brighter and stronger than anything she'd ever felt before. And even better? It stayed with her, settling into a sweet glow that was part of that pillar inside her. The one that was labeled Ryan and she could feel with just a thought.

"Yes," she said. "Yes!"

He surged upward as she threw her arms around him again. It was a laughing struggle to get her to stay still long enough so he could slide the ring on her finger. And then they were kissing, hugging, and Ryan spent a bit more time stroking her belly. All in all, it was the best morning of her life. Only to be beat by every morning after this one.

"I love you," she said as he pressed a kiss to her belly.

"Thank you for giving me everything I've ever wanted," he said. Then he straightened up and kissed her. "I love you."

It was good to be home.

YOU CAN'T KEEP A GOOD BEAR DOWN

Alyssa Nelson doesn't actually believe that Simon Gold is a shape-shifting grizzly bear—until she sees it firsthand. (Aaaaand the award for Totally Surprising Changes goes to Simon Gold!) But Alyssa doesn't have time to deal with the fact that her ruggedly hot, longtime secret crush is a shifter…not when her brother has turned into one, too.

After ten months in bear form, Simon is struggling. He's not ready to deal with anyone, let alone the bold and gorgeous Alyssa. Mine, whispers his bear. But all hell has broken loose in the Detroit shifter community, and it's spreading to humans. Now Simon must face the darkest place of all: where bear and man become one. And the only way he can make it back to his humanity is by finding—and claiming—his mate.

Don't miss *Alpha Unleashed*, by *USA Today* best-selling author Kathy Lyons, available now.

See the next page for an excerpt.

Chapter 1

Bear grumbled, the sound low and deep in his belly. The birds squawked and flew straight up, a squirrel took off through the trees, and best of all, a rabbit leapt high and ran, drawing him away from her babies tucked beneath a nearby tree. He didn't follow. It amused him to watch the forest animals scatter at his smallest sound.

He made another sound, this time a chuff of contentment. He rolled onto his back and scratched his rear leg against the tree. He had an itch there. And another slightly higher up between his thighs. There was a female nearby. One who was coming into his territory unaware that he waited for her. He'd been tracking her for a while now and it pleased him that he would soon have his go at her. She was not fertile yet, but his nose told him it might be soon.

He was puzzling, in his dull bear way, about the best way to catch her when a dangerous sound disturbed the morning air. The growl of an engine. It was the call of the worst predator of all: man. He straightened onto all fours, grumbling at the inconvenience. He could not allow such a creature into his territory. Not when a female was coming. So he shook out his shoulders, hips, and rump, then went off in search of the danger.

He moved with confidence over this land because it was his. He knew the rocks, the smells, and the sounds. He knew, too, that when the engine sound abruptly stopped, the danger increased. It meant that a human was out of his machine and hunting on foot.

Bear prowled closer, moving toward the structure he called his own. He sniffed the air and caught the scent of a human woman. It might have been pleasant if not for the acrid stink of her engine. She was making a great deal of noise, pounding on the building and calling out. He didn't put any effort into processing her words. He'd been a bear too long to want to work that hard. Besides, it didn't matter what she said. This was his place and he would not allow anyone else inside his dominion.

So when she pounded her fist against the structure again, he growled, low and threatening.

She spun around and he smelled terror in her scent. She gasped and moved sideways across his vision. Not at him, but not retreating either. She made sounds, too, ones that were tight with alarm.

He decided to frighten her away.

He took a deep breath and released a roar. Secretly, he was pleased with the full, loud sound. It echoed in the trees and startled birds in the distance. And when he was done, he watched for her to run away with her engine. He would not give chase. He knew from experience that he couldn't catch the human prey when it was surrounded in metal. So he would remain where he was with his teeth bared until she left.

Except she did not run. She stood her ground next to his structure. Tall and proud as if she were anything but tiny compared to him.

Why would she not leave?

He needed to frighten her again. This time he matched her stance. She needed to see how small she was compared to him. He reared up on his back legs and showed his teeth. He spread his arms and let his claws flash in the sun. He was much larger than her. She should run.

Bam! Bam! Bam!

Something hit him. Powerful somethings. Three times, hard in the chest. He stumbled backward, his bear mind sluggish. Pain hit next, blinding him with fury. He roared again as he struggled to regain his footing.

Bam! Bam!

His leg buckled and he went down on his face. The ground slapped his mouth closed but he was already rolling. Or trying to roll. Something was wrong with his breath. The pain whited out his thoughts, though he tried to scramble to his feet. He had to attack the human predator. He must defend his territory. And yet his breath was wrong. The smell of blood cluttered his senses. His feelings gave no clue beyond pain and fury.

My time, his other self said. *Quickly.*

There were other words, other thoughts, but the mind spoke too quickly and bear was unused to hearing it. He felt pain. He felt anger. And he felt those things being tucked away as the mind began to assert itself.

It came on like a trickle of icy water that quickly became a deluge. It dampened the feelings, then turned everything liquid. His emotions, his body, even his sounds became wet and fluid. Thoughts were still too complicated to follow, but the mind knew enough, had practiced enough, to act without forethought.

He isolated the worst pain—hard points of metal—and shoved them from his body made liquid. It was hard work to push them away. His body was too thin in this in-between place, the energy too insubstantial against something so hard. But he worked at it, holding off the freezing of muscle and bone, until the points—the bullets—were out or at least near the surface.

He didn't have enough time. Three bullets fell away, but two others were trapped in his human body when his cells locked into place. Bone, organs, muscle, skin—all human. All that remained liquid was the blood that flowed inside.

"Holy shit," someone whispered. "It's true."

He opened his eyes. No, they were already open. He focused them now, sorting vision into colors, shapes, and meaning. A woman stood above him, a gun trembling in her hand but aimed unerringly at his heart. Her eyes were wide and her breath stuttered in and out with terror.

Someone wheezed, a sound filled with wet pain. Oh damn. He'd made that sound. His rational mind was coming online now. It was processing information with increasing speed and all the conclusions were bad.

He was lying on the ground after being shot five times.

His body still burned, overwhelmed from the sudden shift. It was all painful, so he could not tell what hurt most. He knew there were two more bullets inside him somewhere, but he couldn't remember where. And an outsider stared at him, terrified and still dangerous.

He had to communicate with her. He had to deliver the message that was uppermost in his brain. They were bear's words, now made intelligible by a human mouth.

"Go. Away."

"Simon?" she whispered, the words half gasp, half squeak of terror.

Had he said the words wrong? Was her brain injured? He tried again, putting more force behind the message though it hurt his chest to do it.

"Go. Away."

"You were a bear! I shot a bear!"

"Human." He tried to push up, but the pain kept him from moving far. Instead, he rolled over onto his back, his breath seizing tight as bolts of agony shot through his ribs.

He focused again on his body, itemizing sensations. His ribs weren't broken but—damn—they ached. The bullets. Trapped in the muscles between ribs. Still sensitive from the shift, he could feel them as hard points inside his body. As his human mind took more control, those sensations would dull. He needed to remove the bullets now while he still had bear's magic strong inside him.

"Get. Knife," he said, his voice stronger now that he had a plan.

"What?"

"Dig. Bullets. Out."

"I…You were a bear!" she said.

"Knife!"

She fumbled to obey, rooting into a purse that he now noticed was slung across her muscular frame. She pulled out a decent-sized Swiss army knife and popped open a blade. "Just remember, I've got a gun."

He didn't respond except to snarl as she extended the blade to him. He had to fully stretch out his arm to get it, and the movement made him hiss with pain. But a part of him admired that she was smart enough to keep back.

He palmed the blade, adjusted it, then reached down to feel where the bullets lodged between ribs. This was going to hurt.

"What are you doing?" she asked. Her tone told him she knew exactly what he was going to do, but couldn't believe it.

Neither could he. But the window was fading on his keen physical awareness. He had to cut the bullets out now. So he did, starting with the one pressed on the inside of his left floater rib. He sliced down precisely, releasing his breath in a slow hiss of pain.

"That's not sterile!" she cried. He hadn't the focus to comment. The good news was that shifters on a whole had really good immune systems.

It sucked to dig around with his fingers to get the bullet. He managed it, though it stole his breath and made him weak with pain. He dropped the bullet and his whole arm to the ground with a grunt of disgust.

One more.

He narrowed his focus, but the bullet was higher on his chest, just on the inside of his right nipple. He'd have no dexterity to use his right hand. The pectoral muscle would move the bullet around while he worked, and he didn't think he could do this one-handed.

He opened his eyes. "You. Now."

"What?"

"Bullet. Here." He pointed, and her eyes widened on horror.

"Hell, no! Jesus, just call a doctor!" Then she grimaced. "Call 911. Why the hell didn't I call 911?"

"You. Shot me."

"You were a bear!"

He looked at her, not even bothering to hide his fury. And he knew his silence challenged her because they both knew no one would believe he'd been a bear. Though there were as many as a million shifters in the United States, their existence was a closely guarded secret. He'd probably get into serious trouble for changing in front of her, but he had to survive first.

"Help. Me," he said, panting the words because of the pain.

She stared at him slack-jawed, her cell phone clutched in her fingers. His rational mind told him that anger wasn't getting him anywhere, so he moderated his tone.

"I'll show you. Bullet. Pretty close." He focused on her face and tried to smile. "I'll heal."

"W-what?"

"Look." He brushed aside the wound where he'd carved out the other bullet. The skin had already knit closed. A light tug would split it open again, but this close to a shift, he healed really fast. "Losing time," he said, pitching his voice to a low threat. "Must do this now."

"W-what?"

"Don't argue. Just do."

Annoyance washed through her features, but was quickly smoothed out. Then she hardened her jaw as she glared down at him.

Oh hell. He knew that look. He knew her face, too, but damned if he could remember how. She was so damned familiar, but he couldn't place her.

"I do this for you, you do something for me."

"You shot me."

"You attacked me."

"I roared."

"You were a freaking bear. Now agree or you dig that shit out yourself."

God, he hated negotiation and time was running out. He was already losing awareness of exactly where the bullet was in his body. "Fine. Dig now." Easy to agree when he had no intention of remembering this promise.

She grimaced and dropped down to her knees beside him. Then she tossed aside her purse and wiped her palms on faded blue jeans before taking the knife from his hand. "This is not smart."

There were a lot stupider things, but he didn't have the breath to say that. He used his left hand to point to where the bullet was. "Cut here. An inch."

She set one palm on his chest, surprisingly cool though there were beads of sweat on her forehead. Or maybe that was because his temperature was still running hot from his shift.

Pain sliced through his consciousness as she cut, but he controlled his breath so that his chest didn't jerk under her.

"Find. Bullet."

"I see it. I think."

Really? Good for her. She was ten times steadier than he expected. As if she had some medical training. Or disaster training. "You. Nurse?"

"No, I'm not a nurse, you sexist pig."

Hope spiked. "Doc?"

"You wish." She dug her fingers in and it took all his attention to not react to the pain. He needed to keep his chest still while she worked, but God, he wanted to scream.

"Got it!" she cried as she pulled it out. "It's done. I'm done. You can heal it now."

He looked at her, his breath still coming in short pants. "Not magic trick. No wand—"

"Whatever. Just do it."

He exhaled and his eyes drifted closed. Let her think he was doing some meditation bullshit. His body would heal as all bodies did. One cell at a time in its own time, which, admittedly, was really fast right now. Of course, it didn't hurt that he could center himself fully inside his human body. He could mentally run through a list of his organs as if tapping each one. Heart, lungs, liver, kidneys. He rolled through the whole litany until he hit his skin. In his mind's eye, it sealed together in a seamless line exactly as it should and the blood vessels beneath worked just as they ought. All perfect human normal.

A few minutes later he heard her move restlessly beside him. "Is it done? Are you all better?"

His eyes opened and shot her a look. Now that the pain was fading, he was better able to think. What he thought about now was her face and body. Caramel skin on a muscular frame. Her dark brown hair was pulled tightly back into a thick bun, and there was a broadness to her nose that should have looked odd, but beneath those large chocolate eyes, she looked absolutely perfect. That is if he ignored the hard jut of her sharp chin.

"I know you," he said.

Her eyes widened for moment, then slowly narrowed the longer he stayed silent. "Don't stop there. Keep thinking."

He was, but there was a lot to process. Sure he was absorbing her physical details, but he was also just realizing that it was cool outside and the air smelled of spring. That the birds were back to twittering and their song was about hatching and feeding young barely out of the shell.

"What day is it?"

"Hell if I—" She cut off her words then thumbed on her phone. "The twenty-second." And when he didn't respond, she added, "Of May."

"Damn." The last time he'd been human it had been mid-July.

"What? Is something else wrong?"

No way to answer that. There were a thousand things wrong. He'd been a bear for ten months. He wasn't sure he remembered how to be human. And yet even as those thoughts rolled through his mind, he managed to push himself upright until he sat facing her. He didn't concentrate on the movement. He'd learned young to just let his body work as it willed. The more he thought about it, the more awkward he got. And besides, his brain was busy parsing other things.

Like who she was and what was she doing up here. His cabin was in the middle of nowhere in Michigan's Upper Peninsula. She sure as hell wasn't a local. To begin with, there weren't that many African Americans up here. But she had found him, sure enough. And that dirty Chevy Malibu in his driveway said she'd driven a long way to get here, even though it did have Michigan plates.

"Your name," he said.

"Can't remember? I'm hurt." She didn't smell hurt. She smelled like cheap floral perfume over something sweet and nutty.

"Do you know who I am?"

"Corporal Simon Gold of the Corps of Engineers. Discharged about a year ago."

That was awful specific for someone he couldn't quite remember. But he knew how to do this. He could look at the individual pieces of her body and connect them with a memory. He could, though it took so much focus. In the end, it was her stubborn chin that triggered his memory, though in his mind's eye it was always paired with a mischievous tilt to the head. Her brother—his closest friend—had always been searching for fun.

"You're Vic's little sister." What was her name? "Alyssa."

Though he and Victor had been nearly inseparable for the last few years, they'd never been stateside together. Not until last year…er, two years ago, when he'd spent a wonderful couple weeks seeing the bars of Detroit while Alyssa had alternately harassed or hung out with them. He remembered her being skinny, sassy, and a ton more fun than his tight-jawed, muscular woman before him. And back then, he was pretty sure she'd never touched a gun much less been able to stand her ground and put five rounds into a roaring grizzly bear. "You've grown up."

"You were a bear, so I'm pretty sure you're the winner in surprising changes."

He looked at her calmly, analyzing her features and stance. Her eyes were steady as they met his gaze, but her hands were twitchy and her nostrils kept flaring as her breath came in and out in a short, tight tempo. Not quite panicked, but certainly not comfortable. Since she'd picked up her gun again, he'd do well to keep her heading toward calm, not terrified.

So he shrugged and was pleased when the motion didn't hurt too badly. "I can explain."

"Really? Have at it soldier. Give me the details."

He frowned. "Um, what details did you want?"

"You an army experiment?"

"No."

"Bit by a radioactive spider or something?"

"That's a comic book."

She arched a brow and he huffed out a breath. "I was born this way."

"As a bear?"

"Human. All human normal. My first shift was at sixteen."

She crinkled her nose. "You make it sound like a shift at a donut shop. You mean you turned into a bear?" It was half statement, half question, so he answered it.

"Yes. Ripped my favorite jeans. Hurt like hell. Wandered until I was in Gladwin."

She frowned. "Where?"

"Middle Michigan. State park. Here." He held up his hand in the shape of Michigan and pointed an inch below the base of his index finger.

"So it's a genetic thing? Your parents can do it, your—"

Her questions were making his head hurt. He was trying to do too much too fast. He couldn't remember how to act. How to answer. And he was starting to think too much. Which meant—oddly enough—that his language ability was about to deteriorate as he tried to function as a man and not a bear. "Not automatic. Can't say more." He pushed to his feet, his coordination awkward.

Don't think about it. Just do it.

He balanced on his feet while she scrambled backward. And though he tried to appear casual, he kept a close eye on where she put that gun. Fortunately, it went back into her purse-satchel after she'd thumbed on the safety. Jesus, she was just now putting on the safety?

He started walking to his front door. His gait was slow and jerky, but eventually it smoothed out. He needed to keep moving to remember how to be a man. He'd never gone bear for so long before, and a sliver of alarm skated down his spine at the realization. Ten months as a bear? Back in July, he'd planned to be bear for a week. Why hadn't he gone insane? Why hadn't someone hunted him down as a feral?

He looked at the woods behind his cabin. Out there was the female he had been tracking. The memory held equal parts temptation and horror. What had he been doing?

And yet as he looked at the woods, his steps faltered. The longing to shift back to grizzly hit him square in the chest, less painful but no less potent than the slugs he'd taken ten minutes before. There was a sweetness out in the woods. A song that he couldn't hear any more and he wanted it like a man wanted that perfect feeling he couldn't quite remember. And as he stood there staring, the woman's voice cut into his thoughts. Her tone was hard and sarcastic, but not enough to cover her fear.

"You're not going furry again, are you? I still have rounds left in my gun."

He turned slowly, his eyes narrowing as he again picked out the details of her face and body. Minute details, the more specific the better because it forced him to process information like a man. Her brows were drawn down in a frown. Her shoulders were tight with fear, but determination glinted in her narrowed eyes and the set of her feet. She was equally prepared for fight or flight, and one of her hands rested inside her purse, no doubt on the butt of her gun.

"You saw a bear turn into a man. Why aren't you freaking out?"

A dull flush crept up her cheeks. "I adapt quickly."

"No one's that flexible." She couldn't know. Shifters were a really big secret and bear-shifters even more so. Sure, someone was always catching sight of the werewolves, but that's because there were so many damned dogs. Then understanding hit. She'd already been told. Because her brother hadn't kept the secret. "Victor has a big mouth."

She shifted awkwardly, but her gaze remained steady. "I didn't believe him. I thought he was hallucinating until…" She swallowed and gestured to where Simon had been lying on the ground in a pool of his own grizzly blood. "I thought a bear was attacking me. I didn't think it was you. I didn't…" No one believed until they saw. And some not even then. He growled, a very animal sound. And when the noise felt too good inside him, he abruptly shifted to words. "Go home. Go back to Victor. Tell him I'm in a shit-ton of trouble because he talked." And because Simon hadn't reported that Victor knew he was a shifter.

"I will," she said. Her voice taking on an edge of panic as he made it to the front porch. "But only if you come with me."

He tried to think of an appropriate human expression. He found it a moment later when he turned to look straight at her and then rolled his eyes. Then in case the message wasn't clear, he added words. "No. Fucking. Way."

"You have to," she said as she rushed to follow him up the steps. "He's turning into one of you." Her voice shook as she said it, but the words rang with conviction.

He ignored it as he unscrewed the case around the porch light and pulled out the key that was taped inside. A moment later he was unlocking the door, but she gripped his elbow. Her fingers were tight hard points, but he'd just survived five rounds. Fingers were nothing.

"I'm serious. He's changing into…into a bear or something. You have to help him."

"It doesn't work that way."

"Really?" she pressed. "Are you sure?"

"Of course—"

"Because this looks like a freaking bear to me."

She pushed her cell phone into his face. It took him a second to focus on the screen, but he managed to pick out the details of his once best friend. Vic was crouched against a wall, his eyes wild and clearly terrified. And was his nose longer? The eyebrows were bushier, and no scissors had ever trimmed that beard. Vic was staring in horror at his left arm. It wasn't human, but it damn sure wasn't fully bear, either. It was thick and furry and came complete with a hairless paw and real claws.

That couldn't be real. It just couldn't. It...

Again, understanding clicked into place. "That's makeup." He shoved open his front door.

"It's true!" she cried as she tried to follow him.

He stopped her, his hand flat and implacable right on her...Um, wow. He'd forgotten what human breasts felt like. His palm was higher up on her chest, but he felt the curve of both her breasts and was startled by how distracting they were. And that pissed him off even more.

"Go home. This wasn't funny."

"This is real and Vic's dying. Your best friend is dying!"

"Bullshit." He shoved her hard, right in the center of her chest. She stumbled backward. Not far enough to land on her ass, but enough that he could slam the door right in her face.

And this kind of nonsense was exactly why he'd been a bear for the last ten months. No one screwed with bears. No one banged on their doors or forced them to think. And because humans—every single one—were assholes.

About the Author

Kathy Lyons is the wild, adventurous half of *USA Today* bestselling author Jade Lee. A lover of all things fantastical, Kathy spent much of her childhood in Narnia, Middle Earth, Amber, and Earthsea, just to name a few. There is nothing she adores more than turning an ordinary day into something magical, which is what happens all the time in her books. Winner of several industry awards, including the Prism Best of the Best Award, a *Romantic Times* Reviewers' Choice Award, and Fresh Fiction's Steamiest Read, Kathy has published more than fifty romance novels, and she's just getting started.

Check out her latest news at:
KathyLyons.com
Facebook.com/KathyLyonsBooks
Twitter: @KathyLyonsAuth

CPSIA information can be obtained
at www.ICGtesting.com
Printed in the USA
LVHW111004080319
609858LV00008B/87/P